KILLING FROST

KILLING FROST
JOHN R. RIGGS

A GARTH RYLAND MYSTERY

BARRICADE BOOKS INC. / New York

Published by Barricade Books Inc.
150 Fifth Avenue
New York, NY 10011

Printed in the United States of America.

Library of Congress Cataloging-in-Publication Data

Riggs, John R., 1945–
    Killing frost / John R. Riggs.
        p.   cm. — (A Garth Ryland mystery)
    ISBN 1-56980-053-7 (cl)
    1. Ryland, Garth (Fictitious character) Fiction. I. Title. II. Series:
Riggs, John R., 1945–   Garth Ryland mystery.
    PS3568.I372K55   1955
    813'.54—dc20   95-21901
    CIP
First printing

To Carole

Other titles in the Garth Ryland mystery series:

The Last Laugh
Let Sleeping Dogs Lie
The Glory Hound
Haunt of the Nightingale
Wolf in Sheep's Clothing
One Man's Poison
Dead Letter
A Dragon Lives Forever
Cold Hearts and Gentle People

1

It was manure time in south-central Wisconsin—that time in late February to mid-March of freeze and thaw, clear cold nights and sunny days, when the sap starts to run and the maple syrup pots start to boil, when the cow manure the dairy farmers have spread while the ground was still frozen first begins to waft its aroma throughout the countryside far and wide. It's not the end of winter. Far from it. But after months of cabin fever, of harsh bleak days and even bleaker thoughts, that first hint of spring makes the people of Oakalla, where I live, go a little crazy, walk around barefooted and bare-chested through the snow, and hug and kiss on people they haven't spoken to in years. For me, Garth Ryland, who likes winter less and less each year, manure time is a time for renewal. A time to sort through my thoughts and sort through my tackle box and throw out everything I won't use again this year. A time to hope and a time to dream. A time to clear out the cobwebs and peep my head out of my hole, groundhog style, and see all of my promises left to keep in a world that (maybe) is not such a bad place after all. Not the time I would choose, if I had a choice, for someone to find a body.

My nightmare began when Sheriff Harold Clark stopped by my office at the *Oakalla Reporter*, interrupting what had promised to be my best Monday in weeks.

"Garth," he said, looking Eeyore glum, as was his nature. "I hate to bother you, but I just got a call from Amos Hogue."

Clarkie, as Sheriff Harold Clark was known to most of us in Oakalla, was a short round generally cheerless man, who had a good heart, but a complete lack of common sense. A computer genius, who could have named his price just about anywhere else in the country, Clarkie took himself and his job seriously, but he could never quite command the respect he thought he deserved. Part of his problem was timing. He had the bad luck to follow (after a brief interlude in the person of Whitey Huffer) Rupert Roberts, the only three-term sheriff in the history of Adams County, Wisconsin, and the best lawman that I had ever known. Part of his problem was Clarkie himself. The reason the rest of us in Oakalla couldn't take him as seriously as he did himself was his total lack of street smarts. As my housekeeper, Ruth Krammes, often said about him, "He was an accident waiting to happen."

"What did Amos Hogue have to say when he called?" I asked.

"He said he found a body in that old dump just down the road from his house."

"Did he happen to say whose body it was?"

"He said he couldn't say. He said I'd understand when I got there."

"Let me get my coat," I said.

Once in Clarkie's patrol car, we drove west out of town along Galena Road, crossed Rocky Creek about a half mile out, and went a few miles until we came to Galena, where we turned south along a winding gravel road that was simply named County Road 425 West.

Galena was one of those crossroads towns whose name had stayed after the town had gone. The only things left there now were an abandoned building that had once been a grocery store, a rusting gas pump in front of the building, and on its west side, two large round red metal Coke signs that seemed to fade a little bit more every year.

"That's Oakalla forty years from now," Clarkie had said as we passed through Galena.

"Not if I can help it."

Still in the south after three months of winter, the sun shone full-stream through Clarkie's windshield, making the heavy denim jacket I wore seem cumbersome and unnecessary. But I made no move to take it off. Though the road was mostly clear with only patches of ice, the woods on either side were still steeped in snow—at least six inches of it on the level, more where the wind had found a break in the trees and drifted it. And the shadows, when we passed under the railroad trestle, and then again under a cluster of pines pressed in close to the road, still seemed winter deep.

"How's Eugene getting along?" I asked.

Eugene was Eugene Yuill, Clarkie's deputy, who Saturday before last had jumped down from his grain truck, caught the side of his size fourteen, steel-toed Redwing work boot on an unseen tree root, and broken his left ankle. As a result, Eugene was now manning the sheriff's office while Clarkie was patrolling the streets, which was not at all what Clarkie had in mind when he had hired Eugene seven months ago.

Clarkie scowled as he slowed for a patch of ice. "Eugene is doing a lot better than he lets on. He could drive on that ankle if he really wanted to."

"To what end?" I asked. Having Eugene on the streets was no improvement over Clarkie. It was like substituting Laurel for Hardy.

"It would give me a break at least. I'm getting tired of spending all of my time in this car."

"Try walking, like I do. It might do you good."

"If I had your car, I'd walk, too," Clarkie said.

Discussion closed. Jessie, my ancient brown Chevy sedan, needed no defense. That was because I had none to offer.

We then came to a steep grade where the road narrowed and fell away into deep ditches, and the hills on either side pinched in, leaving a thin backbone of gravel on which to drive. Clarkie fought the wheel all the way up the grade, as the patrol car hit washboard and tried to slide out from under us, and at the top we were nearly sideways before the back end of the car swung around and decided to follow the front end again.

"Hell of a place to lose it," Clarkie said.

I nodded in agreement.

But Clarkie's eyes weren't focused on the ravines on either side of the road. He was staring at the too-tall orange brick house that stood deep in the cedar thicket to our left. A house that looked deserted, and (up until recently) had been deserted.

"I don't know about you, Garth, but that place flat out gives me the creeps," Clarkie said.

I glanced over my shoulder as the house passed from sight. It was a stately old house, and it commanded a great view. But I had to go along with Clarkie. Something about its looks didn't appeal to me either. Though I couldn't agree that it gave me the creeps.

"Aunt Norma says it was once a station on the Underground Railroad," Clarkie said.

"That's what they say about every old house around here. I'll believe it when I see it," I said. My skepticism was based solely on the fact that I had yet to find a house in Oakalla or its surroundings that *had* been part of the Underground Railroad. I was beginning to think that, local legend to the contrary, the Underground Railroad never had run through Adams County.

At the bottom of that same ridge we came to the shell of a deserted house and the charred remains of what had once been a hog barn here in the heart of dairy cattle country. The hog barn had been the scene of the infamous "Hog Roast," as it was known to the members of Oakalla's volunteer fire department—where twelve sows and their suckling piglets had died in a fire one bitterly cold January night, where the fire trucks had gotten mired in the snow and had to be hand pushed out again, where one fireman had cut his hand to the bone and another had stepped up to his knees in a dead sow. Years later, I could still smell the smoke from that fire—the cold-thickened scent of burned hair and flesh, and I could still see the barn's owner, Amos Hogue, warming his hands in the dead sow as part of his life's work went up in smoke.

"I wonder why they don't do something with that place," Clarkie said in disgust as we drove by the blackened barn. "If there ever was an eyesore, that sure is one."

I glanced from the barn to the woods across the road, where stately spruce and pine were interlaced with a network of small streams that had carved the woods into a series of hills and dales, each separate and unique, yet locked together in one perfect whole, like the pieces of a jigsaw puzzle. The difference was like night and day. One grotesque, the other sublime, they stood in stark contrast to each other and made me wonder about their separate histories, how each evolved to where it was today.

"Who owns the barn now, do you know?" I asked Clarkie.

"As far as I know, Amos Hogue still does."

"Figures," I said.

"But you know he bought the place from his cousin Clarence?"

"Before or after the fire?"

"Before, I think. Why?"

"Just curious."

The last time I had seen Clarence Hogue he was driving a new GMC four-by-four and building a new home just west of Oakalla there along Galena Road. Not bad for someone who had been a washout as a farmer and everything else he had tried.

"I'm glad Clarence has finally found his niche," I said.

"What's that?"

"Auctioneering. To hear Ruth tell it, he has a silver tongue. He could sell ice machines to Eskimos, or so she says."

Clarkie didn't say anything. He appeared to be deep in thought.

"Something bothering you, Clarkie?"

He shook his head no. "It would be nice, that's all, to finally find your niche."

A quarter mile down the road we came to the two-story white frame farmhouse where Amos Hogue lived. Unlike the snow that was still white if not pristine in the surrounding woods, the snow in Amos Hogue's yard had assumed a dirty brownish cast, which matched the paint on the house and the silo. Pigeons came and went through the aging red barn's broken windows, and a couple of Duroc sows rooted through the snow in the barn lot for what I assumed were snow-buried ears of corn. Or perhaps they rooted from hope and habit, like a lot of the rest of us.

Clarkie tooted his horn, and a couple minutes later Amos Hogue came out the back door of the house. Amos wore knee-high gum boots, brown Carhart coveralls stuffed into the boots, a red Farm Bureau Co-Op cap with the ear flaps turned up, and a broad smile on his face, as if he had just won the lottery.

"Hop in," Clarkie said.

"You're the doctor," Amos replied.

Even before Amos got into the back seat and closed the door, I smelled the hog manure on him. Some people, Amos among them, said it smelled like money to them. To me, it smelled like shit.

"Where are we going?" Clarkie asked.

"On down the road a ways. You can't miss it."

I glanced into the back seat. "Morning, Amos," I said.

"Morning, Garth. How's tricks?"

"Fine. The last I looked."

Amos Hogue hadn't shaved that morning, or the last few mornings judging by the coarse blue-and-white stubble of his beard. All neck and shoulders, he was a short, broad, powerfully built man, who reminded me a lot of the French Voyageurs in his hardy appreciation of life and his ability to laugh in the face of adversity. And like the Voyageurs, he was a fatalist. *Que sera sera.* An eat, drink, and be merry type, who would rather risk the rapids than make an unnecessary portage. He was also about the crudest man I had ever met.

"My wife been in to see you lately?" Amos asked.

"No. Not lately," I said.

"Fancies herself a songwriter," Amos said to Clarkie, while using his thumbnail to pick some tobacco from between his teeth. "Thought old Garth here would do her up right."

I didn't say anything. It had been nearly two years since I had last seen Alma Hogue, and I still hadn't found the courage to return her cassette tapes.

"What about it, Garth? Did you do her up right?" Amos asked. When I didn't answer, he continued, "I didn't think so. Who would want anything to do with that old bag of bones anyway? Except me?"

I sucked in and kept quiet, afraid of what I might say. Alma Hogue was anything but an old bag of bones. She was a sensitive, intelligent, caring woman, who had had the misfortune to marry Amos Hogue, a man five years her junior. Not that age was an issue to her, but Amos Hogue certainly was.

"Are we getting close?" Clarkie quickly asked. Clarkie, who prized order and serenity above all, hated conflict of any kind.

"Just a few more rods." Amos pointed to show us. "It's in that holler up there."

"The one with all the junk in it," Clarkie said in disgust.

"Where else?" Amos said with a smile.

Clarkie parked the patrol car alongside the road. He and I got out. Amos, however, remained in the back seat.

"Aren't you going with us?" Clarkie said.

"What's the point? I've already been."

Clarkie and I stood in the middle of County Road 425 West. In the hollow just east of us, a small stream wound its way around and through a tangle of old fence rolls and the rusting hulls of discarded pieces of farm machinery that sat hunched in the snow like dinosaurs, frozen there for all time.

"All that stuff ain't mine," Amos yelled out the window at us. "Those bags are all new."

The bags he was referring to were several large plastic trash bags in various colors—white, dark green, chocolate brown, and black—that had been thrown, most of them anyway, only as far as the fence, where they had piled up like the drifts of snow, until it was hard to tell snow from trash. Hard to tell, that is, until we started wading through it.

"Look at this mess," Clarkie said as he kicked a frozen Pamper off his shoe. "What kind of people would do something like this?"

"You might be surprised."

We stopped at the fence while Clarkie scanned the dump ahead. "I wonder why Amos decided not to come along," he said.

Thinking back to the night the hog barn burned, I had to wonder the same thing. It couldn't be because he was squeamish. After he had warmed his hands in the belly of the burned sow, he had pulled off a hind leg and begun to eat it. "Hate to waste the meat," was his explanation as he used his coat sleeve to wipe the grease from his chin.

"I don't know why, Clarkie," I said. "But knowing Amos, you'd better watch your step."

Clarkie went over the fence first. I followed a few seconds later. Though he appeared to be watching his step, Clarkie still managed to stumble over something before he had gone very far. Then he picked himself up and ran as far as he could before the horror overtook him, and he began to vomit.

CHAPTER 2

What Clarkie had stumbled over was a man's naked torso. The man's hands, head, and feet had been severed and he lay there belly up in the snow, like something about to be field dressed. Little blood that I could see. Neither did I see any sign of the missing head, hands, or feet. Apparently he had been killed somewhere else and then dumped there. All of this I determined several minutes later when I could get my brain working again.

"What did you find out, Garth?" Clarkie stood atop a small knoll several yards away. He couldn't make himself move any closer to the body.

"Not much, Clarkie. It looks like he was killed somewhere else and then dumped here."

"So what do we do now?"

"Wait for Ben Bryan to get here." Ben Bryan was the county coroner. Clarkie had called him just before we left my office.

Clarkie shivered, turning his back on what was below. "Why don't we wait in the car?"

"Good idea."

Amos Hogue was waiting for us in the patrol car. Amos was all smiles, so apparently he had gotten the reaction he had wanted.

"He still have his pecker up?" Amos asked.

Clarkie looked to me for help.

"I don't know. I didn't examine him that closely," I said.

"Do, the next chance you get," Amos said. "I swear that man died with a hard-on."

Clarkie wanted to cut and run. I could tell by the look of panic in his eyes. But where would he go?

"You mind if I ask you a couple questions, Amos?" I said.

"I don't mind," Amos said, as he pulled a bag of Red Man tobacco from his pocket and pinched off a chew. "But it seems like, if this is official business, Sheriff Clark here ought to be the one asking the questions."

I reached into my jeans, took out my wallet, and showed Amos my special deputy's badge, the one that Rupert Roberts had given me over a fifth of Wild Turkey several aeons ago. The only reason I still carried it was in the hope that I wouldn't have to use it. But it hadn't worked out that way.

"Imagine that," Amos said as he examined the badge. "What are you, a Junior G-Man or something?"

I closed the wallet and put it away. "Something."

A momentary silence followed. Clarkie, who had a notoriously weak stomach anyway, was still trying to compose himself. Amos had opened the door in order to spit. I was trying to think of the right questions to ask.

"What time did you find the body?" I asked.

Nobody answered. I looked back at Amos, who had misjudged his aim and spit tobacco juice all over the inside of the patrol car's back door.

Amos used his hand to swipe away at the spit, then wiped his hand on his coveralls. "Were you talking to me?"

"Yes."

"Long about eight, nine o'clock, I figure. Breakfast was over and the feeding was done."

I looked at my trusty Timex, which had survived the past few years far better than I had. It was going on eleven A.M.

"Any particular reason why you just happened to wander down here and find the body?" I asked.

"Figured you'd ask that," Amos said, taking time out to spit again. "I would've been there sooner if Alma hadn't stopped me."

"How much sooner?"

"The middle of the night. That's when I heard the car drive by."

Clarkie looked at me with a question in his eyes. Apparently he and I were wondering the same thing.

"Do you always run down here to your dump when a car drives by?" I said.

"Lately I have been. Take a look at this place," he said. "It's worse than the county dump."

"No other reason why you'd go out in the middle of the night and try to chase somebody down?" I asked.

Amos didn't seem to like that question, but neither did he try to avoid it. "You'll have to ask Alma about that one. She's the one who keeps the strange hours."

"What are you saying, Amos, that the car might have been there because of Alma?" Which to me seemed unlikely, since Alma Hogue was not one to fly in the face of convention.

"I'm just saying it's a possibility. And don't forget, about half the houses in this township have been robbed lately."

I heard Clarkie sigh. "I haven't forgotten," Clarkie said.

"Ah, so he speaks after all. Or is that Garth there, throwing his voice, the way he does his weight around?"

Clarkie's face turned red with an anger that matched my own. "You still haven't said why you were in such a hurry to get down here to the dump this morning," Clarkie said, coming to life.

Amos spat again, this time deliberately hitting the door. "I told you why. People have been dumping on my property. Since you won't put an end to it, I intend to."

"It's the first I've heard about it," Clarkie said.

Amos was indignant. "Well, it ain't the first time it's happened, you can sure see that. Why don't you get your fat ass out of town once in a while and see what's going on?"

Clarkie's face turned purple. He was about to blow. "Why don't you get your fat ass out of my car before I lock you up?"

"Glad to. I wasn't liking the company much anyway."

Amos crawled out of the car and started walking home. For spite, he left the back door open, so one of us would have to get out and close it.

"I'll get it," I said.

"Leave it for now. We need to air it out in here anyway."

"At least let me wipe the spit off the door before it dries."

I got out of the car, scooped up a ball of snow in my glove, and used it to wipe off the door. Though warmed by the sun, the snow was still a couple hours away from being just right for fort building.

A tan late-model Oldsmobile Eighty-Eight pulled up behind us and Ben Bryan got out. He was accompanied by his assistant, Dr. Abby Pence-Airhart, who in another week or so, when her divorce was final, would just be Dr. Abby Airhart.

Ben Bryan was a retired mortician, who had become county coroner by default when no one else would take the job. A small, friendly, serious man, who liked contract bridge and classic old cars, he could often be seen puttering around the east end of Oakalla in a Model A Ford pickup. Every December for twenty years now, he had paraded as Santa Claus across the gymnasium floor, passing out candy to the kids, following Oakalla Grade School's annual Christmas pageant.

Dr. Abby Pence-Airhart was the new surgeon at Adams County Hospital and a budding pathologist, who had volunteered to assist Ben Bryan for free in order to learn as much as she could about the job. Just over five feet four inches tall with blue-green eyes and yellow hair, she liked fast cars, spicy food, long drives in the country, and me. She also liked living in Oakalla, and from all reports was liked in return.

"Wasn't that Amos Hogue we just met on the road?" Ben Bryan asked.

"One and the same," I answered.

"What's his problem? He kept walking as if we weren't even there."

"He and Clarkie had a falling out."

Ben Bryan glanced at Clarkie, who still sat brooding in the patrol car. "I'm not surprised. Clarkie's had a falling out with a lot of us lately."

"It's the burglaries," I said in Clarkie's defense. "I think they're starting to wear him down."

"That's his own fault," he said without sympathy.

I turned my attention to Dr. Abby Pence-Airhart, who had a smile for me. "Fancy meeting you here," I said.

"I was thinking the same thing."

She wore a bulky green coat that just covered her rear, jeans, hiking boots, and gray wool gloves. She looked more like a kid about to take a sled ride than the surgeon she was.

"What are you smiling at?" she said.

"You. You always make me smile." Almost always anyway.

"Keep that up and you're going to make me blush."

I didn't know how to tell her it was already too late for that.

"So what do you have for us, Garth?" Ben Bryan said.

I'd forgotten he was there. Abby soon-to-be-just-Airhart had a way of doing that to me.

"It's not pretty," I said.

"It never is," he answered.

I pointed to show them. "He's over there. Just follow the tracks."

"You're not going with us?"

"No. Like Amos said earlier, I've already been."

"That bad, huh?" Abby said.

"You'll see when you get there."

"And where will you be?"

"Here, for now."

I watched Abby and Ben climb the fence and approach the man's torso. Then they both stopped at once, as each turned to look at the other. It was Abby who made the first move after that, as she knelt in the snow to examine the body.

"What's going on?" Clarkie said from inside the car.

"They've found the body."

"And?"

"They're examining it."

"Just like that?"

"Just like that."

"Shit," he said.

"Don't let it eat at you," I said. "You knew how you were about these things when you took this job."

"I just thought it would get easier, that's all."

"Some things never do."

"Tell me about it."

Abby and Ben returned a few minutes later. They looked grim, but not devastated. I guessed they'd both seen worse in their day.

"Well?" I said.

Ben Bryan shrugged. "He's dead."

"That's a comfort."

"What else do you want to know?"

"How long has he been dead, for starters?"

"There's no way of telling. Not until we thaw him out. Maybe not even then."

"Do you think he was killed elsewhere and then brought here?"

"That'd be my guess." He turned to Abby. "What do you think, Dr. Airhart?"

"Unless we can find his head, hands, and feet around here somewhere."

"They weren't anywhere around that I could find," I said.

"What about tracks, leading in and out?"

"Only one fresh set that I could see. What about you, Clarkie?" I said, wanting to draw him in.

"Only one fresh set," he answered. "And they belong to Amos."

"You're sure about that?"

He reached into his glove compartment and handed me a tape measure. "There's one way to find out for sure."

First I examined, then measured, the tracks that Amos had left along the road on his way home. Then I climbed the fence and measured the tracks that I had staked out alongside the body. They were a match.

"Was I right?" Clarkie asked.

"You were right."

"How do you figure?" Ben Bryan asked. "There only being one set of tracks?"

"There was some wind in the night. Snow could have drifted in any other tracks," I said.

"Not much wind," Clarkie said.

"But maybe enough."

"So what's the verdict?" Ben asked.

"Death by natural causes," I said.

"I'll write it up if you'll sign it." Ben was only half kidding.

"What do you think, Clarkie?" I said. "Don't we both have enough to do without taking on something that we'll probably never solve?"

Clarkie wore a strangled look, as he wrestled with his conscience. Like the coroner, he was tempted to whitewash the whole thing.

"Don't I get a vote here?" Abby said before Clarkie could answer. "Or aren't women included in this fraternity?" She wasn't smiling at me now.

"I already know what your vote is," I said.

"Still, I'd like to cast it."

"I'm listening."

She made a face at me, which was the most that she would do with witnesses present. "I vote that we wait until after the autopsy before we decide anything."

I looked at Ben and Clarkie, who both gave me a nod. "Then it's unanimous."

"It was all along, wasn't it?" Abby said with that irrepressible gleam in her eye that I found so attractive.

"Pretty much."

"You're a jerk, you know that?"

I nodded and smiled.

As we were leaving, Clarkie and I met the Operation Lifeline ambulance, which for once was driving within reason and under control. I guessed miracles weren't extinct after all.

"What's up?" I said to Clarkie. "That's the sanest I've ever seen them drive."

"After their last accident, I put the word out. One more and I was going to cite them for being a public nuisance."

"Can you do that?"

"I can sure as hell try."

When we passed Amos Hogue's place without even slowing down, I said, "Don't you want to talk to Alma Hogue?"

"What about?"

"Amos's story about finding the body. I'm not sure it holds water."

"What's the point, Garth? She'll only say what he wants her to."

"I don't think you give her enough credit."

"Then you talk to her. I don't think I can face her or Amos either one right now."

"Why not her?"

Clarkie didn't answer. His face seemed to be growing redder by the second.

"Clarkie, what's up?"

"That dead man's prick, or so Amos says."

"That's no answer."

"It's the best I can do right now."

At the top of the next ridge, I said, "Stop. I want to talk to the woman who lives here."

"Garth, are you crazy? That woman is a witch." He slowed, but didn't stop.

"Says who?"

"She does. She's told several people that."

"She doesn't look like a witch to me."

"What's a witch supposed to look like?"

"Never mind, Clarkie. Just stop the car."

He did as I asked.

"You coming with me?" I said.

"Not this time, Garth. I'd just as soon wait here."

"Jesus Christ, Clarkie. You're the sheriff, not me."

He folded his arms and did his best imitation of a wooden Indian. "I haven't forgotten, Garth."

I made my way through the cedar thicket toward the orange brick house. Whatever sunlight that late February day held, and it was strong enough to eat through the whiskers of snow at the edge of the road, it had yet to penetrate the thicket. Here the snow was light and powdery, the cold pronounced, as the shadows held sway.

The house ahead of me was a renovator's dream, or every kid's nightmare, depending on the eyes of the beholder. Four ponderous white wooden pillars supported a tottery balcony that leaned precariously toward the south where the top of one of the pillars had rotted away, leaving the balcony dangling. Above the balcony and equally spaced across the narrow face of the house were two tall arched windows, both of which had thin diagonal cracks running the length of them, and above them, at the crown of the house, was a white wooden balustrade that gaped in places, like missing teeth, where the balusters had broken off.

Beneath the balcony was a massive black wooden door, and on either side of it an arched window in perfect symmetry with the window above it. The result, as I approached the house, and its face grew higher and higher, its door loomed larger, and its windows seemed to narrow and focus, like eyes, was one of intimidation. In my mind I could blame it all on too many Lon Chaney movies as a kid, but in my heart I knew better.

The door, which had to be at least four feet by ten feet, had iron studs imbedded in it, perhaps for effect, and had been painted black, which made the door look recent and out of time with the rest of the house. I looked for a door knocker. Finding none, I had to use my fist. It was like knocking on a sequoia.

But apparently someone on the inside heard my feeble rappings because the door swung open.

"You rang?" I expected her to say. But she didn't.

The woman before me was in fact not a toad, but she reminded me of one. Pallid skin, a short, thick, doughy body, sleepy, nearly colorless eyes with heavy lids, stringy, seldom-washed hair. She wore a full brown-print dress, moccasins, and Indian beads. I had seen her in town occasionally in the company of Bruce Barger and Jeremy Pitts, two of Oakalla's lesser lights, usually late at night at the Corner Bar and Grill. She hadn't seemed all that friendly then. She didn't seem all that friendly now. Rather, she seemed very annoyed at me.

"Can't you read the sign?" she said, blinking rapidly as if the sunlight hurt her eyes.

"Which one?"

"The one that says 'No Trespassing.'"

"I thought that was for the property down the road."

"There's one in the yard if you were paying attention."

"I must have missed it."

She didn't care one way or another whether I'd missed it or not. "As you're leaving, you'll see it on your way out."

"This isn't a social call," I said as she started to close the door. "I'm here on official business."

"What kind of official business?"

Testing her, I said, "What other kind is there?"

She stopped blinking. Her eyes passed unfriendly and headed down a long dark corridor for somewhere else.

"Let me guess. You're the law, right?"

"Right. I'm the law." At the moment anyway.

"Do you have proof of that?"

I showed her my badge. She was one of the few who ever took the pains to read it.

"It says special deputy," she said. "What's a special deputy?"

"I specialize in murder."

The word seemed to make no impression on her. She could have cared less. "Really? Who's been murdered?"

"We haven't identified him yet. But we found his body just down the road on Amos Hogue's property."

She grimaced as if something had left a bad taste in her mouth. "Why doesn't that surprise me?"

"Do you know Amos?" I asked.

"We've met. He's my landlord, or at least thinks he is."

"You don't think he is?"

A horn tooted before she could answer. Apparently Clarkie was ready to move on.

"Who is that on the horn?" she said.

"Sheriff Clark."

She stiffened. Something had put her on the alert. "Then why isn't he the one asking the questions?"

"Because he thinks you are a witch."

"I am."

I let that pass.

"I really am."

"Good for you, but that's not why I'm here. What I need to know is if you heard or saw anyone driving this road late last night?"

"How late?"

Amos Hogue had said the middle of the night. How late was that?

"Midnight or so," I said, guessing.

"I was in bed by midnight."

"Earlier then?"

"No." She stared at the cedar thicket, which effectively blocked all view of the road. "I couldn't see anything from here anyway."

"From your balcony, you could."

"If I wanted to risk a broken neck."

She yawned. Evidently I was boring her. "Is that all?" she said.

"Yes. I guess so." I wasn't ready to leave, but I didn't know what else to ask her.

"Good. Don't call again." She went inside and closed the door.

I stood a moment on her doorstep, wondering why I disliked that woman so, then walked on back to the patrol car.

"Okay, what's going on?" I said to Clarkie the minute I was inside. "Why did you blow the horn?"

"I got cold sitting here."

That was a lie and we both knew it. It was so warm in there that Clarkie had unzipped his jacket.

"Just drive," I said in disgust. "The sooner I get back to work the better."

"I'm not holding out on you, Garth," Clarkie said, as he started the patrol car and put it in gear.

"Then what are you doing? Why didn't you want to stop, and don't tell me it's because what's her name there is a witch?"

"She *is* a witch."

"I know. She told me. But that's not why you didn't want to stop or go to the door with me."

We were gathering speed, splashing through puddles that had been iced over only hours before.

"What is her name anyway?" I asked.

"She calls herself Stella."

"She have a last name?"

"Not that I know of."

"Then how does she sign her checks or get her mail?"

"You'll have to ask her, Garth. I haven't paid all that much attention to her."

"I'll bet."

Angry, Clarkie turned my way. As he did, he jerked the steering wheel and we almost went off the road. "What's that supposed to mean? Do you think the two of us have something going, is that it? I swear, Garth, the most I've seen that woman is two or three times in my life. And she spooked me each time I did."

"Watch where you're going," I said as we started off the road on the other side.

"It's the truth," he insisted.

"Okay, it's the truth. But you're still holding out on me."

"Ask me anything you want to know about her, anything at all, and I'll tell you what I know."

"How long has she been in the Oakalla area?"

"A couple-three years. Maybe more, maybe less."

"That's exact," I said.

He ignored me.

"Where was she before she came here?"

"I don't know that."

"She have any relatives around here?"

"I don't know that either." We came to Galena and turned right toward Oakalla. "Why all the questions about her?" he asked.

"You said to ask anything I wanted."

"I mean what's your point, except to try to prove that I'm holding out on you?"

It was hard to explain gut feelings to Clarkie, a man not really in tune with his inner self. But something about the woman Stella stuck in my craw. Perhaps it was the underlying hostility I felt from her from our first moment on.

"She's hiding something, Clarkie. Don't ask me why, but I can usually tell when someone is."

"She is hiding something, Garth. I told you she was a witch."

"God damn it, Clarkie, I don't care whether she's a witch or not!" I shouted. "That's not what she is all about."

Evidently I hurt his feelings because he didn't say anything more all the way back to Oakalla.

CHAPTER 3

After a cheeseburger with fried onions, a glass of milk, and a piece of pecan pie a la mode at the Corner Bar and Grill, I walked to my office at the *Oakalla Reporter*, where I began calling my sources to see what had happened in and about Oakalla over the weekend. The topic of the day, as it had been every Monday lately, was the continuing string of robberies that had plagued Adams County for the past few months. The MO was always the same. The robbers would stake out a house, wait until its occupants left for the day, or the evening, then kick in the back door if the house was locked, ransack the place, stealing guns, jewelry, electronic equipment, and cash. Virtually all of the robberies had occurred at out-of-the-way places where there was little likelihood of the robbers being seen by neighbors, or by a passing motorist. Since the robbers had been successful so far and not one of the robberies had been solved, it seemed likely that the robberies would continue.

That was the topic of today, but when the word got out about the headless, handless, footless body that we'd found, the robberies would be all but forgotten.

At five P.M. I packed it in and started the six-block walk home. Probably I would come back later that evening, but for the time being I wanted a change of scene. As I walked west along Gas Line Road, I noticed the chill in the air now that the sun was on its way down. And in the longest shadows, the puddles born at midday had started to glaze over with ice again.

Home was near the heart of Oakalla, two blocks north of the intersection of School and Jackson Streets, which was the main intersection in town. Home included a large concrete front porch with four concrete pillars and a concrete railing around it, a much smaller two-step back stoop, a brick fireplace that we used more in the fall than we did in the winter, two bathrooms—a full bath upstairs and a half bath downstairs, a basement, three bedrooms, several closets, a dining room, kitchen, living room, utility room, and Ruth Krammes, my housekeeper, who tonight stood in the kitchen with a cast-iron skillet in one hand and a paring knife in the other. At five-ten, none of it fat, with shoulders every bit as broad as mine, Ruth makes an imposing figure whether armed or not.

"Mouse or burglar?" I said.

She glared at me as she set the skillet on the stove. "Neither. I got caught up in a thought and forgot what I was doing."

Ruth is an iron-willed and rock-jawed Swede somewhere in her seventies, who has been my housekeeper

ever since I bought the *Oakalla Reporter* and moved to
Oakalla over a decade ago. Through the years she and I
have forged a friendship that is not likely to fail now that
we both are a little longer of tooth and shorter of time
than we used to be. A gambler at heart, as am I, Ruth is
the one person I know who truly is not afraid to bet it
all on one fickle roll of the dice.

"What thought were you caught up in?" I asked,
as I hung my coat in the hall closet, then sat down at
the kitchen table and began sorting through the day's
mail.

"My niece, Sara. My youngest sister, Faye's daughter. She's planning on marrying Donald Priest."

I found a bill that I thought I'd paid and opened it.
That's what I like about utility companies. Make every
payment for a decade and you get no thanks in return.
Miss a payment by a week and they threaten to cut your
power off. Banks, too, have a notoriously short memory.

"Is there something wrong with Donald Priest?" I
said.

"The man's half Indian, that's all." She opened the
refrigerator door and dug around in the meat drawer until
she found the round steak. "Who knows what he's liable
to drag in the back door? Or when?"

"In the form of what?"

I had given up on the mail. What friends I had didn't
write many letters. Neither did I, come to think of it.

"In the form of whatever he happened to shoot that
day. Or catch. Or trap. Or run over with his pickup. One
thing that girl will never have to worry about is running
short of meat."

"Why don't you buy her a freezer?" I said as a joke.

She took the Crisco down from the cupboard and used a wooden spoon to transfer a glob of it into the skillet. Then set the flame on medium high and waited for the Crisco to get hot.

"I went up to Bass Appliances today with the intention of doing that very thing. But all the freezers that they had in there weren't big enough to hold a good-sized turkey, let alone a moose or two. I asked him what happened to the big one that he used to have in the back, you know, the one Aunt Emma thought about buying for the conservation club, and he said they sold it three or four years ago. I asked him if he could order one like that for me, and he said his company didn't make them that big any more."

Ruth walked over to the sink, stuck her finger to the faucet, and returned with a drop of water that she flicked into the skillet to test the Crisco. They could probably hear the pop and sizzle all the way uptown.

"Hot enough," she said, as she laid the round steak into it.

After she'd browned the round steak, she peeled and halved some potatoes, put the potatoes in with the steak, added some water, covered the skillet, and set it in the oven. An hour later we'd eat.

"So how did your day go?" she said as she sat down at the table.

"Have you heard what we found in Amos Hogue's dump?"

If she hadn't, it would be a first. Ruth and her compatriots, which included friends and several dozen relatives scattered about the state, had a communications network that was second to none.

"No head, hands, or feet from what I hear," she said.

"You heard right."

"I wonder why that is?"

"Probably so nobody can identify him."

"Do you think he's from around here?"

"I don't know. We'll have to see who's missing."

"We?"

"Clarkie, I should have said. It's his case until he says otherwise."

"Then it will never be solved."

"It might not be anyway. Not if we can't identify the body."

She sat with both elbows on the table, her hands folded, and her chin resting on her hands. "Do you think this body has anything to do with all the robberies we've had lately?" she asked.

"It could. I don't know. What do you think?"

"Let me chew on it for a while," she said. "But the one thing about these robberies that everybody keeps forgetting is that they have been going on for years now. It's just here lately that we've had an epidemic of them."

She was right. For the past several years isolated homes around Oakalla had been burglarized on an average of about three or four a year. But the deluge had started only about six months ago. What had changed in Oakalla at that time? I put the question to Ruth, who obviously had been thinking about it.

"I don't know. But something did," she said with certainty.

"That's your answer?" I said, disappointed.

"Until I can come up with a better one."

"Then maybe you can help me out with something. What's the story on that property, there where the hog barn burned several years ago? Didn't that belong to Clarence Hogue at one time?"

Clarence Hogue was Amos Hogue's first cousin. He was also Amos Hogue's chief critic and had recently called the DNR in on Amos for maintaining an unsanitary hog lot.

"It belonged to Clarence until he went bankrupt," she said. "Then he had to sell out to Amos."

"Why to Amos?"

"Because he was the only one to make an offer on it."

"Why was that?" I persisted.

"Because no one else wants to live across from Amos Hogue."

Another question had been eating at me all afternoon, ever since Stella, the witch, had raised it. "Then who owns the big house on the hill? You know, the one that the self-proclaimed witch lives in?"

"I assume Amos does. He owns about everything else in Hogue Valley."

"Hogue Valley? I never heard it called that before."

"That's because you're not as old as I am."

"What does that have to do with it?"

"Here. I'll show you."

She went to our bookshelves in the living room—the ones that I had built on either side of the fireplace several years ago when I still had time for that sort of thing, and she returned with a copy of the 1910 *Adams County Atlas*. She leafed through it until she found the page that she wanted and handed the atlas to me. I laid it down on the table where I could study it.

Immediately I was struck by two observations. There really was a place named Hogue Valley once upon a time. What a place it was!

"Was it really this beautiful?" I asked, unable to get over the harmony and grandeur of it.

"To my eyes, it was the prettiest place in the county." Which was saying a lot because Ruth handed out compliments about as often as she did hundred dollar bills.

"I wish I could have seen it then."

"You'd have been right in your element, that's for sure," Ruth acknowledged. Unlike me, she held no reverence for the past.

For the next few seconds I lost myself in time, as I sat gazing at what had once been the Hogue Valley farm. The orange brick house on the hill, complete then in all of its splendor, with an equally magnificent barn that stood on the crest of the ridge behind it, belonged to Cecil Hogue, Senior. The house at the foot of the hill, a neat two-story frame house, the one that now stood vacant beside the blackened hog barn, belonged to Cecil Hogue, Junior. Wooden worm fences partitioned the farm into pastures and meadows where sheep, cattle, and horses grazed ever so contentedly, and several streams, five of them in all, wound their way through the meadows past stately pines and limestone outcroppings, as a horse and buggy and a Model T Ford sat facing each other on County Road 425, while their drivers seemingly exchanged pleasantries. In real life, I had seen such a magnificent farm only twice before. One, a few miles east of Wolf Creek Pass in Colorado; the other on U.S. 60 between Frankfort and Lexington, Kentucky.

"It's hard to believe," I said, closing the atlas, "how far down it's gone since then."

"Remember, Garth, that's a drawing, not a photograph," Ruth pointed out. "Our mind's eye is not always what's really there."

"Still," I said. "Still. What a marvelous place it must have been. And to think, Amos Hogue owns it all now. How could that happen, Ruth? Old Cecil Hogue, Senior, must be rolling over in his grave."

"Do you want an answer?"

"If you have one."

"It's not so hard to figure out. Cecil Hogue, Senior, had just one son, Cecil Hogue, Junior. Cecil Hogue, Junior, had two sons, Ben and Marvin Hogue. Ben Hogue had a son and a daughter, Clarence and Cassandra Hogue. Marvin Hogue had only a son, Amos Hogue. You start with a section of land, which is 640 acres, divide that in two, which was what Ben and Marvin Hogue did, and you get 320 acres apiece, which was Amos's lot when his father, Marvin, died, and which was Clarence Hogue's lot when his father, Ben died. Amos bought Clarence's lot from him, so now he owns it all."

"Aren't you forgetting somebody, Ruth?"

"Who's that?" Up until then, she was very well satisfied with herself, and it showed.

"Cassandra Hogue, Clarence's sister, or didn't she get a share?"

Ruth had to think about that. "I guess not. She must have left before Ben ever got around to dividing it up."

"Left for where?"

"San Francisco, the last I heard."

"Just like in the song?"

Ruth had sat still for about as long as she could stand to. She got up and began to set the table.

"What song is that?" she asked.

"'When you come to San Francisco, be sure to wear some flowers in your hair.'"

"Yes. That sounds right."

"You mean it fits her?"

Ruth already had the plates down and was reaching for the silverware. "Yes. It fits her."

"Do you remember what Cassandra looked like?"

"Why?"

"Just curious."

Ruth set a fork to the left of my plate, a knife and a spoon to the right. "She was a cute little thing. No bigger than a minute, if I remember right. But after her mother died, she sort of went wild, and there wasn't much her father could do about it."

"Not who I was thinking of, then."

"Who were you thinking of?"

"The witch that's living there in the house at the top of the hill. She's considerably bigger than a minute."

"People can change over time."

"So I hear."

Ruth had momentarily forgotten about setting the table. "Her age is about right, if we're thinking of the same person."

"She's the one who runs with Bruce Barger and Jeremy Pitts."

"That's the one. Sour as week-old cream."

"Maybe it was all a lie," I said.

"What was?"

"The song. Maybe she didn't meet any gentle people there."

For supper we had the steak and potatoes, shell-out beans with bacon, and canned peaches for dessert. I was on my way out the door when the phone rang, so I stopped to answer it.

"Hello," I said.

"Garth, it's Abby. How about if I buy you a beer later?"

"Sure. What time?"

"I should finish my rounds by nine. How about nine-thirty at the Corner Bar and Grill?"

"I'll be there. What about the autopsy?"

"That's what I wanted to talk to you about."

"See you then."

"Abby?" Ruth said after I'd hung up.

"Abby."

"Has she heard anything from Doc?"

Doc was Dr. William T. Airhart, Abby's Uncle Bill and Oakalla's most famous citizen. He and his setter, Daisy, were spending February in Sun City, Arizona, with an old friend of Doc's, who needed a checkers partner to help get him through the winter. Doc was doing so over Abby's and my protests. We weren't protesting the fact that he had gone to Arizona for a month, but that, at age ninety, he had driven the whole way himself.

"I think he's getting bored," I said. "In Doc's words, there's not a hell of a lot to do out there but play checkers and read obituaries."

"How's Abby getting along without him?"

I could tell by the look on her face that we were about to get to the crux of the matter.

"You mean now that we have his whole house to ourselves?"

"I don't recall mentioning your name."

"No. But that's the direction we were heading. So to answer your question before you ask it, no, we're not playing house in Doc's absence."

"Then that's sure a change from the past," she said with a smug look on her face.

"I'll be at my office if Clarkie calls," I said. Ruth and I could never discuss my morals without at least one of us losing his temper.

"Why would Clarkie call?"

"I just have the feeling he's going to."

"You can't keep bailing him out forever, Garth. One of these days he's going to have to stand on his own two feet."

"I know that. He knows that. But it hasn't happened yet."

"Neither is it going to happen if you keep coming to his rescue every time."

I reached into the closet and took out my coat, which like me, was starting to show its winters. "What would you have me do, Ruth? As Clarkie goes, so goes Oakalla. I can't let it go down the tubes just because he's not up to the job."

"You can't forever save him from himself either."

"Then I repeat, what would you have me do?"

"Let go of him, Garth. Let him stumble, let him fall. Let him drag this town down with him if you must, but let go of him."

"I can't do that, Ruth. I can't take that chance."

"Then it's you who'll suffer the consequences."

On that cheery note, I left for work.

CHAPTER 4

For the next two hours I sat in my office, laying out that week's edition of the *Oakalla Reporter*. Though mornings were my best time to work, I usually got more done at night because I had fewer interruptions. Also at night I was less likely to peek out my north window to see what might be happening along Gas Line Road. Though on a night as clear and clean as this one, I forgave myself one small break, to step outside and stare at the stars.

At nine-fifteen that evening I went in the side door of the Corner Bar and Grill and immediately headed for the corner booth that Abby and I had come to call our own. But it was already occupied by Bruce Barger, Jeremy Pitts, and the toady one who called herself Stella. Since I was already headed in that direction, I saw no point in stopping.

"Mind if I sit down?" I said.

Jeremy Pitts glanced uncertainly at the others, then scooted over to make room for me. "It's a free country," he said.

"No thanks to you pigs," Stella said to me.

It was the first time I had ever been called a pig. I didn't know quite how to take it.

"You've got Garth all wrong here," Bruce Barger said in my defense. "He's not a pig. Not a real one anyway."

Stella's pale eyes were small and hard, like two drops of sleet. "He knows what he is. So do I."

"What will it be, Garth?"

I looked up to see Hiram, the bartender, standing next to me. He must have sensed what was about to happen and moved to prevent it. Lucky for me he did because I was about to deck my first woman.

"Nothing right now, Hiram," I said. "Maybe in a few minutes."

"How about the rest of you?" Hiram said.

Nobody answered. Then Stella got up and went to the rest room. We all seemed to breathe a little easier.

"Budweiser for me," Bruce Barger said.

"Make that two," Jeremy Pitts echoed.

"You sure you don't want anything, Garth?" Bruce said, trying to make peace. "It's on me."

"Thanks, but no thanks."

"She didn't mean anything by it."

"That's where you're wrong, Bruce. She meant everything by it."

I got up and took a seat a couple booths away. Hiram returned with two Budweisers and set them on the table, but neither Bruce nor Jeremy made a move toward them. Stella remained in the rest room, or wherever it

was that she had gone. Then Abby came into the barroom and I could feel my anger start to lift.

"Are you all right?" she asked as she slid into the
booth across from me.

"I am now."

She flashed a smile at me and took off the same heavy
green coat that she had been wearing earlier that day. She
also wore the jeans and hiking boots that she had been
wearing that morning, and a powder-blue turtleneck
sweater. I liked her sweater. It went well with her yellow
hair and her rosy-red cheeks. And her perky breasts that
I was trying hard not to stare at.

"Who's the lovely couple in our booth?" she said.

"Bruce Barger and Jeremy Pitts."

"Which is which?" she said as she took a pack of Win-
stons from her purse and lighted one.

"Bruce is the redhead with the scraggly beard and
flannel shirt. Jeremy is the brunette with the ponytail and
the gold earring."

Bruce wore torn jeans, laceless high-top tennis shoes,
and a perpetual look of astonishment on his face as if,
somehow, life was always one step ahead of him. Astonishment, followed by brief flashes of cunning in those rare
instances when he thought that he had just figured it all out.

Jeremy wore a black T-shirt, a soiled black leather
jacket and cap, his jeans tucked inside black biker boots,
gold chains on his jacket, and a tattoo of a skull on his left
earlobe. Both he and Bruce were in their early thirties and
had lived their entire lives in Oakalla. Though perenni-
ally unemployed, they always seemed to have money to
spend. Welfare money, I guessed, which didn't endear
them to me.

"They're both guys, I take it," Abby said.

"Yeah. They're both guys." Though, because of his long hair and slight build, Jeremy could be mistaken at first glance for a woman.

"What are they doing in our booth?"

"Drinking Budweiser, it looks like."

Then Stella returned from the rest room and took her seat beside Bruce. If she noticed Abby and me sitting there, she didn't acknowledge it.

"Another of life's beautiful people," Abby said for my ears only.

"You're just mad because they're in our booth."

"Aren't you?"

"Yes. Mad as hell, in fact."

"Then let's rumble!" she said, starting to stand up.

I thought she was serious and had started to rise with her when I saw the smile in her eyes. "You're nuts. You know that," I said.

"Part of my charm."

"Agreed."

Hiram came over to our booth, and we each ordered a draft of Leinenkugel's. Meanwhile Bruce Barger, Jeremy Pitts, and Stella were deep in conversation. I wished I could have listened in.

"You seem preoccupied," Abby observed.

I nodded and told her what I was preoccupied about. "The woman who just sat down lives in the big orange brick house there along the road where we found the body today."

"And you think she has something to do with it?"

"I wouldn't go that far. But she has something to hide. I'm sure of it."

"Why do you say that?"

"Something in my guts tells me so."

"No other reason?" she said, not quite believing me.

"She just called me a pig."

"Pig as in cop, or pig as in oink-oink?"

"Pig as in cop. She doesn't like me. The feeling's mutual."

"But you're not really a cop, Garth."

"Try to tell her that."

I heard the thump of heavy footfalls heading our way, then saw the swinging doors that separated the barroom from the dining room fly open, as Clarence Hogue strode into the barroom and cast a wild look about. A big, rugged man with coal-black hair and long Elvis-like sideburns, Clarence usually had considerable aplomb, particularly under fire, and a good-old-boy smile that assured you that all was well, even when you knew better, but neither was in evidence tonight. Something had spooked Clarence to the point of panic.

Clarence started for the bar, saw me, did a double take, then came my way. "You seen Sheriff Clark anywhere around?" he said.

I shook my head no. "How about you, Abby?" I asked.

"Not since this morning," she said.

Clarence ran his hand through his thick black hair and tried to calm himself. As he did, I noticed that Stella, Bruce, and Jeremy had ended their conversation and all were now staring raptly at Clarence, as if perhaps he were the first messenger of the Second Coming.

Seeing their interest in him, Clarence slid into the booth beside me. I had to scoot over to keep from getting sat on.

"A shot of Ten High, Hiram!" he yelled. "Make it a double."

"Is something wrong, Clarence?" I said.

He glanced at Abby, then lowered his eyes. He wouldn't talk with her there. Partly because she was a woman, but mainly because he didn't know her.

"I'll be back in a minute," Abby said, heading for the rest room.

Clarence used that opportunity to take over her seat. Neither he nor I was all that comfortable sitting there cheek to cheek.

"She's the new surgeon in town, right?" Clarence said.

"Right."

"She looks like a dandy."

"She is."

"Smokes, too," he said, picking up the butt that she had left behind. "I've always liked that in a woman. They seem to get with the program faster, if you know what I mean."

I knew what he meant, but didn't give him the satisfaction of telling him so.

"You said you were looking for Sheriff Clark," I said.

Clarence glanced uneasily at the booth behind me. "They'll let anybody in here," he said, and not in a whisper either. "Don't you people have homes?"

I was curious as to how Stella would react to that. I didn't have long to wait, as she raised her middle finger for all to see.

"Same to you, witch," Clarence said.

Hiram brought Clarence his double shot of Ten High. Clarence downed it in one swallow and ordered another, and the color began to return to his face. "Man,

I needed that," he said as he wiped his mouth with his hand in much the same manner as his cousin Amos had earlier that day.

As I thought about it, there were a lot of similarities between Clarence Hogue and Amos Hogue. Clarence had just spent more time polishing his act.

Hearing noises behind me, I looked around just in time to see Jeremy Pitts leave by the side door. Bruce Barger and Stella waited for the check, which Bruce paid. Then they left together through the swinging doors that led into the dining room and then outside.

Hiram brought Clarence his second shot of Ten High. Clarence tossed down about half of it, then rested his meaty hand on the table with the shot glass still in it. Now that the trio had left, Clarence seemed to relax, and found his good-old-boy smile again.

"Sheriff Clark," I said. "What was it you wanted to see him about?"

"I figure that's between him and me." He scanned the barroom. "Your lady friend must have gotten lost."

"I think she's waiting for us to finish our business."

He raised his shot glass, drank the rest of the Ten High, and sat his glass back down on the table. "It's finished as far as I'm concerned." Then he rose and left the same way he'd come.

A moment later Abby returned to the booth. "Is it safe?" she asked.

"I think so. What did you find to do in there all that time?"

"Read the walls. When I wasn't coming up for air."

"Stinks in there, huh?"

"Yeah. Like somebody just burned a rope."

It took a moment for that to sink in. "Stella?"

"That'd be my guess."

I shrugged. "I guess it's no big deal."

"Not where I come from anyway."

We waited out the silence that came between us. There are some things that you would rather not know about the person you love, even if they don't matter now.

"What did you find out about the body that we found earlier today?" I finally asked.

Abby looked discouraged, which was not her usual pose. Like Ruth, she could handle the ebb and flow of everyday life much better than I.

"Not much. I can tell you that."

"You were hoping for more, I take it."

"I was hoping for a lot more."

"Did he die with an erection, as Amos Hogue said he did?"

She turned about the brightest shade of red possible. "No," she said. "Why would he say that?"

"Wishful thinking perhaps."

"He did die with a full stomach, more blood in him than I thought he would have, an anchor tattooed on his left forearm, and the name Maggie T. tattooed on his right forearm."

"Why more blood in him than you thought he would have?"

"Because . . ." She paused over the brutality of what she was about to say. "Because whoever dismembered him used a saw. That had to take some time. He had to be bleeding the whole time it was going on."

"Maybe the cold acted as a coagulant," I said.

"That's the only thing I can figure."

"Is that the only thing that bothered you about him?"

She shook her head. "No. His skin seemed awfully rubbery to me, but maybe that was because he had been frozen."

"Rubbery?"

"Rubbery. You know, the way celery gets when you leave it in the refrigerator for too long."

"Is there anything else that could cause that besides his being frozen?"

"There probably is. But I don't yet know what."

Noticing the silence, I looked around. We were the only ones left in the barroom. Even Hiram had temporarily disappeared.

"Where is the body now?" I asked.

"Uncle Bill's. Down in his morgue." Abby's Uncle Bill had been Adams County coroner up until he had retired at age seventy-five.

"Why not at Ben Bryan's?" Which was where I would have preferred for it to be.

"Because it's my case now, not Ben's."

"Why is that?"

She shrugged. "Because, quite frankly, Ben doesn't know what to do with him. Neither do I, but I'll be damned if I'll just let him sit there and rot, which is what would happen if I didn't take him."

"I don't like his being there in your basement."

"I don't particularly either." She smiled at me. It was meant to be reassuring, but I wasn't reassured. "But what can he do to me now? I mean, even if he could rise from the dead."

"I still don't like the idea."

She reached across the table and took both my hands in hers. "Well, you'll just have to get used to it." Then she yawned, though she tried to hide it.

"I get the message," I said.

"Sorry. But it's been a long day."

Hiram came back into the barroom. I paid him and we left. The night outside was cold, but not bitterly so. It felt good to be on the move again.

"I wonder where all the cars went?" Abby said.

"What cars?"

"The ones that were parked in front of the City Building when I came in. I thought maybe there was a fire or something."

"Farm Bureau meeting, I think, if I remember my calendar right." That might also explain where Clarence Hogue had been before he rushed into the barroom. If so, it might do me well to find out just what went on at that meeting.

Hand in hand, we walked in silence the rest of the way to Doc Airhart's house. It was nice to be isolated by the cold, to have the streets of Oakalla to ourselves. It made talking seem all that more unnecessary.

"Well, here we are," Abby said as we arrived at her front door.

"So it appears."

"The corpse was in his early thirties and seemed to be in good health," she said, as if she had been reading my thoughts. "And he probably had hair about the color of mine."

"That's something to go on at least."

"Not much."

"Have you told Sheriff Clark what you know?"

"Ben said he'd take care of it."

I looked longingly inside where a light burned in the dining room.

"You could come in, you know," she said.

"I know."

"Even spend the night, if you didn't mind sleeping on the couch."

"I sleep better in my own bed."

"It's only ten days. Then my divorce will be final."

"What then?" I said.

"I don't know. You know that once we start, there's no turning back."

"I'm not sure there's a turning back now."

"You know what I mean."

I nodded. I knew what she meant. It wasn't the act of making love, but the idea that gave us pause. We knew that it would happen in its own sweet time, but that's what we wanted for it—its own sweet time, not something that we took just because it was there.

"We'll know when it's right," I said.

She put her arms around me and pursed her lips, guppy-like, to be kissed. "I can hardly wait."

Ruth already had the coffee on when I made my way down the stairs the next morning. Though not yet up, the sun at least had broken through the dusk on the eastern horizon and warmed the sky with its pink glow. Since Ruth was busy mixing pancakes for breakfast, I picked up the 1910 *Adams County Atlas*, which still lay on the table, and began to read where I'd left off.

"I'll be damned," I said. "Clarkie was right."

"About what?"

"It says here that Hogue Valley was once a station on the Underground Railroad."

Ruth wasn't impressed. "So is every other big old house in Adams County."

"That's what I told Clarkie yesterday. But this is the first time I've ever seen it in print."

She poured some vegetable oil onto the griddle and waited for it to get hot. "Don't believe everything in print. You of all people should know that."

"It also says here," I said, ignoring her swipe at me and the *Oakalla Reporter*, "that Cecil Hogue used to stand in the cupola of his barn and watch his trotters circle the track that he had built east of the barn. Imagine that, Ruth, if you can."

"I can. I saw the track once when I was a girl. Or what was left of it."

"Whatever happened to it?"

"It went the way of the rest of Hogue Valley, I guess."

The phone rang. Since I was the closest, I answered it. "Ryland here."

"Garth, it's Harold Clark. I wanted to catch you before I went to work."

"What's up, Clarkie?"

"Have you talked to Ben Bryan yet?"

"I talked to Abby last night."

"Same as, then. So you know what we're up against."

"I have a pretty good idea."

"It doesn't get any better on my end either. No one matching the dead man's description has disappeared anywhere within three hundred miles of Oakalla within the last week."

"That we know of."

"That goes without saying."

I looked to the southeast where the sun was about to make its appearance. Orange now, the sky promised another beautiful day.

"So what are you going to do about it?" I said.

He hesitated, then said, "I thought I'd turn it over to you. I'm up to my ears in other things right now."

"Such as?"

"The robberies for one thing. Then something else came up last night."

"Clarence Hogue?"

Again he hesitated before answering. "How did you know about that?"

"Clarence came into the Corner Bar and Grill looking for you last night. I assume he found you?"

"He found me." But that's all he would say.

"It didn't have anything to do with the body, did it?"

"No. It didn't have a thing to do with the body."

"Or the robberies?"

He didn't say anything.

"You still there, Clarkie?"

"Still here. But not for long. I have places to go and people to see."

"Same here."

I was about to hang up when he said, "Garth, you will help me on this body business, won't you?"

"I'll do what I can, Clarkie."

"Thanks. I knew I could count on you, Garth."

A half hour later Ruth and I sat at the breakfast table, each drinking a third cup of coffee after a breakfast of sausage and pancakes.

"So what are your plans today?" I said.

She eyed me suspiciously. "Why?"

"If you aren't too busy, I have a job for you."

"Which is?"

"To find out all you can about the robberies."

"I thought our illustrious Sheriff Clark was handling that detail."

She took a drink of coffee and turned another page in the 1910 *Adams County Atlas*. For someone dedicated to forgetting the past, Ruth knew more about Oakalla's history than almost anyone I knew. Save for Ruth's Aunt Emma, whom Ruth didn't count because she was kin.

"Clarkie *is* working on the robberies," I said. "But I have to wonder if they don't have something to do with the body we found."

"What makes you think that?"

"Timing as much as anything else. What else is going on around here that shouldn't be?"

"Probably more than either one of us want to know," she said without looking up.

"On a large scale."

She closed the Atlas and leaned back in her chair. "Nothing that I can think of. But I still think you're reaching for straws."

"Better than reaching for nothing."

"Where will you be if I learn anything?"

"At my office."

"I'll see what I can do."

I smiled. I'd hoped she'd say that.

The walk to my office was a pure delight. The sun was now all the way up and too dazzling to look at for long, while the cold seemed to condense the sun's brilliance and aim it at the snow.

I spent most of the morning on the phone, taking advertisements for that Friday's *Oakalla Reporter* and collecting local interest information from some of the many sources that I had cultivated over the years. In between phone calls, I was jotting down notes for my weekly syndicated column that now reached nearly all of Wisconsin and even had made some inroads into the neighboring states. It was nice to be recognized for my work, but even in Wisconsin, my name still wasn't a household word.

Ruth called at exactly eleven forty-five AM. She knew me well enough to know that by noon I'd already be on my way to the Corner Bar and Grill for lunch.

"Here's what I have for you. Make of it what you will," she said. "Of the last ten robberies, nine of the houses were insured by Jerry Patterson."

"What about the other robberies?"

"Hit and miss. There doesn't seem to be a pattern to them."

"Then it's probably a coincidence that nine out of the last ten fell in Jerry Patterson's lap."

"I'm aware of that. But you said to try to find out something and I did." She hung up.

Ten minutes later I left for the Corner Bar and Grill with three cassette tapes in my coat pocket. An hour after that I walked along Jackson Street to the far west end of Oakalla and entered Jerry Patterson's insurance office, which was really a converted room on the front of his house. Jerry Patterson used to live on a small farm at the east end of town. He also used to have a secretary, and his office used to be downtown above the First Farmers Bank. But that was before the hard times hit.

"I'll be with you in a minute." Jerry didn't look up. He was busy typing what looked like an accident report.

The hard times had started innocently enough about twelve years ago when Jerry's wife, Janie, then a beautician, fell for apparently no reason and couldn't get up.

In the tests that followed it was discovered that Janie Patterson had multiple sclerosis, but she was given reason to hope that with medication and therapy she could lead a fairly normal life. The fates had other plans though. Things went from bad to worse, and five years later Janie was dead and Jerry was nearly bankrupt. So he sold his small farm, let the lease go on his office uptown, and he and his son, Teddy, moved to the small house on Jackson Street where Jerry now lived.

All of us who knew Jerry wished him well. It seemed that after so much heartache he deserved to catch a few breaks in life. Again the fates intervened. Three years ago September, Teddy Patterson, a state finalist cross-country runner on scholarship at the University of Wisconsin in Madison, was killed just before dawn while running along University Avenue. A woman on her way to work hit him. She had dropped a hot cigarette ash in her lap. By the time she brushed it off and got control of her car again, Teddy Patterson was dead.

"Garth!" Jerry Patterson said as he rose to shake my hand. "I didn't realize it was you."

Jerry Patterson stood about five-ten, had a medium build, curly reddish-brown hair that he used to wear in an Afro, and one of those round, ruddy, forever-young faces that never seem to age. He and I had been friends ever since I had insured my house and the *Oakalla Reporter* with him. We had even fished for bluegill together a couple times on Grandmother Ryland's pond and for catfish on Rocky Creek a time or two in front of his cabin, but we were too busy with other things, it seemed, to take that fishing trip up north to muskie country that we had always talked about.

Jerry's grip was firm, and his smile, as always, was genuine. He seemed especially delighted whenever I came into his office, perhaps because I gave him so much business.

"What can I do for you today?" he asked.

Jerry sat back down and clasped his hands behind his head. I noticed that he still wore his wedding ring and that the eight by ten of him and his family was still on his desk.

"I'm not here to buy any more insurance," I said.

"I figured you weren't. But you could use more. I've told you that before."

"You and everybody else in the business." I took the nearest chair which, like everything else in the office except for the knotty pine paneling, had made a few trips around the block. "What I'm here about is the rash of robberies that we've been having lately," I said. "It probably comes as no surprise to you that nine out of the last ten were in homes insured by you."

"No surprise at all," he said, holding up the form that he had been typing. "If I didn't know better, I'd think that the thieves were trying to put me out of business."

"Is there any chance that is what's happening?"

He shook his head, looking grim. "No. It's a coincidence, that's all. At least that's what I have to think."

"That's what I figured. But I still had to ask."

He forced a smile. "Now why don't you ask me your next question."

"Which is?"

"If I'm somehow involved in the robberies."

"Are you?" I asked him point blank, which was the way he seemed to prefer it.

"No. Though I won't say it's not a tempting game to play."

"How so?"

"Well, from my end it would be very easy for me to know who had what in their homes worth stealing. It wouldn't be hard then to find someone to steal it and someone to fence it. In fact, that would probably be the easy part. Keep that in mind along with the fact that people are notorious for under-insuring their valuables, like jewelry, which is understandable, since we as agents save our company money that way in case there is a theft. So if there's a claim and we pay off and some of the valuables are later recovered, they then become the company's property. Or my property, if I decide not to tell the company about it."

"Could you get away with that?"

His smile left no doubt. "I could sure as hell try."

"But have any of the stolen items been recovered?" I asked.

"Not to my knowledge. Not any of those that I insured anyway."

As I looked around his office, which was nearly bare, going on Spartan, I decided that if Jerry Patterson was skimming money from his claims, he wasn't spending it on furnishings.

"Doesn't it seem strange to you, that none of the stuff has been recovered?" I said. "Where could it all be anyway?"

"Chicago, Milwaukee, Madison. Take your pick."

"They've got cops there, too."

"Yes. But lots and lots of places to fence it."

"You don't think that it all could be around Oakalla somewhere?"

He gave it some thought. "Now that you mention it, Garth, that is a possibility. It does seem strange that not a single thing has turned up."

"So where is all of it?"

He smiled and shrugged. "Your guess is as good as mine."

I'd risen to leave when I remembered something else I'd wanted to ask him. "Jerry, were you at the Farm Bureau meeting up at the City Building last night?"

"I was there," he said, not appearing eager to talk about it.

"I just wondered what went on?"

"The usual. Every year costs are up and prices are down, or so it seems. A bitch session. That's what it usually amounts to."

"No mention of the robberies or the body that we found on Amos Hogue's property?"

He found some papers on his desk to shuffle. "There was some talk about that."

"Which? The robberies or the body?"

"Both."

"Which was it that got Clarence Hogue so stirred up?"

He shook his head. He wouldn't tell me. "I'm sorry, Garth, but Clarence is a client of mine, too. You'll have to ask him that."

"Never mind. It's not worth the trouble."

I was almost to the door when he said, "Garth, there is something that I can tell you. It might mean something. It might not."

"I'm listening," I said.

"A couple days ago, it was right about noon I think, I was here in my office working when I heard a car door slam and saw this man get out. I didn't pay too much attention to him, but when the car drove on, and he just stood there along the street, I had to wonder what he was up to. But when I opened the door to ask him his business, he took off south along West Street."

West Street was the westernmost north-south street in Oakalla. It T'd into Galena Road three blocks to the south.

"What did the man look like, do you remember?" I said.

Jerry closed his eyes and put his right hand to his brow as he thought. "Medium height, sort of a stocky build," he said. Then he opened his eyes again. "Wearing a coat something like what you've got on. Only I think it might have been black instead of blue. A blue, or black, watch cap, and carrying a dark-blue satchel, like the one I had in the Navy.

"What color of hair?"

"Blond, I think. But I was looking into the sun at the time."

"And you say he was heading south on West Street?"

"Yes. The last I saw of him anyway."

"Thanks, Jerry. At least it's food for thought."

"That's what I thought." Now that I was here, he seemed reluctant to see me go. "We're still going to have to get up to the Flambeau one of these days," he said.

I glanced around his office at the muskie lures hanging by their treble hooks every few feet. Some of them were bigger than the bluegill in my grandmother's pond.

"One of these days," I said.

A few minutes later I stopped by home to pick up Jessie and to tell Ruth where I was going. Ruth was lying on the couch, reading a copy of *Archeology* magazine.

Apparently she had just finished the dishes because the drain board was still wet.

"I just got down here," she said, "so don't say anything."

"I wasn't planning to. I just stopped by to tell you that I was going out to Hogue Valley, that's all."

"For what?"

If I told her the whole truth, I'd never hear the end of it. "To look around. See if I can find anything that we might have missed yesterday."

"What brought this on?"

I told her about the man that Jerry Patterson had last seen walking south on West Street.

"Do you think he's the man whose body you found?"

"I think it's a possibility. Jerry said he was carrying a blue satchel and wearing a blue or black watch cap. Abby said that the man we found had the tattoo of an anchor on his left forearm. It all seems to fit."

"Navy, you mean?"

"Yes."

"What would somebody from the Navy be doing way out here?"

"I have no idea. But call Clarkie for me, will you, when you get a chance? Tell him what Jerry Patterson told me."

She returned to reading her magazine. "When I get a chance." A moment later she looked up again, perhaps because I still stood there. "Was there something else, Garth?"

"Jerry Patterson," I said. "Is there any chance that he's involved in these robberies?" I didn't think so, but I wanted to be reassured.

Her look said it all. "Do you even want me to answer that?"

"He's fallen on hard times. Janie's MS nearly wiped him out. Then Teddy was killed. If I were he, I might be thinking of taking some shortcuts about now."

"But you wouldn't, would you?"

"I don't know, Ruth. I've never been put in that situation."

"We don't change, Garth. Or rather life doesn't change us. Not inside, where it counts."

"It's changed me. Not for the better either."

She sat up and laid her magazine aside. Now that I'd interrupted her tranquillity, I was about to get both barrels.

She said, "You just think that, because like me, you're getting some age on you and can't do all of the things you used to do. Or in your mind be all of the things you thought you'd be when God first set the table. But you don't sell your soul because of it. You take what life gives you and go on, thankful for that. Thankful that the world didn't end yesterday and you still have something to complain about."

She rose and went into the bathroom. Discussion closed.

CHAPTER **6**

Jezebel, alias Jessie, waited for me in the garage. Jessie was the ancient sedan that I had inherited from Grandmother Ryland, along with Grandmother's small farm and the money to buy the *Oakalla Reporter*. A dowager, who ran only at her own convenience, Jessie had thwarted all of my attempts to keep her running for more than a month at a time and, subsequently, all of my attempts to kill her. More than one in Oakalla, Ruth chief among them, had urged that I get rid of Jessie in favor of a newer, more dependable car but, whether out of loyalty or obstinacy, I wasn't yet ready to cast her aside and thus end that chapter of my life. So, while longing for the day that she would go to that great junkyard in the sky, I put up with her, and she in her own way put up with me.

69

I drove west on Jackson Street, then south on West Street to its junction with Galena Road. There I got out of Jessie and asked the people in the nearby houses if they had seen anyone matching the stranger's description early Sunday afternoon. None had.

I got back in Jessie and drove east on Galena Road until I came to Bruce Barger's battered white Chevy pickup four houses down on the right. Bruce Barger was nowhere in sight, however. Neither did he answer his door when I knocked, though I was certain that he was home. Neither did his neighbors answer their doors when I knocked. I was starting to feel unwelcome.

Clarence Hogue wasn't answering his door either. I determined that after knocking several times with no response.

Clarence had bought the old Miller place just west of Oakalla, bulldozed a lot of trees, reshaped the old brick farmhouse into what looked like a Tudor mansion, and started to put in a pond in front of it. The effect was striking. Before I could drive Galena Road all the way to Rocky Creek bridge and not notice a thing. Now, I couldn't drive it without seeing Clarence's house and wondering when he was ever going to get his pond finished.

I climbed into Jessie and started for Hogue Valley. All the while I kept shuffling the three cassette tapes now lying on Jessie's seat.

Alma Hogue was a tall, thin, almost frail-looking woman with soft brownish-white hair, a narrow friendly face, and soft sad eyes. Fifty at her last birthday, she and I had become acquainted three years ago when, unexpectedly, she had carried a guitar into my office at the

Oakalla Reporter and asked me to listen to a song that she had written.

Shyly, her eyes never leaving the guitar, and so softly that I could barely hear the words, she had then sung me a love song, which, as love songs went, wasn't bad.

"What do you think?" she had asked when she finished. She still wouldn't look at me.

"Pretty good."

"But not great?"

"No. Not great."

"I want it to be great."

What followed for the next few months was a weekly appearance by Alma Hogue at the *Oakalla Reporter*. She always came carrying her guitar, wearing a long, plain, sparrow-brown dress and white low-cut tennis shoes, and driving an old green GMC pickup splattered with mud and hog manure. And she always sang me a love song— all of which were good, none of which were great.

For the first few weeks, I enjoyed her company and her songs—up until the time that she looked up from the guitar, gave me a smile, and never lowered her eyes again. She had not said whom the songs were for. I had always assumed that they were for someone else, actually a fictional someone that she had dreamed up in her lonely kitchen there in Hogue Valley. But when I caught that first glimpse that they might be for me, I began to retreat. A sensitive, observant woman, Alma noticed my retreat and mistook it for rejection. So the visits, which became increasingly rare and more painful for both of us, finally stopped. But not before she gave me three cassette tapes to listen to in my spare time.

Had I listened to them? I didn't think so. Though she would never know that.

Alma Hogue came to the back door, wearing a blue print apron over her plain brown dress, white low-cut tennis shoes, and two small silver barrettes on either side of her forehead to keep her hair from falling down into her eyes. Though not striking, she was in truth a pretty woman, who reminded me of a rose a day past full bloom. But it was her vulnerability that most appealed to me and from which I ran the hardest, since every wounded bird that I ever had sheltered and then put back in the nest had turned around and pecked me.

"Garth," she said in that slow musical drawl of hers, "it has been a while, hasn't it?"

"Yes, Alma, it has." I reached into my coat pocket and handed her the three cassette tapes. "I thought you might want these back."

She took them, reluctantly it seemed. "You needn't have bothered. I'd even forgotten you had them."

An awkward pause followed. It almost felt like a breakup, that I was giving her keepsakes back.

"Amos is out in the farrowing barn, if you're looking for him," she said. "We've got some sows due to pig any day now." She tried to make it sound as if it were a joint enterprise, as if her heart and soul were into hogs the way Amos's were.

"Actually I came to talk to you."

"About what?"

"A number of things."

"But not my music?"

"No. Not your music."

She seemed relieved. "Have a seat, then. I'll see what I can do about making us some coffee."

I took a seat at the table while she put some water on to boil. One look around her kitchen told me it hadn't seen too many improvements lately. The cracks ran deep in the plaster walls and the floor's brittle green linoleum had started to break away in places, showing the plywood beneath. Overhead, the white Formica-like ceiling sagged in the center, like a middle-age paunch, and the round fluorescent lamp attached to it sagged right along with it. Cabinets, stove, sink, and refrigerator all showed wear, and all appeared to be at least twenty years old.

Still, all in all it was a comfortable kitchen. Not a cozy kitchen, though. Cozy was Ruth's kitchen and Grandmother Ryland's kitchen, where along with the snug and the warm was a sense of security that you felt the instant you walked in there. Not only that you felt, but that you knew way down deep in your soul.

"Do you take cream or sugar?" Alma asked, as she served us each a cup of instant coffee.

"Both," I said.

She set a spoon and the sugar bowl on the table, then poured some two percent milk into a small cream pitcher and set it on the table. I doctored my coffee while she sat staring at hers.

"Amos prefers instant," she said as way of an apology. "So that's all I keep around any more."

"Instant is fine." I said. "It's what I live on at work."

"I hate instant coffee," she said, just before taking her first drink of it.

"How long do you think Amos will be in the barn?" I said.

"Not long enough." A hint of color appeared in her cheeks. "Why? What did you have in mind?"

I didn't say anything. Either way I went, I'd lose.

"Well, now that we have that settled," she said, looking away. "What is it that you wanted to ask me?"

I blew on my coffee, then took a drink of it. It gave me time to find my center again.

"Sunday night," I said. "Amos said that he heard a car drive by in the middle of the night and wanted to follow it to see what it was up to, but that you wouldn't let him. Is that the way it happened?"

Her look was noncommittal. "If that's what Amos said, then it must be so."

"What's your version of it?"

She took another drink of her coffee, grimaced in disgust, then set the cup as far away as she could reach. I doubted that she would pick it up again.

"I think we've both been a little jumpy lately because of all of the robberies that have been taking place around here. I know Amos has. Though I don't know why." As she glanced around the kitchen, her sadness seemed to deepen. "I mean, what would they find to steal here?"

"Doesn't Amos keep any guns around the place?"

"An old twenty-two that he uses to shoot hogs with. That's about all."

"What about money?"

She brightened, as if understanding something for the first time. "I completely forgot about that. He has jars of it hidden everywhere around here."

"Is there any in the house?"

"I don't know. I've never looked."

Her eyes said that she was afraid to look. But whether she was afraid that she might be caught or afraid that she might find it and thus be tempted by it, they didn't say.

"Does anybody else know about the money?" I said.

"Not unless Amos has told them. I haven't."

"But it is possible that other people might know about it?"

She smiled at me. I wished I could have known what she meant by it. "Anything's possible, Garth. We've both lived long enough to know that."

"So do you think that Amos's concern Sunday night was more over his money than the fact that somebody has been dumping on your property?"

"I didn't until now, but yes, that's what I think. Besides, nobody's dumped on us in weeks. Amos was just up there Sunday evening checking. Or at least I think it was our truck I saw."

"Why don't you start at the beginning."

She scanned the kitchen, as if looking for something. "You don't happen to see a pack of cigarettes anywhere around, do you? I thought that Amos's cousin Clarence left the tail end of a pack when he was here this morning. It would be just like Amos to hide them from me."

"Clarence was here?"

"Yes. He and Amos had quite a row about something."

"You don't know what?"

"No. I didn't hear most of it."

Alma got up and went to the waste basket, where she found a partially smoked cigarette and lighted it. Then she stood, keeping an eye out for Amos as she smoked it.

"God, how I used to love these things," she said. "But Amos didn't approve of a woman smoking, so I gave them up."

She hadn't given them up entirely, it seemed to me. "It's not the only thing you've given up for Amos."

"As you well know."

Alma had promised to marry her childhood sweetheart as soon as he returned from the service, but she got lonely in his absence and started seeing Amos on the sly. Amos was sixteen, she twenty-one when she got pregnant. Despite the scandal, they decided to get married, but lost the baby in its sixth month. Childless since then, they had lived for over thirty years in what was on her part a loveless marriage. Fear was what kept her from divorcing him. Fear of Amos. Fear of being fifty, and alone.

"Back to Sunday," I said. "How is it that you don't know whether it was your truck or not that you saw at the dump?"

"For one thing, it was nearly dark when I got home. For another, I wasn't paying all that much attention."

"Where had you been?"

She suddenly came to life, as her face took on a whole new evangelical look. "The Rocky Creek Baptist Church. We usually have a pitch-in dinner following morning services, then Bible study and another short service after that. It makes for a very full day."

"So it shows."

"I can't tell you the good it does me to get to spend a day away from here among people that I care about. Besides, it's the only day that Amos lets me drive the car." Which, if I remembered right, was a dark-blue Buick Electra, Amos's one nod at luxury.

"You came home from church and went into the house, after noticing that someone was parked down by your dump. Was it a car or a pickup that you saw?"

"A pickup, I think. But I'm not sure."

"Light or dark?"

She went to the sink, where she doused the cigarette that she had smoked all the way down to the filter. Then she threw the cigarette back in the waste basket and opened the back door a crack to let the smoke out.

"I really can't say, Garth. As I said, it was nearly dark."

"Did that vehicle then drive by here later?"

"It might have. But in the meantime I had turned the TV on and was watching it."

"When did Amos make his appearance here in the house that evening?"

She seemed distracted by something outside, or maybe her intuition said that trouble was on its way. "An hour or so after I got home. I asked what he had been up to, but he didn't much want to talk about it."

"But you are the one who later that night kept Amos from chasing down the car that drove by here?"

"I told him that I thought it was stupid to climb out of a warm bed and go out into the cold," she said. "But I didn't hogtie him or anything to keep him here."

"Was the car driving by here slowly? Was that what alerted Amos?"

"Yes. Very slowly, it seemed."

The back door banged open. I smelled Amos Hogue at almost the exact instant that I saw him. He was carrying an armload of what looked like stove wood.

"Jesus Christ!" he bellowed. "Doesn't anybody but me close doors around here?" Then he saw me and lost his grip on the wood, which slid out of his arms and went rolling across the linoleum. "Well, well," he said. "Ain't this cozy? I thought, judging by the car outside, you were one of Alma's old woman friends from church."

"Afternoon, Amos," I said. "I was just leaving."

"You're damn right, you are. No man talks to my wife in my own house, unless I know about it, and that includes you."

I had forgotten all about the cassette tapes that I had delivered to Alma Hogue. But she hadn't. In a move so deft that I hardly noticed it, she swept the tapes off the table and into her apron. Then feigning sickness, she bent over to hide the tapes and ran out of the kitchen.

"And drinking my good coffee to boot," Amos said, kicking a piece of wood out of his way. "Why didn't she serve you some of that decaffeinated crap that she tries to foist off on me all the time?"

I heard a door close, and within seconds after that, I heard a stool flush.

"Morning sickness," Amos said, losing some of his anger. "It happens every time she catches sight of me."

I studied him, saw the sadness on his face, which he had evidently caught from Alma. Or perhaps she had caught it from him.

I stood, intending to leave, but Amos Hogue, all two hundred burly pounds of him, blocked my way.

"What are you doing here, Garth?"

"Just clearing up some details about the man you found in your dump yesterday. I wondered if Alma might have seen something you missed."

"Such as?"

"The vehicle that looked a lot like your pickup parked there by your dump late Sunday evening."

His face registered his surprise. "That's news to me."

"Then it wasn't your pickup?"

"Hell, no, it wasn't my pickup. Why would I drive a quarter mile down the road when I could just as easily walk?"

I had no answer for him, since I chose to walk at almost every opportunity. "Then do you have any idea whose pickup it might have been?"

"Nobody that I can figure." Then his face darkened, became angry. "Unless it was somebody dropping off that body."

"I wondered about that."

"But whoever that might be would have to have nuts down to his knees to be doing that in the daylight."

"Or be awfully desperate," I said.

Amos wasn't buying that. "How desperate can a man be who just cut off another man's head, arms, and feet? We're not talking desperation here, Garth. We're talking about a cool customer, who doesn't have a nerve in him."

As much as I hated to, I had to admit to myself that he was right. I started walking for the door. Amos stepped aside to let me pass but, as I did, he grabbed me by the arm and stopped me. Even through his thick cotton gloves, I could feel the power in his hands.

"As much as it hurts me to say this, somebody's been porking my wife, Garth, and I ain't so sure that it's not you. So if you want to keep things cozy between us, after this you'll let me know first off when you come onto my property."

I shook free of his grip, though it took more of an effort than I wanted it to. "I'll be sure to, Amos. As soon as you promise not to find any more bodies lying around."

"I mean it, Garth. Law or no law, which you really ain't if we get technical about it, nobody comes on this property without me knowing it." Since I didn't say anything, he followed me outside to repeat it. "I mean it, Garth."

I had an answer all ready for him, but with Jessie I had learned the hard way not to fire any salvos unless I was within walking distance of home. Otherwise, I might eat my words.

Instead, I changed the subject. "Alma said you and Clarence got into it earlier today. I didn't realize that you two were back on speaking terms."

Amos used the toe of his right gum boot to scrape a glob of hog manure off the left one. Then he switched feet and repeated the process.

"We're not on speaking terms," he said. "He came out here to voice his opinion, and I told him where he could put it."

"His opinion about what?"

"Private matter, Garth." His smile was unconvincing. "None of your concern."

I nodded as if I really believed him. "And Alma was gone all Sunday afternoon, is that right?"

"All Sunday morning, afternoon, and evening. If that woman spent any more time in church, she'd grow wings."

"Which left you alone here."

His eyes narrowed, grew suspicious. "What direction are we headed here, Garth? Of course I was alone here. I am every Sunday. Except for when I drive into town to get a Sunday paper. That dinky little thing that you put out won't start many fires."

"What time do you normally go into town?"

"Depends on when I get the feeding done and what else I have to do. It could be anywhere from ten until two."

"What about last Sunday?"

"I'd say it was close to noon. Why?"

"Somebody saw a hitchhiker heading south on West Street at about that time. I wondered if you'd seen him along Galena Road either on your way into or out of town."

"No. But I can tell you someone who might have seen him. That fat witch who lives in the home place up on the hill, and those two scuzz-balls she hangs out with. They were all standing around their white pickup when I drove by."

"Your renter, you mean?"

He gave me a shrewd look as if wondering how I came by that information. "Yeah. That's what I mean."

"Do you really own that property up there?"

"As long as she thinks I do, that's all that matters."

"Who does own it, then?"

"I figure Clarence still does." ·

"You didn't buy it when you bought his other property?"

"Nope. Just that one-twenty where the hog barn was. He said that's all he had to sell."

It seemed odd that Clarence wouldn't sell all of his land and be done with it, but I'd figure that out later.

"Have you ever taken a close look at your renter?" I asked.

He studied me, searching for my meaning. "No. Why?"

"Do, the next chance you get, then tell me what you think."

A smile crept onto his broad face and stayed there. I felt as if we'd just shared a lewd joke. "It's not possible it's Cissy Hogue, is it?" he asked.

"Cissy?" I asked.

"That's what we all used to call Cassandra when she was little. Cissy."

"But she and the one who calls herself Stella could be one and the same?"

"Anything's possible, I guess. But you sure wouldn't have thought it then. A size three, I think that's what she wore. And good looking enough to turn my head."

"She is your first cousin, isn't she?"

"Hell, Garth, what difference does that make? It's not like she was my sister or anything. Of course, if I had a sister looked like that...." His lewd smile returned. "Well, who knows?"

I got in Jessie and rolled my window down. "Remember what I said about looking her over."

"First chance I get, I'll do that. In fact, I think I'll head up there now." But he made no move in that direction. "After you get gone from here, of course."

"Give me time to stop there first."

"Glad to, Garth. Glad to." He sounded almost genial.

CHAPTER 7

But Stella wasn't home. Either that or she wasn't answering her door.

After leaving Amos Hogue, I had driven south to the dump where the body was found, crossed the fence, and widened my search from the day before to see if I could turn up anything that might belong to the dead man. On my third circle I did find something—a dark-blue watch cap half buried in the snow. But why was it there so far from the body? Had it fallen from someone's pocket and then the wind had skidded it across the crusted snow? Possibly. There was enough wind on Sunday to do that. Sunday evening anyway. I didn't know about midnight.

After a further search of the dump had turned up nothing else of note, I had turned Jessie around in the next wide spot on the road and driven to the house on the hill where Stella lived. On my way past Amos and

Alma Hogue's house, I noticed Amos standing at the back door watching for me. Whether he was curious about what I might find at his dump or afraid I might sneak back and try to "pork" Alma in his absence, I couldn't tell. But I did note, after waiting out of sight around the next curve, that he seemed in no hurry to follow me to Stella's doorstep.

Back in town, I went directly to my office at the *Oakalla Reporter*, worked until six, then drove home. As I put Jessie in the garage for good that night, I breathed a sigh of relief. Hogue Valley and back without that first hint of trouble. It had to be some kind of record. Or omen.

After supper I tried to call Abby at home, got her answering machine, then tried to reach her at the hospital, where they put me on hold. Five minutes later I was still on hold, so I hung up. I'd try to reach her later.

Meanwhile Ruth had started clearing the table and stacking the dishes on the sink. "Where to tonight?" she said.

"I'll be at my office until late, so don't wait up on me."

"I wasn't planning to." Then she noticed the frown on my face. "Something bothering you, Garth?"

"The watch cap that I found at the dump today. I can't explain its being there."

"Maybe it fell off when they cut off his head," she suggested.

"I don't think they cut off his head there."

"Well, maybe they were carrying it in their pocket and it got caught in a bramble or something."

"I thought of that. But then how did it get to where I found it? It must be at least a hundred feet east of where we found the body."

"Like you thought, the wind could have blown it there." Once the dishes were stacked, she collected the silverware and cooking utensils and put them into the sink to soak.

"I suppose it could have."

"How do *you* think the cap got there?"

"My gut feeling? Someone put it there on purpose. But why, I don't know."

"You will one day."

"I don't know, Ruth. Unless something breaks soon, I don't think we'll ever solve this one."

"Ten dollars says we will."

"You're on."

It felt strange to do that, since I had never bet against myself before. What felt stranger was the ease with which I'd done it.

"Hang in there, Garth," Ruth said. "Better days are ahead."

"That's what you said last year."

"Was I wrong?"

I thought about Abby and all that she had brought into my life. "You weren't wrong."

"So what's the problem now?"

"When I figure it out, you'll be the first to know."

Outside, the night was as clear and bright as the previous three had been. Three days of sun, followed by three nights of stars. After the coldest, gloomiest winter on record, it *did* seem like spring.

What was bothering me? Part of it was the body in Abby's basement that I wished had been dumped somewhere besides Oakalla. Part of it was the winter, which had gotten into my bones and stayed there. Part of it was my age, which had begun to show itself in the dust on my temples, and in my beard whenever I let it grow for more than a day. Most of it, however, was the realization that life had not gotten any easier as I had gotten older. Somehow I always had thought that it would; now I felt betrayed, that like Robert Frost, it had played a great big joke on me.

My phone was already ringing when I opened the door to my office. Good thing it was Abby, or I might have kicked my chair the rest of the way across the room.

"Is something wrong, Garth?" she asked.

I was bent over rubbing my shin. "Office surfing," I said. "I don't think I'm cut out for it."

"You *will* explain that later?"

"If you really want me to." I straightened up and tried to walk it off. "What I called you about earlier," I said. "Is that I wondered if you could stop by here on your way home from the hospital? I have something for you."

"It might be late."

"How late?"

"Ten or so."

"I'll be here."

After I hung up, I continued to lay out that week's edition of the *Oakalla Reporter*. But it was one of those nights that none of the pieces seemed to fit, and after a couple hours of frustration, I gave up and went outside. So still and cold that I could blow breath balloons, the night seemed to be drawing ever tighter into itself, as if by folding its arms and pulling its knees up to its belly, it could keep from freezing to death.

Then, from somewhere close, I heard the crack of a .22 rifle. It shattered the stillness and any hope that I had of getting any more work done.

A few moments later, Abby drove up in her dark-red Honda Prelude and started walking my way. She didn't see me until she was nearly upon me. When she did see me, she stopped immediately.

"Garth, is that you?"

"It's me."

"What's wrong? You sound funny."

"Nothing, I hope. I thought I heard a rifle shot a little bit ago, but I might have been mistaken."

"You don't act like you were mistaken."

I shivered. "Let's go inside."

Back in my office, I warmed up some water on my hot plate and fixed Abby and me a cup of instant coffee. Tonight she wore gray wool slacks, a blue-green ski sweater that matched her eyes, and the look of weariness that either a long day or a short night can bring.

I handed her coffee to her. She sat down on my oak desk facing me. I sat down on my swivel chair. Both the desk and the chair had come from my father's dairy back in Godfrey, Indiana. They were almost as much a part of me as I was.

"You said you had something for me," she said.

I scooted her legs aside, opened the top middle drawer of my desk, and handed her the plastic sack that contained the watch cap that I had found earlier that day.

"Where did this come from?" she said.

"The dump where we found the body." Then I told her about the hitchhiker that Jerry Patterson had seen around noon on Sunday.

"Do you think it's his?" she said.

"I think it might be."

"I don't like this, Garth."

"I don't either. It almost seems like a plant to me."

She said, "I mean the whole thing. I'm not enjoying my home nearly as much as I used to with that body in the basement. Something about him makes me uneasy."

"Besides the fact that he has no head, hands, or feet?"

She looked solemn, concerned to the point of worry. "Yes. Besides that. It's almost as if his mutilation has robbed him of his soul. That he won't rest, and neither will I, until he's whole again."

"That's a tall order," I said.

"I know," she said without confidence.

"Well, don't let it eat at you too much. I've already bet Ruth ten dollars that we don't solve the case."

She glared at me in anger. "Why in the world did you do that?"

I didn't get a chance to answer, as Clarkie burst into my office. Though I had seen him at his worst more than once, I had never seen him look quite so pale, or so terrified.

"Garth, I need you both to come with me. There's been a shooting."

I felt my heart ricochet off my ribs. "Who's been shot?"

"Jeremy Pitts. His sister just found him."

"Damn," I said.

Though Clarkie drove us the block and a half to Lori Pitts' house in record time, we could have walked and saved ourselves the ride. Jeremy Pitts was dead. I knew it the moment that Abby knelt on the kitchen floor and put her ear to his chest. Still, she covered his bloody mouth with hers and tried to breathe life back into him. When that didn't work, she cupped both hands over his heart and shoved down hard. I thought I heard a rib crack and had to look away.

Meanwhile Operation Lifeline and Ben Bryan had arrived. All of us stood watching helplessly, as Abby tried to make a dead man's heart beat again. When it became obvious that it wasn't going to happen, I reached down and put my hand on her shoulder.

"I know," she said. "But I had to try."

Then she got up and did a very unprofessional thing. She buried her face in my chest and began to sob.

"What are you standing there for?" Ben Bryan said sharply to the paramedics. "Get him to the hospital. We'll be along in a second."

Meanwhile I walked Abby around the body and outside. Her sobbing had stopped. But she still had yet to raise her head to look at me.

"What's happening to me, Garth?" she said in a muffled voice. "I've seen lots of people die, some of them kids, but I've never lost it before, at least not in public."

"It's Oakalla," I said. "When someone falls, it's like losing one of our own."

She raised her head. Along with the pain, I could see worry in her eyes. "It's not healthy to be so consumed with a town," she said, speaking for both of us.

"I know that. But I can't help myself."

"Neither can I, I'm afraid."

I waited outside while the paramedics put Jeremy Pitts into the Operation Lifeline ambulance and left for the hospital. Ben Bryan and Abby then followed in Ben's Oldsmobile Eighty-Eight.

When I went back into the house, Lori Pitts, Jeremy Pitts' sister and the owner of the house, sat on the living room couch, talking to Clarkie. Short, small, and dark, with long black hair, like her brother, wearing jeans and a black sweatshirt, and a tiny gold star in the lobe of each ear, Lori Pitts looked enough like Jeremy to be his twin. But she was in fact at least five years younger than he and at least five times more ambitious. Her old black Peterbilt truck cab was parked outside in the driveway. An independent trucker, she had probably just come in from a long distance haul.

Seeing me, Clarkie said, "Why don't we start over, Miss Pitts, so that Mr. Ryland can hear?"

"Hi, Lori," I said.

"Hi, Garth."

In the not too distant past, Lori Pitts and I had shared some late-night, hard-luck stories at the Corner Bar and Grill. Born poor, she had worked hard all of her life and still couldn't get more than a whisker ahead. Born curious, I had asked questions all of my life and still hadn't found THE ANSWER, or anything approaching it. So we drank drafts of Leinenkugel's, ate Beer Nuts, and commiserated.

"Long time no see," she said.

"I've been busy with work."

"That's not what I hear."

I shrugged and didn't comment. Lori and I had been good drinking buddies, but nothing more than that.

"I'm sorry about Jeremy," I said.

She glanced away. "Yeah, well, so am I. But it was bound to happen some day, considering his life style and all."

"Are you the one who found him?" I asked.

She turned back to me. Hard and dark, and intensely alive, her eyes reminded me of the bright keen eyes of a

crow. Lori Pitts was part Cherokee and part medicine
woman, who when you told her where it hurt, would tell
you what earth remedy to use to heal it.

"Yes, I'm the one who found him," she said. "I'd just
walked in the door when I saw him lying there."

I glanced at Clarkie to see if he wanted me to continue the questioning. But Clarkie wouldn't look at me.
He didn't appear angry at me, or preoccupied, but guilty
of some enormous crime.

"Tell me exactly what you saw," I said.

She took a moment to make certain that she didn't
miss anything. Lori Pitts was cool under the circum-
stance, a lot cooler than I would have been.

"Blood everywhere it seemed," she said, "though
really not all that much, I suppose. The phone was off
the hook and dangling on the floor. There was a hole in
the window. I could feel the cold air rushing in..." She
hugged herself, as if she could still feel it. "The funny
thing is, at first I was worried more about the window
than I was about Jeremy. 'A thousand mile haul and I
come home to a goddamn busted window.' Those were
my exact first thoughts."

"Where were you hauling from?" I asked.

"Didn't you hear what I just said?" Angry at herself,
she was now angry at me.

"I heard what you said. Do you know what my first
thoughts were after my son died? 'Thank God.' Not for
him because his suffering had ended. But for me because
mine had."

"But you didn't hang up the phone and tape a goddamn piece of plastic over the window before you knelt
to hold him, did you?" she shouted at me.

Without a word, Clarkie rose zombie-like from the couch and went outside. He and I would have to talk. Soon.

"Where were you hauling from, Lori?"

"Amarillo."

"And you say the phone was off the hook?"

"Yes."

"And Jeremy's body was where we found it?" Which was in front of the sink in reach of the phone.

"The exact same place." Her voice had gone dead. It was like talking to a computer.

"So do you believe that he was on the phone when he was shot?"

"I don't know. What do you believe?"

I glanced around the living room, at the Bedford stone fireplace and mantel, the gray shag carpet and matching gray sofa and easy chair, the blue-gray figurine lamps, a colonial man and a colonial woman, at each end of the sofa. Lori had spent the past five years and most of her money fixing this place up. I wondered if she would ever look at it through the same eyes again.

"I believe I'm about done asking you questions," I said.

"Good. Because I'm about done giving you answers."

"Except I need to know two things. One, do you know of anyone who might have reason to kill Jeremy? Two, what was he doing in your house tonight?"

"That's easy," she said. "I asked him to stay here while I was gone. I was afraid my pipes might freeze up or something, like they did last month."

"Did he often stay here while you were gone?"

"In winter he usually did. Not so much in summer."

"Where did he stay when he wasn't here?"

"Here and there. But usually at Bruce's."

"Bruce Barger's?"

"What other Bruce is there?"

"And the first part of the question, why someone would want to kill Jeremy?"

"I can't think of any reason," she said. But her eyes said differently.

"Well, if you do think of a reason, let Sheriff Clark or me know."

She nodded, but made no further commitment. "Am I free to go?"

"Do you have some place to go besides here?"

"I can find a place. If worst comes to worst, I can always sleep in my truck."

"Then you're free to go. Just don't go too far for now."

"And if I do?"

"Just don't. It'll make things a lot easier on all of us."

She gave me a look that I wished I could read. "That's easy for you to say."

She got up from the couch and wasted no time heading for the door. By the time I made my way outside, she and her old black Peterbilt cab were already gone.

Clarkie sat in his patrol car with the motor off. I couldn't even see inside for all of the frost on the windows.

"Do you mind getting out and helping me hunt for a shell casing?" I said after opening the passenger-side door.

"I already looked," he answered. "I couldn't find one."

"Where did you look?"

"Over by that apple tree where the shot came from."

"How do you know that the shot came from there?" Right next to the apple tree was the thick concrete wall of the storehouse for the cheese plant uptown.

Clarkie looked sullen and withdrawn. He didn't even want to be bothered. "Because, judging by the angle of the bullet where it came through the window, that's about the only place that the shot could have come from."

I walked over to the apple tree to see if he knew what he was talking about. He did. Then I returned to the patrol car where Clarkie still sat as I'd left him—arms crossed, a bullish look on his face.

"What are you pissed off about anyway?" I asked. I'd had about all of Clarkie that I could take for one day.

"I'm not pissed off," he said.

"Then what are you?"

He didn't answer.

"Clarkie, what the hell is going on?" I said, losing my temper. "Your town's falling down around you, and you sit there like a great big dummy with your thumb up your butt."

He wouldn't look at me. He wouldn't even try. "That's because I *am* a great big dummy," he said. "It's my fault that Jeremy Pitts got killed tonight."

"You can't be everywhere at once. Even Rupert Roberts couldn't do that."

"No. But I could have been here."

I looked east across Park Street at what once had been Jerry Patterson's happy home. Now abandoned and up for sale for at least the third time in seven years, it had begun to show the signs of neglect. The neighborhood, it seemed, wasn't what it used to be.

"How is it that you should have been here, Clarkie?"

"Lawrence Hogue came to me late last night and said that after the Farm Bureau meeting there was some tough talk about forming a vigilante committee and ending these robberies once and for all."

"How ending them?" I asked when he didn't go on.

"By shooting the robbers."

"You mean catching them in the act and shooting them?"

"No. Just shooting them."

It took me a moment to process that. Then I asked, "What does that have to do with what happened here?"

"Jeremy Pitts was one of the robbers. Bruce Barger and that witch who calls herself Stella are the other two."

"Do you have proof of that?"

"If I can ever find where they're hiding all of the stuff they've stolen. I think it's in that old brick house where Stella lives."

At least one thing became clear. "That's why you didn't want me to go up there yesterday. You didn't want me to spook her."

He didn't say anything, so I knew that I was on target.

"Why didn't you tell me that yesterday?" I said. "I would have backed off if you'd asked me to."

"Because I wanted to solve this case by myself, without your help."

He made no apology. I didn't expect one. He was the sheriff of Adams County, the one taking all of the heat right now. Not me.

"What is your proof that they are the robbers?" I said.

"An anonymous caller told me they were. He even told me where they were hiding the stuff they stole."

"So why haven't you looked there?"

"I need a search warrant. I can't get one without reasonable grounds. An anonymous phone call doesn't qualify as reasonable grounds. I know, because I tried for a search warrant and was turned down."

"Then it sounds like you've done about all you could," I said.

"Except to tell anyone else what I knew."

"You're the sheriff, Clarkie. You have to call them as you see them."

"Then you're not mad at me?"

"I'm mad as hell at you. But I'll get over it. Will you? That's the question." I closed the door of the patrol car and started walking south along Park Street.

By the time I'd closed up the *Oakalla Reporter* and walked home, I'd cooled down enough to call Abby. She must have been close to the phone because she answered right away.

"Hello?" She sounded unsure of herself.

"Abby, it's Garth. Sorry to call you so late, but I needed to."

"I'm glad you did. I was just getting ready to call you."

I smiled, remembering an old joke about a woman who is told by her doctor not to make love any more because it will kill her. So she sleeps upstairs in the bedroom and her husband sleeps downstairs on the couch until the fateful night that they meet on the stairs.

"Honey," she says, "I was just coming downstairs to commit suicide."

"That's good," he answers, "because I was just headed upstairs to kill you."

I told the joke to Abby and we both had a good laugh.

"Any ideas on who killed Jeremy Pitts?" she asked.

"No. His sister might have, but she's not saying."

"I know *what* killed him. It was a .22 long rifle. Or at least that's my guess."

"If we find the rifle, can you match the slug?"

"No. It's as flat as the proverbial pancake."

"Then how do you know it's a .22 long rifle?"

"Because I weighed it."

"Kidneys."

"Of course."

I smiled. It was hard to go one up on her.

"There's something else you ought to know. A hair sample from that cap you gave me matches the hair on the man in my basement."

"Why doesn't that make you happy?"

"I want the rest of him, Garth. I just don't want his hat and trunk."

"I know you do."

"But you don't think we'll find them, do you?"

"No. But I think our odds are better than they were just a few hours ago."

"Do you think there's a connection between the two deaths?"

I looked outside at a sky full of stars. Reassuring to know that they were still there, and that I could still see them, and wonder.

"Yes."

"Is that a yes I'm sure, or a yes I hope so?"

"A yes I think so. The deaths came too close together for me not to think that they are related."

"Are they tied to the robberies?"

"It looks like it." Then I told her what Clarkie had told me.

"Poor Clarkie," she said when I finished. "He tries so hard."

"You're not angry with him?"

"No. Why? Are you?"

"I could have strangled him earlier tonight."

"He does his best, Garth. That's all you can ask from him."

"But is his best good enough?"

"Considering all the grief he gets, sometimes I think so."

"He brings a lot of it on himself."

"Don't we all? Goodnight, Garth. Sweet dreams."

"You too."

She hung up. I did, too, eventually.

CHAPTER 8

The next morning at the breakfast table Ruth and I had our first real argument in a long time. The ironic thing about it was that she, who had once called Clarkie "the sorriest excuse for a sheriff since Chicken Little" was defending him, while I, who had been his staunchest (and sometimes only) supporter in Oakalla, wanted his head on a platter.

We were interrupted by a knock on the door. Hat in hand, Clarkie stood outside, looking like a lost pup.

"May I come in, Garth?" he asked when I opened the door.

I pointed the way and he came on inside.

"Ask him if he wants a cup of coffee," Ruth said from the kitchen.

"Would you like a cup of coffee?" I dutifully asked.

He shook his head no. "What I came to ask was if you'd like to ride along on some stops I'm going to make?"

"Where did you have in mind?"

"Bruce Barger's house, for starters."

"Let me get my coat."

Lori Pitts' old black Peterbilt cab was parked behind Bruce Barger's battered old white Chevy pickup in Bruce's drive. Clarkie looked at me at the same time that I looked at him. We neither one liked the implications.

"What do you suppose that means?" Clarkie said.

"There's only one way to find out."

To get to Bruce Barger's front door, we had to climb three wooden steps, then walk several feet along a wooden porch, passing a large single-pane window on the way. The porch railing and posts were painted brown, the rest of the house a bright metallic yellow that looked as if it would glow in the dark. But all in all, the house seemed in good repair, which for one of Wilmer Wiemer's rental houses was saying something.

"Garth, if you don't mind, I'd like to do the talking," Clarkie said when we got to the front door.

"Then why am I along?"

"To ask anything that I might miss."

"Fair enough."

Bruce Barger came to the door wearing a white V-neck T-shirt and baggy gray sweat pants. No shoes or socks. No expression of perpetual wonder. Red-eyed and unshaven, Bruce Barger looked grim, as if he'd caught on to life at last.

"May we come in?" Clarkie said.

He stepped aside to let us in. Apparently he had been expecting us.

The first thing that I noticed about the house was how bare of furnishings it was. The second thing was how warm it was. In just his sweats and T-shirt, Bruce was still overdressed.

"Is there any place to sit down here?" Clarke asked, shedding his jacket.

Though we were apparently in the kitchen, an overhead light, sink and card table were the only things in view.

"There are some chairs in the next room."

We followed him into the next room where four folding chairs, none of which matched each other or the card table in the kitchen, were staggered about the room, one of them facing a small color television and with a remote control lying on its seat. There were blinds on the windows, but no curtains. A pole lamp, an ash tray, and the bleached remains of a potted plant. Clarkie sat on one of the folding chairs. Bruce and I sat on the hard beige carpet.

"Bruce, who is it?" someone asked from upstairs. It sounded like Lori Pitts, and she sounded anxious, as if she were afraid of the answer.

"The law," he answered.

That was the last we heard from her.

"You know that Jeremy Pitts was killed last night?" Clarkie said.

"I know."

Bruce bowed his head and ran his hands through his shaggy red hair. Knowing and accepting were two different things.

"Do you have any idea who might have killed him?" Clarkie had brought along his note pad and was writing down Bruce's answers.

Bruce put both hands behind his neck and stared at the floor. "No. No idea whatsoever."

"You're sure of that?"

As Bruce raised his head to look at Clarkie, I saw anger on his face, and fear.

"Yes, goddammit, I'm sure of that. What are you here badgering me for? Why aren't you out there tracking down whoever did it?"

Bruce got up and began to pace around the room. Whatever was eating at him wouldn't let him rest, even for appearance's sake.

"To find out who killed him," Clarkie patiently explained, "we have to have some place to start. Since you were his best friend, we're starting with you."

"And I told you I don't know anything." There was a whine to Bruce's voice that I didn't much care for.

"What about all the robberies that have been taking place lately? Do you know anything about them?" Clarkie said.

Bruce stopped his pacing, as if struck with a sudden vision. "So that's what this is all about. You don't really give a shit who killed Jeremy, do you? You just want to hang my ass." His voice had plenty of volume, but no power, like that of a kid who just wants his way. "Well, be my guest. Be my frigging guest. Take a good look around this place and tell me what you see."

"What do you think, Garth?" Clarkie said.

"I think we should take him up on it."

Clarkie rose from the chair and walked to the foot of the stairs. I got up off the floor and followed him.

"Miss Pitts, I hope you're dressed," Clarkie said. "Because we're coming up."

Lori Pitts didn't wait for that to happen. Wearing last night's clothes, jeans and a black turtleneck sweater, and carrying her black suede cowboy boots, she hurried down the stairs and past us into the bathroom, which was located just off the kitchen.

"Don't let her go anywhere," I said to Bruce. "Don't you go anywhere either."

"I wasn't planning on it."

There were two rooms upstairs, both makeshift bedrooms, with only a blanket hung in the doorway between them. There was a mattress in each room, a sleeping bag on one of the mattresses, and a sheet, blanket, and pillow on the other. The sleeping bag looked relatively clean. The sheet, blanket, and pillow all were so filthy that they had a furry greenish cast to them. What looked like cereal bowls had a thick layer of dried milk in the bottom of them and spoons stuck in the milk. Glasses had been used as spittoons and then left on the floor, half-filled with tobacco and saliva. Cracker crumbs were everywhere, including on the mattresses and in cracks of the floor where the carpet ended. And sometime within the past year someone had tried to fix macaroni-and-cheese in an electric skillet, burned the lot of it, and left the remains on top of an old floor model Zenith color television. The television had been rigged with coat hangers and aluminum foil and plugged into an extension cord along with a lamp and the skillet.

I glanced at Clarkie, whose shade of green about matched that of the sheets. "Seen enough?" I said.

"How can people live like this?"

He covered his mouth with his hand. For a moment, I was afraid he was going to vomit.

"Good question, Clarkie." But not one I had an answer for.

Downstairs Lori Pitts and Bruce Barger each sat on a folding chair, but not quite facing each other, like two characters in a mood play, acting out their alienation. I didn't think Lori and Bruce were acting.

"Satisfied?" Bruce asked.

"You have a basement in here?" Clarkie answered.

"I don't think so. Do we, Lori?"

"No," she answered. "We don't."

I wondered what had brought Lori here? Surely not a bond of love, or even friendship. She seemed repelled by Bruce Barger, as if she couldn't wait to hit the door and start running.

For once in his career, Clarkie didn't take someone at his word. He went into the kitchen, searched for a stairway that might lead to a basement, and returned to the living room, looking defeated. Whatever he had hoped to accomplish here hadn't happened.

"Don't leave town," Clarkie said. "Either one of you."

"What do you consider town?" Bruce asked.

"You figure it out."

Good, I thought. Nothing like being specific.

"Are you ready, Garth?" Clarkie asked.

I took that as my cue that I could talk now. "Almost. I just wondered if either one of you owns a twenty-two rifle?"

"I don't," Bruce said. "I don't know about Lori."

"I don't either," Lori said. "But I keep a loaded .38 in the cab with me at all times."

"For protection, I assume?"

"You assume right."

"Well, let me ask this, then. Bruce, do you remember seeing any strangers in your neighborhood about noon on Sunday?"

Bruce shook his head. "I wasn't even here Sunday."

"I have a witness who says differently."

"Then he's a liar. You can ask..." He panicked as he momentarily lost his train of thought. He had started to say, you can ask Jeremy. But Jeremy was dead. "You can ask Stella. We were out at her place."

"You and Jeremy?"

"That's right."

"What time did you get there?" Then I added a small lie. "And I hope it matches the time that Stella gave us."

Bruce's look of panic grew. Like most habitual liars, he had no real feel for when someone else was telling the truth.

"Okay, it was early in the afternoon when we got to Stella's. But I still didn't see any strangers around here before then."

"Blond, well-built guy, wearing a watch cap, and carrying a dark-blue satchel," I said. "We found him the next day in Amos Hogue's dump."

I was watching both Bruce and Lori for their reaction, and got more than I bargained for. Lori got up and ran for the bathroom. Bruce sat there stunned and milky white, as if someone had hit him in the guts with a sledge hammer.

"Jesus," was all he managed to say.

On our way out, I stopped to tap on the bathroom door. "We're leaving now, Lori. Be sure to stay close, as Sheriff Clark said."

I got no answer.

Back in Clarkie's patrol car, we drove west on Galena Road. Clarkie sat darkly brooding, and as silent as a stump. I wondered what I had done now.

"Why is it, Garth," he finally said, "that no matter what I do, you always manage to make me look like a fool?"

"It wasn't my intention."

"No. But that's the way it always turns out."

"Would you like to let me out and you go on from here?"

He had slowed the patrol car to little more than a crawl, as if that's what he had in mind.

"What would that solve?" he said.

"At least you wouldn't have to feel like a fool."

He stopped the car in the middle of the road. I looked around, but no one was behind us. "The best thing for all concerned would be for me to resign as sheriff. I've given it my best shot, Garth. Nobody can say I haven't. But sometimes your best isn't good enough."

"I can't argue with that, Clarkie."

I didn't like saying that. He didn't like hearing it. "Then you think I should resign?"

"I think that it's not my decision. But I don't think it's a decision that you should make today, or even a week from today. Give yourself a chance at least to redeem yourself in your own eyes."

"What's the point?" he said sadly. "From the first day I took this job, nobody in Oakalla, except for maybe you, thought I was up to it. Now even you are having your doubts."

"I am," I said. "And last night I felt even more that way. But today at Bruce Barger's you handled yourself well. You acted like you were in charge, even if perhaps you didn't feel like it."

"You're right. I didn't."

He drove on. A quarter mile later we pulled into Clarence Hogue's new stone driveway, where we stopped again.

"But I'm not stupid, Garth." His face reddened at the thought. "And sometimes I know more than even you give me credit for."

"I've never said you were stupid, Clarkie. For that matter, you know a lot more about a lot of things than I do."

"Except people. That's it, isn't it, Garth? I'm not a student of human nature, like you are. All I know are percentages and probabilities, not the face of evil when I see it."

I saw Clarence Hogue round the corner of his Tudor mansion and head for his maroon-and-silver GMC pickup. "Nobody knows the face of evil very well, Clarkie. Not even when we see it in the mirror."

Clarence was driving fast to get around us with apparently no intention of stopping. But Clarkie let off the brake just in time and effectively cut off Clarence's escape, as he skidded to a stop inches from Clarkie's patrol car.

"What the hell are you doing?" Clarence asked, as he jumped from his pickup. "You damn near hit me."

"Morning, Clarence," Clarkie said, keeping his cool. "If you don't mind, I'd like to ask you a couple questions."

Clarence wore shiny brown leather cowboy boots, stiff new Levi jeans, a shiny brown leather jacket, and a thirteen-gallon cowboy hat—his idea of what the well-dressed auctioneer should wear. But his good-old-boy smile had run out of megawatts.

"Sale today?" I asked, forgetting my place.

"Sale tomorrow. I'm checking out the merchandise today."

I tried to recall any Thursday farm sales advertised in last week's *Oakalla Reporter* or any sale bills to that effect, but couldn't. But I kept my peace for now. I'd already asked one question too many.

"This won't take long," Clarkie said, almost apologetically. "All I need to know is who was heading up the vigilantes at Monday's Farm Bureau meeting."

Clarence looked perplexed, as if he'd never heard of a vigilante before. "I'm afraid I don't know what you're talking about, Sheriff Clark."

"You know damn good and well what I'm talking about, Clarence. It's what you chased me all over town to tell me Monday night."

I glanced up at the sky, which was about as blue as sky could be, looked to the west where a dark row of pines rose in peaks against the snow. Manure time in Wisconsin. There was nothing like it.

"I still don't know what you're talking about, Sheriff Clark. Monday night I went straight home after the Farm Bureau meeting."

Clarence was looking right at me when he spoke, as if defying me to set the record straight. But this was Clarkie's show.

"You know that's a lie," Clarkie said.

Clarence shrugged as if to say, so what?

"Was that all, Sheriff Clark?" Clarence flashed us his good-old-boy smile. "I'm already late as it is."

Clarkie was making no move to stop him. It took more than I had to let Clarence just drive away.

"Then you won't mind if we look around the place while you're gone?" I said.

Clarence's smile began to fade. Meanwhile Clarkie gave me a befuddled look, which wasn't encouraging.

"Why would you want to do that?" Clarence asked.

I waited for Clarkie to jump in and take it from there, but it didn't happen. "We just want to make sure that everything is up to the county building code," I said. "Isn't that right, Sheriff Clark?"

Clarkie was right at the point of saying, "What code?" when he caught himself. "That's right. With all of your square footage you might be in violation of Ordinance 97, which governs additions to existing buildings."

"That's bullshit and you know it," Clarence said.

"So are your answers, Clarence," I replied.

"I don't have to stand here and take this."

"Fine. I think Sheriff Clark has his own tape measure in the car."

Clarence first looked at Clarkie, then at me. "There is no goddamn Ordinance 97!" he said.

I shrugged. "Maybe so, maybe not. But there are a whole lot of other ordinances that we haven't even looked at yet."

Clarence's eyes strayed momentarily to his recently completed Tudor mansion, then to his unfinished pond that had a backhoe sitting at its edge, waiting for a driver. He had to be mortgaged to the hilt. And as the old saying goes, you can't fight City Hall.

"My cousin, Amos," Clarence said through clenched teeth. "He's the one you need to ask about the vigilantes."

"Thanks, Clarence. You've been a big help."

We climbed into Clarkie's patrol car, turned around in Clarence's drive, and left. The last I saw of Clarence Hogue, he was still standing where we'd left him.

"You did it again," was the first thing Clarkie said to me as we traveled west on Galena Road.

"What are you after, Clarkie, style or results? Who gives a damn who does what as long as we get at the truth?"

"Because you're the one who always gets the results. And I'm the one who always looks bad." He had his jaw set, the way he did whenever he felt backed into a corner.

"Jesus, Clarkie," I said, exasperated at him. "It's not my fault you asked me along."

He leaned forward and put a death lock on the steering wheel. We rode the rest of the way to Hogue Valley in silence.

CHAPTER 9

As we approached Amos Hogue's house, I noticed that the look on Clarkie's face had changed. No longer sullen, he appeared nervous, like a suitor calling on his lady love at her home for the first time. And when Alma Hogue answered the door and her eyes went from mine to Clarkie's I swore I saw a spark of something there.

"Is Amos home?" Clarkie couldn't get the question out fast enough.

"He's in the barn," Alma said.

As Clarkie hurried off in that direction, I waited to talk to Alma alone. Something had happened to her since we had talked yesterday. Her all-pervasive look of sadness had changed to one of fear.

"Alma, are you all right?" I asked.

"I'm fine, Garth. Why do you ask?"

"You don't look fine to me. What happened here yesterday after I left?"

"Nothing. I swear it, Garth."

"Amos didn't hit you or anything, did he?"

She rolled up the sleeves of her dress. Her arms looked pitifully white and thin. "You don't see any bruises, do you?"

"Some bruises don't show."

Tears came to her eyes, but she quickly blinked them away. "So I hear. You'd better go, Garth. I think Sheriff Clark's waiting for you."

I turned around to see Clarkie standing at the door of the barn, looking lost. "So he is."

"Garth?" she asked as I was starting to leave. "What's all this about? I mean what are you and Sheriff Clark doing here together?"

"Someone was murdered in Oakalla last night."

"Who?"

"Jeremy Pitts. But I don't think you know him."

She put her fist to her mouth and closed her eyes. "Oh," was what she said.

"What was that all about?" Clarkie asked when I got to the barn.

"Alma and I are old friends. We had some catching up to do."

"That was all you were doing, catching up?" he seemed worried about the answer.

"That's all, Clarkie."

Inside the barn we found Amos Hogue carrying a dead piglet in each hand. These he deposited in a pile of several other dead piglets, some of which looked as if they had been there for more than a day.

"Scours," he said, taking off his gloves and putting a chew of tobacco in his mouth. "Shit themselves dry. Once they get it, you might as well knock them in the head."

"Did all of these have scours?" I asked about the pile of dead piglets.

"Most of them. A couple were runts of the litter that couldn't find a tit to suck on." He spat on the floor and used his glove to wipe a dribble of tobacco juice off his chin. "So what brings you boys out here so early on this fine morning?"

Clarkie started to speak, then had to wait for a pig to stop squealing. Reaching for an ear of corn, it had gotten its head stuck in a metal gate and for a moment couldn't get it out again.

"Stupid bastards," Amos growled. "I should raise cows like everyone else around here."

I looked around the barn, which was primitive by even most hog barn standards. No steel automated feeding pens for Amos. No power washer for keeping the concrete walkways clean. No ventilation system and ceiling fans. Just a couple of overhead lights and a bare earth floor, most of which was ankle-deep in hog manure.

"We came to ask you a couple questions," Clarkie said to Amos. "About the shooting in Oakalla last night."

"Who got shot?" Amos said. He spat at and hit a hog that had stuck its nose through a nearby gate.

"Jeremy Pitts."

"That long-haired fag that runs around with Bruce Barger? Then they ought to pin a medal on the guy that shot him."

"Talk is that he might be you," Clarkie said.

Amos stared at Clarkie as he might have a toad that just peed in his hand. "Who told you that? It was Brucie boy, wasn't it?"

"Brucie boy?" Clarkie was already lost.

"Bruce Barger."

"What do you have against Bruce Barger?" Clarkie asked.

"Nothing that a couple sticks of dynamite wouldn't cure. The night my hog barn burned, who do you think I saw driving up and down this road at least twice that day and once that night? Brucie, and his little fag-buddy, that's who."

"I thought the fire was an accident," Clarkie said.

"That's what the fire department said. They said one of my sows knocked over one of the space heaters I had in there and set the straw on fire. But where I had those heaters setting, there's no way, short of flying, that a sow could have reached them."

The barn erupted in squeals as a hog got rooted away from the feed trough.

"Why would Bruce Barger and Jeremy Pitts want to burn down your hog barn?" Clarkie asked.

"You might ask my cousin, Clarence, about that. He's the one who's been buddying up to them all of these years. If he wasn't my own flesh and blood, I might think there was something queer going on."

"Let me get this straight," Clarkie said. "Are you saying that Clarence had Bruce Barger and Jeremy Pitts burn down your hog barn?"

"I'm saying that somebody did."

"Why? What did he stand to gain by it?"

"To get even with me for buying his property out from under him for one thing. To maybe ruin me for another." Amos's grin spread from ear to ear. "But as you can see, I'm still here." He patted his stomach. "And not missing many meals at that."

Clarkie seemed at a temporary loss for words, so I tried to help him out. "When you said *somebody* had Bruce and Jeremy burn down your hog barn, does that mean you're not sure it was Clarence?" I asked.

"Funny you should ask that, Garth. A day or two after the fire along comes Wilmer Wiemer, wanting to buy me out. At his price, which was chicken feed. Of course I refused. Then a couple more days after that, I get this anonymous phone call, wanting to do the same thing, only his price is lower than Wilmer's. I told him that if I planned on giving it away, I'd give it back to the Indians, where it came from in the first place."

"Noble of you," I said.

"That's what I thought."

"You have any idea who the caller was?" Clarkie said.

"Damned if I know. But he sounded hoarse, like he had a wad of chew stuck in his throat."

I watched a pig root an ear of corn out of the manure and eat it. I would remember that the next time Ruth fixed pork chops.

"You know we have a witness who says you were threatening Bruce Barger and Jeremy Pitts after the Farm Bureau meeting on Monday," Clarke said.

Amos as much as laughed in our face. "I did no such thing and you know it. What I said was that we ought to arm ourselves and shoot the thieving scums that were stealing us blind. At no time did I mention Brucie boy or his fag-friend by name."

"It amounts to the same thing," Clarkie said.

"Try to tell a judge that."

Amos was enjoying himself too much. I hated for it to be at our expense.

"Then you wouldn't mind showing us your rifle?" I said.

"What rifle?" A look of caution crept into Amos's eyes.

"The one you keep around to shoot your hogs with."

"That old thing," Amos said with a laugh. "Hell, it won't even shoot straight beyond a couple yards or so. I have to put it right up to the hog's head for it to do any good."

"Still, we'd like to see it," Clarkie said.

Amos gave it some thought, then said, "It's around here some place." Then he struck out for the other end of the barn as if he really intended on looking for it. "But you have to remember that I shot a sick hog with it yesterday."

We followed him to the other end of the barn and back again. Amos looked genuinely perplexed. "I don't know where it could've gone," he said. "Maybe Alma knows."

"Does she ever use it?" I asked.

"Sometimes. To shoot a sparrow that's been crapping on our car, or a stray cat that's overstayed its welcome."

"I thought it didn't shoot straight," I said.

"It doesn't for me. But Alma's a regular Deadeye Dick with it."

We all three went back up to the house, where Amos didn't even bother to try to wipe the hog manure off of his boots before going inside. Alma waited in the kitchen where I'd left her. I wondered if she had moved the whole time I was gone.

"Mother, have you seen my old twenty-two around anywhere?" Amos said. "The boys here seem to think it might have been used to shoot that long-haired friend of Brucie Barger's last night."

Alma's eyes widened. "No. You had it the last time I saw it."

Amos gave her a harsh look. "To shoot that sick hog with yesterday. Remember?"

Visibly shaken, Alma pulled out a chair from the table and sat down on it. "I think so. Was that yesterday, Amos? Time seems to pass so slowly lately."

"Alma's not been quite herself of late," Amos said in explanation. "A touch of the flu is what I think it is."

A touch of conscience was what it seemed like to me.

"Of course, you were both here all night last night?" I said.

Alma and Amos exchanged glances. His said that she had better back him up.

"All night," Amos said jovially. "There's nothing that Mother and I like better than spending an evening alone together. Isn't that right, Alma?"

Though he smiled, I could hear the threat in his voice. So could Alma. Instead of answering, she rose from the table and went into another room. A moment later I heard a door close and lock.

"She didn't used to be like that," Amos said, his mood turning dark. "Until she and a certain newspaperman turned cop that we all know started getting together at his place of business."

I wondered how he knew. For sure Alma hadn't told him, so he must have followed her into town at least one of the times that she came to see me. It made me wonder what else Amos Hogue knew and was keeping secret.

"Is that true, Garth?" Clarkie said.

I gave him a look that said to keep his mouth shut. But the horse was already out of the barn.

"Of course, it's true," Amos continued. "He ain't denying it, is he?" Amos opened the back door for us to leave. "I'd ask him all about it if I were you, Sheriff Clark, once you two are back in your squad car and off my property."

Clarkie hung his head and started for the door. I had no choice but to follow him.

"Head south," I said to Clarkie once we were inside the patrol car.

He did as I asked.

"Stop here," I said when we came to the dump where the body was found. "And don't try to follow me."

I climbed out of the squad car and made my way through a hole in the fence across the road from the dump. With its myriad springs, majestic pines, and clumps of cedars, this section of land was once a lot like the rest of Hogue Valley. But Amos Hogue had ruined it, or rather his hogs had. They had killed the trees and rooted everything else down to bare earth, until they were all that was left.

I climbed a hill, stayed on its back side as long as I could, then angled down through a clump of dead cedars toward Amos Hogue's barn. Manure time in Wisconsin took on a new essence when you were downwind of Amos Hogue's hog lot. Not that faint earthy smell of dairy farm that reawakened old memories and pulled you up by your heartstrings from the winter doldrums, but the vile smell of confinement, the smell of hogs forced to wallow in their own excrement. And it didn't smell any better up close. Wading knee deep in it amidst squealing hogs. Nearly losing your breakfast and your shoes.

At the barn door I waited a moment before going inside. Amos Hogue was nobody's fool, although he sometimes tried too hard to give me that impression. Neither was he a gentleman in any sense of the word. And certainly not someone that I would want to surprise in his own barn.

I thought I heard a door slam, gave myself a couple more minutes, then went on inside the barn. Nearly stepped on a hog half-buried in muck. Nearly stepped on another one while dodging the first. Grunts and squeals all about. Alarmed, several more hogs rose up on their haunches to see what was going on. I stopped and stood very still. All I needed at this point was a stampede.

While standing there, I heard someone come into the barn through another door. I crouched down and tried to make myself invisible as he made his way toward me. A nearby hog grunted at me. A friendly grunt, it sounded like. A "welcome to the hog shit" grunt.

Seconds later Amos Hogue came into view, gave that part of the barn a cursory glance and, apparently satisfied that all was well, went back the way he'd come. I heard him climb a ladder, then heard his footfalls in the mow above me. I took that as my cue to move.

But before I could clear the muck and get to a proper hiding place, I heard him on the ladder again. A moment later I heard him grunt as he dropped to the floor. I flattened out against a metal gate and peered through its rails to see what was happening. Nothing, as it turned out. Amos Hogue had left the barn.

Within seconds I made my way to the door that Amos had exited and glanced outside. Amos was heading for the woods to the west, carrying what looked like a rifle in his right hand. Then the back door of the house opened and Alma Hogue stepped outside.

She didn't see me. That was because her eyes were on Amos his entire way to the woods. I eased back into the barn, closed the door behind me, and left.

CHAPTER 10

Clarkie didn't speak to me when I returned to the patrol car. He didn't even mention how badly I stunk. I supposed that I should be grateful that he was still there at all.

We drove in silence past Amos and Alma Hogue's house, the fire-blackened hog barn, and on up the hill. "Stop here," I said on our way past the Hogue home place.

"Why?" Clarkie said, as he slowed, but didn't stop.

"I thought that you might want to talk to Stella, or whatever her name is."

"About what?"

"Jeremy Pitts' death."

"I don't want to talk to her."

"Then I do."

Clarkie stopped the patrol car, but made no move to back it up to the orange brick house, which was by now a good two hundred yards behind us. So I got out and walked. The fact that it was by now a semi-warm brilliantly blue February day, the kind of day that I had been longing for since last October, didn't make the walk a foot shorter, or my mood a watt brighter. So I really didn't expect much from Stella, the witch. She didn't disappoint me.

"Back again?" she said on opening the door.

"Back again."

She held her nose. "Now you even smell like a pig."

I didn't deny it.

Today Stella wore a brown rawhide dress that came to her ankles, a string of brown-and-white Indian beads, moccasins, no make-up that I could see, and that same old combative look on her face that apparently hadn't been softened any by Jeremy Pitts' death.

"I suppose it's too much to ask if I could come in?" I said.

"Do you have a search warrant?"

"No."

"Then, like the rest of the pigs, you'll have to stay outside."

I studied her as she spoke—her pursed lips, her pale murky eyes that reminded me of swamp water and the scaly things that lived there, her sallow skin, her dull brown hair. Nothing personal, her face seemed to say. She just hated me on general principles.

"You know, of course, that Jeremy Pitts is dead?" I said.

"I heard," she answered. "Does that make you happy? That Jeremy is dead?"

"Not very," I said. "How about you, Stella? Does it make you happy that Jeremy is dead?"

"Fuck you," she said.

I shrugged. "You don't seem to be in mourning. So he couldn't have meant much to you."

"Don't you judge me! Don't you ever judge me!" She screamed it, like someone who had been judged before.

"Then don't call me a pig."

"Oink, oink," she said, just before she slammed the door in my face.

A few minutes later I got back inside the patrol car. Even though the engine wasn't running, it was almost hot in there. Clarkie had his eyes closed and seemed to be dozing in the sun.

"Home, James," I said, trying to lighten things up a little.

Clarkie sat up in the seat, too quickly to suit me. He had been playing possum, waiting for me to make the first move.

"Did you say something, Garth?"

"Yes, God damn it, I said let's go. There's nothing more to learn here."

"If there ever was."

"It speaks," I said. "'Tis a miracle."

Clarkie started the patrol car and put it in gear. The sour look on his face said that he was about to lapse into silence again.

"I'm sorry for what happened, Clarkie," I said. "I didn't intend to hurt your feelings. But there at Amos Hogue's place, you hung me out to dry. That's not something you do to your partner."

"Is that what we are, *partners*?" There was as much hurt as scorn in his voice.

"I thought we were."

"And I thought partners were supposed to be equal."

"Not all the time, and not in the same way. The best you can hope for is to balance each other out, help each other over the rough spots. It's sort of like marriage, or so I've been told."

We came to Galena and turned east toward Oakalla.

"Or cancel each other out," Clarkie said. "Like you do to me."

"I can't help it if you don't always know what questions to ask," I said. "Like I said earlier, would you rather I just let you blunder through and we get nowhere?"

"I would rather...," Clarkie stared straight ahead. He was close to tears. "I would rather that you showed me some respect once in a while."

"I do."

"When?"

"Whenever I think you deserve it."

"This uniform doesn't mean anything to you?"

"Not a hell of a lot."

"It did when Rupert Roberts wore it."

Finally we were at the heart of the matter.

"That's because Rupert Roberts *was* sheriff, not someone who was trying to be sheriff."

Tears came into Clarkie's eyes. He looked as crestfallen as I'd ever seen him look. "Don't you think I know that, Garth?"

We drove in silence for a while. Why, I wondered, when the skies finally cleared and the sun came out, couldn't peace abound? At the very least, life could save all of its misery for the cold dark days of winter.

"Alma Hogue," I said to Clarkie. "What's the story with you two? Every time you even think about getting around her, you seem to turn to Jell-O."

"There's no story, Garth. Alma Hogue and I were once lovers."

"When?" Alma was at least ten or so years older than Clarkie.

"When I was sixteen. I used to carry her groceries out to the car for her there at Heavin's grocery. One thing led to another, and before I knew it, we were there in the back seat of her car going to town."

"Did Amos ever know about it?"

"I don't think so. He would have killed me if he had."

Clarkie and Alma. I had to smile at that combination. Gentle souls each of them, but with a side to them that no one knew.

"What ended it?" I said.

"Amos got wind of it and started coming in to town with her to buy groceries. After that, it just wasn't the same."

"It never is, Clarkie. Not once the thrill is gone."

"Tell me about it. But I still can't be around her without getting goose bumps. She was my first, Garth. And my best."

I nodded, feeling that it was just as well that Alma and I had never gone that far.

A couple minutes later Clarkie stopped the patrol car in front of my house. "Do me a favor, will you, Clarkie? Call San Francisco and see what you can learn about Cassandra Hogue. Or Cissy Hogue. Or some variation thereof."

"Who's Cassandra Hogue?"

"I think she might be the one who calls herself Stella."

"The witch?"

"Yes. The witch."

"What is it that you want to find out about her?"

"Whether she has a police record for one thing. And what that record is."

"Why?"

"You seem to think she's capable of robbery. I want to find out if she's capable of murder."

"Jeremy Pitts?"

"He and the body we found in Amos's dump. Even if she's not responsible, she might know who is."

"I never did like her," Clarkie said after some thought.

"That makes two of us, Clarkie."

"I'm still not sure if I want to keep this job or not," Clarkie said as I was about to leave. "Nothing happened today to change my mind any."

"It's up to you, Clarkie. I've said all I'm going to on the subject."

"But I do feel better now that it's out in the open."

I nodded. I wished I did too.

The first thing I did when I got inside the house was to go into the bathroom and take off my shoes, socks, and jeans. "Don't ask," I said to Ruth as I handed them out the bathroom door to her.

"I don't need to."

While Ruth took my clothes to the washer, I went upstairs to get clean ones, along with another pair of shoes. But even then, I could still smell the hog crap on me.

"Where to now?" Ruth asked when I came back downstairs.

"Wilmer Wiemer's office."

"To learn what?"

"Why he's so interested in Hogue Valley."

"And after that?"

"Lunch and the *Oakalla Reporter*."

"What have you learned so far today?"

I told her in brief then about Amos Hogue heading for the woods with a rifle in his hand.

"You don't think he was going squirrel hunting?" she said.

"No. I think he was going to hide his rifle."

"Why?"

"That's a good question, Ruth."

"You don't think he used it to shoot Jeremy Pitts, do you?"

I shrugged. "Where Amos Hogue is concerned, anything is possible."

"Speak of the devil," Ruth said.

"What do you mean?"

I turned around. Amos Hogue stood at our front door with one huge hand all raised to knock.

"Should I invite him in?" I said.

"Over my dead body."

I went to the door. Amos appeared upset about something. He also appeared to be hiding something behind his back.

"Is this what you were looking for when you were sneaking around my barn a little while ago?" he said.

"Is *what*, what I was looking for?" I said, half expecting him to hand over his rifle.

Instead he handed me a man's foot and ankle, or what the hogs hadn't eaten of it. "Merry Christmas," he said, then turned and started down the steps for his pickup.

"Where did you get this, Amos?" I yelled.

"Where do you think I got it?" He turned around to face me. "If I didn't know better, I'd think you put it there."

"Someone will be out this afternoon to search the place."

"Come ahead. I've got nothing to hide."

"Except a .22 rifle."

"You'll never find it now. I can guarantee that. Maybe if you'd asked polite, but you didn't."

"You've got a short memory, Amos. We did ask politely."

"Then came sneaking back onto the place. You ain't only a wife stealer, Garth. You're a back stabber. And I got me no use for either one of those." He got into his pickup and drove away.

"You heard?" I said to Ruth as I carried the foot back inside with me.

"Most of it." Her eyes were on the foot. "What do you plan on doing with that?"

"I thought you might call Abby and have her come pick it up. In the meantime, I'll take it down to the basement."

"What's she going to do with it?"

"That's up to her. But take my word for it, Ruth. She'll be glad to get it."

"She's a strange one, that girl," Ruth muttered as she started for the phone. "But I guess that's only natural, seeing who she's paired with."

I smiled in spite of myself. Only natural, I thought. Then, holding the foot out at arm's reach, I started for the basement.

Wilmer Wiemer was the owner of Oakalla Savings and Loan, the Best Deal Real Estate Company, several rental houses in Oakalla and several farms around Oakalla, and anything else that he thought might turn a profit some day. A small, dapper man with silver hair, tailored suits, a Lincoln Continental, and a million-dollar smile, Wilmer was one of those fly-by-night people that I liked wholeheartedly, but trusted not at all. And what I liked most about him were his style, wit, and enthusiasm, and the fact that he didn't apologize for what he was.

"Garth!" he said, pumping my hand, like that of a long-lost friend. "When was it you were last in here?"

We stood inside Wilmer's office at the savings and loan. In contrast to Wilmer, it was spare and functional with nothing up its sleeve.

"It was last July, if I remember right," I said.

"That's right. All that business about the missing Samuel boy. How did that ever turn out anyway?"

"We found him."

The smile left Wilmer's face. He remembered now. Then he shuffled some papers on his desk and found his smile again.

"So what's on your mind today, Garth?"

"Hogue Valley is what's on my mind. I hear tell you might have an interest in it."

"Have a seat," he said, gesturing to the pair of slat-back Shaker chairs that stood facing his desk. "They don't look comfortable, but they are."

I sat down on one of the chairs, which was not unlike sitting down on a rock. But maybe Wilmer's body required less comfort than mine.

"What is it about Hogue Valley that you want to know?" Wilmer said. "Besides my interest there?"

Never one to give himself away, Wilmer would tell me what I wanted to know as long as it didn't cost him anything.

"For one thing, what is it worth? For another, who owns it, really?"

Wilmer took his time in answering. He wasn't yet sure what my angle was.

"Not much, is what it's worth," he finally said. "Not if you've been out there lately and seen all those hogs running around."

I felt the color creep into my face, as I wondered if Wilmer could smell the hogs on me. Because I still could.

"It's a beautiful valley," I said. "If the hogs weren't there, surely somebody would be interested in buying it."

"The problem is, the hogs *are* there, Garth. And as long as they're there, nobody will touch Hogue Valley. Me included."

"If they weren't there?"

Wilmer flashed his million-dollar smile. "That's another matter altogether."

"And Amos Hogue is the one who owns it, right?" I said, fishing as I went.

"He owns most of it. Except that one-twenty where the old homestead sits..."

"Who owns that?" I said interrupting him, to my everlasting regret.

"Cissy Hogue, the last I heard."

"Had you also heard that Cissy was back in Oakalla and calling herself Stella now?"

"No. I hadn't heard that," Wilmer said. But I didn't know whether to believe him or not.

"Tell me this, then," I said. "What would happen to Hogue Valley if something were to happen to Cissy Hogue?"

"I don't know that something hasn't already happened to Cissy Hogue," Wilmer said. "It was my understanding that she hadn't been heard from for years."

"Then who pays the taxes on her property?"

"That might surprise you," he said.

"You?" I took a guess.

Wilmer's smile said he appreciated the compliment. "Clarence Hogue, Cissy's brother."

"Do you know that for a fact?"

"I know that for a fact."

"So Clarence is the one who has been standing between Amos and all of Hogue Valley?"

"That's what it looks like, Garth."

"Then let me approach it from another direction. What would happen to Hogue Valley if something suddenly happened to Amos Hogue?"

"Providing Alma Hogue would sell out?" Wilmer asked.

That was a possibility I hadn't considered. "Yes. Providing that Alma would sell out, which I think she would."

Wilmer's face said that he wasn't as sure as I was, perhaps because he was looking at it with money in his eyes. "Then there would be the maddest scramble around here that you've ever seen. There's not a real estate company in the county that doesn't have its eye on Hogue Valley."

"Including yours?"

"Knowing me as you do, what do you think, Garth? But like I said, as long as Amos Hogue and his hogs are there, you might as well be trying to sell off Death Valley, which," he added for effect, "is what I hear it's become lately."

"You didn't hear wrong."

Wilmer shook his head, as if a mutilated body was even too much for him to stomach. "They keep on going the way they are, nobody around here is going to get within rifle-shot of Hogue Valley, let alone think of putting a bid on it."

"Maybe that's their plan," I said.

"Whose plan?"

"Whoever killed the man and left him there. Maybe he's giving back to Amos Hogue some of his own."

Wilmer chewed on that thought for a while. "Maybe" was all he said.

After lunch at the Corner Bar and Grill, I walked to my office and began to sketch out my syndicated column for Friday's *Oakalla Reporter.* I knew what I wanted to write about, but so far hadn't tried to put my thoughts down on paper. As it turned out, I could have saved myself the trouble. All I could think about that Wednesday afternoon was what had happened the past couple days. Two bodies, and now an arm had turned up. It made me wonder what might be next.

A little after four I called the sheriff's office and got ahold of Eugene Yuill. Eugene seemed glad for the phone call.

"Garth!" he said. "There's a world out there after all."

"Slow day, huh?"

"Tell me about it. And I thought hauling feed was slow going."

133

"Is Clarkie around?"

"No. He's at home waiting for a fax from San Francisco. He said if you called for you to stop by on your way home from work."

"He'll be there at home, then?"

"Unless something comes up in the meantime."

"Have you heard anything from Ben Bryan or Dr. Airhart about that foot Amos Hogue found?"

"It's my understanding that Ben and Dr. Airhart are out there now, looking around."

"Thanks, Eugene."

"You bet, Garth."

I hung up, called Jerry Patterson, and got a busy signal. Called again in a couple minutes, got through, but no one was answering the phone. I was ready to give it one more ring when he came on the line.

"Farmers Home Insurance, Jerry Patterson speaking." He sounded out of breath, as if he had come from the other end of the house.

"Jerry, this is Garth Ryland. I didn't call at a bad time, did I?"

"No. I was just on my way out the door to see a client."

"This will keep, then."

"I've got a couple minutes. My client's not expecting me until five."

"You're sure?"

"I'm sure, Garth. Fire away."

"What makes you think I have a question for you?"

"I know you, Garth."

I didn't know why that bothered me, but it did. Perhaps because he was right.

"I do have a question for you," I said. "Do you remember when you said that the stealing and the fencing were the easiest parts of the burglaries? I was just wondering what the hardest part would be, then?"

"Getting it to a fence."

I looked out my north window and was surprised to see that shadows already covered most of Gas Line Road. I had to remind myself that this wasn't spring, but only its appearance.

"What's so hard about that?" I said.

"Nothing is hard about it if you do it in the city. But in a community as small as Oakalla, somebody is bound to notice if you're on the road in and out all the time."

"Apparently nobody's noticed so far."

I watched some kids walk down Gas Line Road on their way home from school. Two were carrying books. One was dribbling a basketball.

"Maybe they haven't moved the stolen property yet."

"Maybe they haven't."

But I still didn't buy his explanation about the comings and goings being hard to hide. Even in Oakalla, who the hell cared where you went once you left home?

"What's your explanation?" he asked.

The kid with the basketball was dribbling circles around the kids with the books until one of them kicked it into the nearest yard.

"I don't have one. Unless they're looking to move the stuff all at once and then get the hell out of here. It would be simpler that way, and I guess you're right, probably safer."

"I thought you'd come to see it my way."

"Have you ever thought of running for sheriff, Jerry?"

The question came right out of the blue. I didn't know that I was going to ask it.

"Not really. Why?"

"Clarkie's thinking about resigning. If he does, I'm not sure what we're going to do."

"Have him stick it out until May. Then we'll talk."

"What happens in May?"

"I'll have my thirty years in. I'll be a free agent, so to speak."

"You're not staying with the business?"

"I don't think so, Garth. Too many bad memories go along with it."

"The same could be said for Oakalla."

The kid had retrieved his basketball and was running to catch up with the others, who had turned the corner at Berry Street and were headed north.

"I'll give it some thought," he said, without elaborating. "Was that all, Garth?"

"I guess so. You did know that Jeremy Pitts was murdered last night?"

The silence that followed seemed as cold and deep as the shadows outside. A minute passed. Possibly longer.

"No. I didn't know," he said. "How did it happen?"

"Somebody shot him through a window."

Another silence, this one not as long.

"Where?"

"At his sister's house. Your old neighborhood."

The kids were now out of sight. Only the shadows remained on the street.

"That's not possible, is it, Garth? I practically raised those two kids."

"Something to keep in mind, Jerry, if we suddenly need a sheriff."

At five I closed up shop and walked to Clarkie's house. Clarkie lived in a small white bungalow with a red tile roof and a wide welcoming porch at the corner of School Street and Maple Street, and cant-corner across Maple Street from the City Building. The inside of the house included a kitchen, utility room, living room, bathroom, and two bedrooms, one of which Clarkie used to house his computer and the other electronic gadgets that he had accumulated over the years.

Clarkie had once made the statement that he could lose himself in his computer room and not come out again for weeks. Had I lost myself in there, it only would have been because I couldn't find my way out again.

Clarkie sat at his computer, looking about as contented as a man could look. He reminded me of me, as I sat down at my office desk each morning and began to plan the day ahead.

"What's that for?" I said to Clarkie.

I was looking at the flier lying on top of his printer. MISSING was printed at the top of it, and there was a picture of what appeared to be Lori Pitts in its center. I knew that Clarkie could do about anything with his computer, but I didn't know that Lori Pitts was missing.

"What's what for?" he said. He was preoccupied with punching keys.

"That flier on Lori Pitts. I didn't even know she was missing."

He stopped punching keys and gave me a puzzled look. "What flier on Lori Pitts?"

"This flier on Lori Pitts." But as I picked it up to show it to him, I realized that while it was a remarkably close resemblance, it wasn't Lori Pitts. "That's spooky," I said.

Clarkie wore a satisfied smile, as if he were a step ahead of me. "I thought so, too."

"Who is she?"

"Her name is Christy Morton. She disappeared from the campus at Montevideo early last fall and hasn't been seen since."

Montevideo was a small college town about twenty miles southeast of Oakalla. The campus belonged to Wisconsin Wesleyan University.

"Teacher or student?" I found it hard to lay the flier down despite the bad feeling that it was giving me.

"Student. She was sort of an odd duck, so there's some question about whether she was abducted, or took off on her own."

"In what way an odd duck?"

"A loner from what I understand. She didn't have many friends there at school, or any boyfriends to speak of. She spent most of her time either in her room or at the library. So for a while no one really noticed that she was gone. Not until her parents called the university, asking about her."

"Do you mind if I keep this? I'd like to show it to Ruth." Clarkie was pleased with himself. "Go ahead. There's plenty more where that came from."

I momentarily laid the flier aside. But I knew that I would pick it up again and again before I was through with it.

"Anything from San Francisco?" I asked.

Again Clarkie looked pleased. He was in his element and enjoying the swim. "You want to read it or do you want me to read it to you?"

"Just give me the particulars."

He picked up a couple sheets of paper, scanned them, and set them back down again. "The particulars. Cassandra Hogue, alias Cissy Hogan, alias Stella Hansen is currently wanted by the City of San Francisco and the State of California for burglary, battery on a police officer, and unlawful flight to avoid prosecution. Last seen in Daly City, San Francisco, California, October 28, 1991. Believed accompanied by Kurt Voege, alias Karl Voger, alias Kirk Vopeen, also wanted for burglary and unlawful flight to avoid prosecution."

"Can we back up a step?" I said.

"As far as you like."

"Any prior charges or convictions?"

"A weapons charge in..." He picked up the sheets of paper and read over them. "...1972. Charges were dismissed. Pleaded guilty to distributing marijuana in 1978 and 1984. Received probation both times."

"What was the weapons charge for?"

Clarkie laid the papers down on his computer and swung around in his chair to face me. "The way my source explained it to me, she was a member of a militant group called the Mainliners, which was a would-be Weatherman group, except not nearly so well organized. Because of her age, they let Cassandra Hogue go, but prosecuted most of the rest of the group. Which for all practical purposes ended it, since by the time they got out of prison, the Vietnam War or whatever it was they were opposing was long since over."

"So what happened to her between 1972 and 1978 when she was arrested again?" I said.

"Supposedly she fell in with a local biker gang, which, according to my source, is where she met Kurt Voege.

They've been together ever since, or at least up until October 1991."

"Describe Kurt Voege to me."

I thought that he might have to refer to the papers again, but I should have known better. Clarkie's memory was almost as good as that of his computer.

"Thirty-eight years old. Six feet, one hundred eighty pounds, blond hair, blue eyes, nasty disposition. The way I got it, he was the enforcer for the motorcycle gang, and later for Cassandra Hogue when she went into business for herself."

"Selling drugs, you mean?"

"Among other things. My source said that and the burglaries were just the tip of the iceberg."

"Who is your source by the way?"

"A detective sergeant in the San Francisco police force. As far as he's concerned, if we can charge Cassandra Hogue, we can keep her."

"Do you have a recent photograph of her?"

He spun around on his chair, picked up a sheet of paper, and handed it to me. The resemblance was unmistakable.

"She looks an awful lot like Stella, the witch," I said.

"She looks *exactly* like Stella, the witch," he corrected me.

I continued to read on down the sheet of paper.

"What is it, Garth?"

"Kurt Voege, Cassandra Hogue's partner in crime. I can't see any tattoos listed anywhere. For a biker, that seems unusual."

"Maybe they overlooked them."

"Not likely."

Clarkie took the paper from me and read over it again. "That still doesn't mean it can't be his body that we found."

"It doesn't mean it is either," I said, feeling disappointed. "I'll tell you what you ought to do, Clarkie. The nearest federal judge is in Wisconsin Rapids. First thing tomorrow morning, you ought to be sitting on his doorstep, asking for a search warrant."

"I already called him," Clarkie said. "He'll have one waiting for me."

"Be sure he does. We don't want Stella Hogue skipping out on us."

"I thought about that, Garth. But where would she go?"

At the time neither one of us would have ever guessed.

CHAPTER 13

At home Ruth was fixing supper—Polish sausage, fried potatoes, creamed corn, and beet salad, it looked like to me. I laid the Christy Morton flier on the kitchen table and went into the dining room to make a phone call. If Ruth noticed that I was home, she was doing a good job of hiding it.

"Abby, it's Garth," I said when she answered. "I was afraid you would already be at the hospital."

"Garth who?" she said. I couldn't help but notice the chill in her voice.

Then I realized what was wrong. "So, how did your trip out to Amos Hogue's go?"

Silence.

"Not well, I take it."

"How could you, Garth," she finally said, "send me out to that cesspool without even a warning? Do you realize that I've taken a bath and two showers since I've been home, and I still can't get the smell of hog shit off of me."

"Trust me. It'll go away on its own. I can hardly smell myself at all now."

"So you *do* know what I'm talking about?" She seemed to be thawing a little.

"I was up to my waist in it earlier today."

"Looking for what?"

"The rifle that might have killed Jeremy Pitts. But that's beside the point now. I'll never find it."

"Welcome to the club," she said, sounding discouraged. "Ben and I didn't find any more body parts either. I have to wonder if the hogs didn't eat them."

"That is a possibility," I said. "What about the foot that Amos found? Does it match the body in your basement?"

"Perfectly. That's what makes it all so frustrating. Four more pieces to go and I'll have a whole man again."

I didn't know how to tell her that I didn't think that would ever happen now. "Well, maybe this will help," I said.

I told her about Cassandra Hogue, and then about Kurt Voege, saving his description for last. But she didn't ooh and ah as I hoped she would.

"It sounds like he could be our man," she said.

"Even without the tattoos?"

"It's possible that he got the tattoos after he left San Francisco."

"Is there any way of dating tattoos?"

"I'm not aware of it. Not unless they're fresh."

"And his isn't?"

I felt something crawling up my neck and turned to see Ruth staring at me. Apparently she knew I was home all along.

"Not that I can tell. Nothing about him seems fresh, but don't ask me to explain that because I can't."

I waited for Ruth to notice the flier on the table and wasn't disappointed in her reaction, which was much the same as mine had been.

"Garth, there's something else that I should have told you. The meal that our man ate before he died consisted of some kind of fish. Deep fried, the way you'd get it in a restaurant. French fries and slaw. And lots of it."

I was watching Ruth, who was reading the flier for the second time. "That doesn't sound like lunch to me. It sounds more like supper."

"Explain yourself, please."

Ruth glanced up from the flier and gave me a "hurry up" look. But I was in no hurry.

"You remember that Jerry Patterson saw the man that we found in the dump about noon. Up until now I had assumed that he had been killed shortly after that. But maybe he was killed later on that night."

"And maybe he eats his big meal at noon. Or used to anyway."

"The question is, where did he eat it?" I said. "It wasn't at the Corner Bar and Grill because I've asked about him every time I've been in there."

"What's the closest town to Oakalla where he could get a meal like that?" she asked.

"It's not a town. It's a restaurant. Poor Willy's over on U.S. 51 about fifteen miles east of here."

"I think I'll give it a call," she said.

"Let me know what you find out."

"It might have to be later. I'm already late for my rounds now."

"Whenever. It's always good to hear your voice."

"Yeah. I know the feeling."

Ruth was waiting to pounce the moment I hung up. "Where did this come from?" she said, as she held up the flier.

"Clarkie gave it to me. He thought I might find it interesting."

"Who is she?"

"Nobody that I know. I just think she looks an awfully lot like Lori Pitts. Evidently so does Clarkie. What about you, Ruth?"

"Close enough to make me wonder."

Ruth returned to the stove, where she began taking up supper. I helped in my usual manner by staying out of her way.

"It makes me wonder if we aren't all seeing things. What could a college girl missing from Montevideo possibly have to do with Lori Pitts, a truck driver from Oakalla?"

"That's what I want you to find out."

She set the Polish sausage on the table, followed by creamed corn and fried potatoes. The beet salad went directly in front of me because she knew that's where I would start.

"Why me?" she said, as we sat down at the table.

"Because I've got a hundred other things to do."

"And I don't?"

"And I don't have the network you do," I said, continuing on as if I hadn't heard.

"What is it that you want to know about her?" Ruth took a piece of Polish sausage and handed the platter to me.

"Anything that you can find out about her. Particularly if she has any ties to Oakalla."

"And if she does?"

"Then we'll go from there."

We passed corn and potatoes back and forth until we both had our plates full. "What was this business about Cassandra Hogue that you were telling Abby about?"

Between bites, I told her.

She had eaten most of her supper before she said, "You should be out there with a search warrant right now."

"Tomorrow is soon enough. As Clarkie said, where can she go?"

She raised her brows, but didn't say anything more about it. Psychic that she sometimes was, she must have known that events would prove her right.

CHAPTER **14**

Shortly after midnight, while still mulling over Ruth's words of warning, I had gone to bed with a bad feeling in my guts and awakened with the same feeling. I went downstairs, put on a pot of coffee, and stood staring out the window at the beginning of sunrise. Copper on the horizon, overlaid by the palest shade of blue, the sky gave way to rose, then a darker dusky blue that would still be night everywhere to our west.

Ruth came down the stairs, gave me a bleary-eyed look, poured herself a cup of coffee, and sat down at the kitchen table where I had sugar and half-and-half waiting for her.

"You see anything out there?" she asked.

Reluctantly I turned away from the window. It was hard to describe a sunrise, even to a friend. "Nothing that I haven't seen before."

149

"When is Clarkie supposed to get here?"

"Your guess is as good as mine."

I poured myself a cup of coffee, doctored it to my satisfaction, and sat down across from her. Ruth had been in bed when I came in at midnight, so we hadn't exchanged notes.

"What did you find out from Abby?" she asked.

"Nobody at Poor Willy's remembers the man in question. But it's a busy place on Sunday, so he could've been there, and nobody noticed him." I took my first sip of coffee. The first sip was always the best. "What about you, did you find out anything on Christy Morton?"

"I found out that her grandfather lived in Oakalla."

"Who's that?"

"Andy Metzger. He died of prostate cancer last August."

I remembered Andy Metzger as a kindly, gentle old farmer who had sold his dairy herd about ten years ago and then moved to Oakalla a few years after that when his wife died. He was one of the faithful who used to loaf up at the Marathon service station with Sniffy Smith, Dub Bennett, and that cadre of grand old men whose numbers seemed to shrink every year.

"What do you know about Andy Metzger?" I said.

"I know he has a dingbat for a daughter, and a son-in-law who's not much better. Both of them professors, I think, somewhere in Illinois. You know the type, Garth. Book smart, but stupid about most everything else."

"So what was their daughter doing here, if they both teach in Illinois?"

"Think about it, Garth. What safer place is there to send your daughter than Wisconsin Wesleyan? Especially a daughter who's as addle-brained as you are?"

"Who told you that?"

"My niece, Ruth Ann, my sister Ellen's girl. She and Rachel Metzger, the girl's mother, grew up together. Even went as far as the University of Chicago together, where Ruth Ann dropped out after the first year because she couldn't stand city life."

"Does Ruth Ann have any idea what happened to Christy Morton?"

"She figures she flew the coop. According to Ruth Ann, that was probably her only chance to lead a normal life, by getting away from her family."

"So has her family heard anything from her?"

Ruth glanced outside where the sun was just up. "No. Not that I know of."

"How does Ruth Ann explain that?"

"She said the girl might be a little strange, but she's not stupid. She'll stay hidden as long as it suits her."

"So there's no connection between her and Lori Pitts?"

"Not that anyone knows of. Except the fact that they're third cousins. Andy Metzger and Frank Pitts, Lori's grandfather, were first cousins, which would explain the resemblance between the girls."

"But not much else," I said.

"No," she agreed. "Not much else."

A car pulled up out front. Then someone honked. "Have to go, Ruth," I said as I rose from the table. "But do me a favor, will you? Don't give up on Christy Morton just yet."

"I wasn't planning to."

Clarkie honked one more time before I got my jacket on and made it out the front door. True to his word, he already had been to Wisconsin Rapids and had returned with a search warrant.

"It looks official," I said, examining it.

"It is."

"Then let's go."

Neither Clarkie nor I had much to say on our way to Hogue Valley that morning. In my excitement, as we rode through the frosty bottoms with the moon going down and the sun coming up, I was reminded of those long-ago hunting trips—when my roommates at the University of Wisconsin and I would pack ourselves, three shotguns, and a whole load of expectations into my fifty-six Ford and head for Grandmother Ryland's farm. Opening day of pheasant season. There was nothing like it, hadn't been anything like it since. Except serving Stella, the witch, a search warrant.

"What do you think we'll find once we get there?" Clarkie said, as we came to Galena and turned south on County Road 425 West.

"Maybe nothing."

"What do you *hope* we'll find, then?"

"The missing loot from the robberies. And as long as I'm hoping, the dead man's hands, foot, and head." Which would tie everything up all neat and tidy and give Abby her whole man to bury.

"You don't sound very confident."

I didn't know how to tell Clarkie that whatever confidence I might have had was being eroded by the bad feeling in my guts. Besides, it was another beautiful day. Four in a row, by my count. That seemed too good to be true.

The bad feeling in my guts said I told you so when we discovered Lori Pitts' black Peterbilt truck cab hidden in the cedar thicket a few yards from the orange brick house. It tightened into a knot when we approached the front door and found it standing wide open.

"This doesn't look good," Clarkie said.

That seemed to belabor the obvious.

"Should we knock?"

"Why bother?" I said. "We have a search warrant."

The air inside the house seemed every bit as cold as the air outside, and it didn't take a genius to deduce that there was no heat on in here. I wondered what kept the pipes from freezing when I discovered that there was no running water and no electricity on in here either. Every switch that I tried didn't work. Not only didn't work, but had nothing to work on. The place had been stripped of light bulbs, lamps, and everything else electrical.

A long tall narrow hallway with a hardwood floor and plaster walls and a plaster ceiling led all the way through the house to the back door, which also stood open. Branching off from the hall was a front parlor with a hardwood floor, one high narrow window, an orange brick fireplace that matched the outside walls, and a white lace curtain yellowed with age.

Directly across the hall from the front parlor was what I assumed was once the library, even though no books remained in there. Walnut shelves had been built all around the room from the floor on up to higher than I could reach, and the floor in front of the chimney had been bricked, as if a stove had once sat there. But where had all the books gone? Not to the library, I bet.

The back parlor was identical to the front parlor, except that its window was smaller and had no curtain. Across the hall from the back parlor was the kitchen, and it was there that we saw our first signs of habitation.

First a down sleeping bag, like the one in Bruce Barger's upstairs, rolled up beside a large, ornate, wood-burning range with an enameled exterior and a small square of glass in its oven door. Then a bag of groceries, spilled across a yellow chrome Formica table and onto the floor. Several cans of soup and tuna were in view, along with boxes of spaghetti and macaroni and cheese. More cans of soup and tuna were in the cabinets above the sink, along with cans of pork and beans, a jar of peanut butter, and more boxes of spaghetti and macaroni and cheese. In the sink were two hard plastic plates and coffee cups that looked as if they had come out of the same dump as the table. Pots and pans on the drain board, dirty silverware in the bottom of them, dish soap, scouring pads, and a half-filled bucket of water that was either dish-water, drinking water, or both.

A white wooden door hid a darkened staircase that led upstairs. I found a switch just inside the staircase and flipped it several times, but no light came on.

"You have a flashlight in the car?" I asked Clarkie. "I'd sort of like to see where I'm going."

"I'll be right back."

While I waited for Clarkie, I searched the kitchen and found something that worried me. There on the yellow pine floor amidst the cans of soup and tuna was what appeared to be a small pool of blood. I knelt down to examine it. It was tacky, neither completely dried nor completely frozen.

"What's going on?" Clarkie asked on his return.

I showed him the blood on the floor. Like me, he had to stick his hand into it to convince himself that it was real.

"Where do you think it came from?" he asked.

"I wish I knew, Clarkie."

We went up the stairs with Clarkie in the lead, since he was the one carrying the flashlight. About two-thirds of the way up the stairs was a small, almost square door about four feet by three feet that led into a narrow, but deep room that once was probably used as a storage room, but was now bare of everything but cobwebs and rafters. Something made me stop at the door and go no further, which was probably my claustrophobia kicking in. Though I knew better, the room seemed to shrink before my very eyes until it was the size of an ice cube.

"I wonder where everything in this house went?" Clarkie said as he continued to shine his flashlight around the empty room.

"We might ask Clarence Hogue the next time we see him."

"Do you think he auctioned it off at one of his sales?"

"I wouldn't put it past him, Clarkie. He had to come up with the tax money somewhere."

"Not to mention that new house he built."

"Yeah. My thoughts exactly," I said, glad to move on.

At the top of the stairs was a long narrow room to our left, separated by a wall and a doorway from the much larger room to our right. The large room had no windows and no lights, except for a bare bulb right at the top of the stairs, which as I already knew, didn't work. The small room had two tall windows facing west that I had seen from the outside, and along with the crack in each one, was a small hole in the glass in one bottom corner, a large collection of wasp nests on its sill and on the rafters, bird droppings everywhere, and what looked like a rat hole in the floor. Neither of the rooms was furnished and neither appeared to have any source of heat. The Hogue home place, as I was starting to believe, was all facade.

"Did people really used to live like this?" Clarkie asked.

"Like what?"

"No central heat. No running water."

"They still do."

He shook his head in disbelief.

"But this place has electricity, which means it probably had running water once. It's just not turned on. And there's electric baseboard heat in some of the rooms. I'll show you when we get downstairs."

"There's no heat up here, though?"

I borrowed his flashlight and shined the room. "Not that I can see."

We followed the large room through a doorway into another small room that apparently was Cassandra Hogue's bedroom. Flannel sheets, two red wool blankets, and a thick patchwork quilt covered a small pine bed that was snugged up against the east wall. A gray-and-red shag throw rug lay on the floor beside the bed, and a little red wagon held an assortment of dolls at the foot of the bed. Clothes, most of them dresses from the 1960's, hung on a steel rod in a makeshift closet, and a pair of tennis shoes, a muddy pair of Army boots, a pair of leather sandals, and a pair of rubber thongs were lined in a tight row at the outside edge of the closet. There were no posters on any of the walls. No prophets, poets, zealots, or rock stars— and no words of wisdom from the ages.

I walked to the closet, took out a bright red miniskirt, and compared it to the large brown tent dress that lay draped over the room's single chair. More than their size numbers seemed to separate them. More even than the weight of two decades. I could feel the difference as I hefted one and then the other. It was the difference between body and soul.

"Something bothering you, Garth?" Clarkie said.

I laid the tent dress down and hung the mini-skirt back in the closet. "A lot of things, Clarkie."

He took off his sheriff's hat and scratched his head. "I wonder where all of that stuff they were supposed to have stolen went?"

"I wonder where Cassandra Hogue and Lori Pitts went? You have any ideas?"

He shook his head. With his hat off, and his bald spot showing, Clarkie looked a little older, but no wiser, than he did with it on.

We went downstairs and out the back door to a small brick building that served as a well house, and currently an ice house for Cassandra Hogue. Inside were a pitcher pump, a bucket of water for priming the pump, a wooden box partially filled with party ice, and a jar of mayonnaise, a jar of kosher dill pickles, a bottle of catsup, a package of bologna, a package of hot dogs, and two packages of pepper loaf on the ice. A case of Pepsi and a case of Coors Light sat side by side on the floor of the pump house, but neither case had been opened.

"What do you think, Garth?" Clarkie was as much at a loss as I was.

"I think we'd better do some more looking."

Clarkie went back into the house while I searched the woods behind the house. Still frosty, the leaves crunched underfoot, as did the banks of snow buried in the cedars.

But I saw no fresh footprints there, and no sign of either Cassandra Hogue or Lori Pitts.

I went back into the house where I met Clarkie on his way out again. The look on his face said that he'd had no more luck than I.

"They have to be some place," Clarkie said.

"They probably are."

"I mean here."

"It doesn't look that way."

"Then where could they have gone? Lori's truck cab is still here and, as far as I know, Cassandra Hogue doesn't own a car."

"Maybe they walked. Or were carried."

"I hope not, Garth. I don't think I could take another body just now."

I nodded. My sentiments exactly.

On our way back to the patrol car, we stopped at Lori Pitts' truck cab and were surprised by what we saw. Someone had broken out the driver's side window, and safety glass lay sprinkled all over the inside of the cabin, like pellets of hail. Clarkie opened the door and climbed into the cabin, then leaned on back toward the sleeper.

"Anybody home?" he asked.

He got no answer.

"Check the glove compartment," I said. "Remember that Lori Pitts said she always kept a .38 handy."

"It's not in there," Clarkie said a moment later.

"What about her log book?"

He found it and sat there on the seat thumbing through it. "What am I looking for, Garth?"

"Tuesday night she said she had just come in from Amarillo when she found Jeremy. I wondered what her log book said?"

Clarkie thumbed through it until he found the last few entries. "She wasn't lying, Garth. She left Amarillo at 10:10 AM on Monday, and spent the night at a truck stop in Kansas City, Missouri."

"It never hurts to check," I said.

"I can't argue with that." He put the log book back and got out of the cab.

Clarence Hogue's was our first stop on our way back to Oakalla. Today Clarence wore a John Deere cap and Carhart coveralls, and carried a Stihl chain saw. Clarence had big hands, big knuckles, and big bones, and carried the twenty-inch chain saw as easily as if it were a Tinker Toy.

"Are you landscaping today, Clarence?" I asked.

"Just cleaning up some of the brush around here. Getting it out of the way of my emergency spillway."

"Where's the spillway going to go?"

"Right about where you and fat boy are standing."

Clarkie and I exchanged glances. It didn't take much to set Clarkie off, this morning in particular. Already I could see a storm coming.

"Who are you calling fat boy?" Clarkie said.

"Who do you think? Every time I step outside my front door I see you two here. I'm getting tired of it."

Clarence started the chain saw and began walking toward us. At the same time Clarkie's hand slowly slid down his hip until it rested on the butt of his gun. I shook my head no. If he drew it, he might have to use it. Instead, I stepped aside and gave Clarence the room he needed.

"Your sister's missing," I said as he went by.

He stopped. I watched his shoulders sag. "I know that," he said without turning around. "She's been missing for over twenty years."

"Since last night," I said. "Sheriff Clark and I just left there."

He turned around to face me. "Just what are you trying to pull, Ryland?"

"Your sister, Cissy Hogue, alias Stella the witch, is missing."

"That fat slob is not my sister!" he shouted.

"Have it your way, Clarence, but she's still missing. And who knows? Maybe they'll come for you next."

He revved up the chain saw as if he meant to use it and took a step my way. "God damn you. Get off my property. You and fat boy both."

"Think it over, Clarence," I said, not giving any ground. "You change your mind, give Sheriff Clark or me a call."

"That'll be a cold day in hell." Clarence stood about a yard away from me, just close enough for me to feel the threat of the chain saw.

"Ready, Sheriff?" I said.

Clarkie's hand was still on the butt of his gun. "Ready."

"Think about it, Clarence," I said as I stepped around him. "Think about it."

We were already at Bruce Barger's before I realized that I was sweating. Profusely for me, who usually didn't sweat much. Enough to soak my shirt and give me a chill when we stepped out into the air again.

It took about five minutes' worth of hard banging before Bruce Barger came to the door. We knew he was home because his battered white Chevy pickup was still in his drive, and Bruce never went anywhere without it.

"What do you want?" he said, his voice husky and sullen. Bruce appeared to have been asleep.

"Some answers, Bruce," I said.

He shrugged. "Then you've come to the wrong place. I gave up looking for answers years ago. Questions, man. Now those I've got a shitload of."

"For instance?"

He scratched his scruffy beard and then around the collar of his T-shirt, which smelled as if it had about a week's worth of wear on it. "Like why do you two keep coming around here and giving me grief? I mean, it's not like I've ever done anything to either one of you. So it can't be anything personal, can it?"

"No, Bruce. It's nothing personal."

"What is it, then? You just don't like me for who I am. If that's the case..." Bruce was starting to look persecuted. "That's really lame, man."

I looked at Clarkie, who wanted to jump on Bruce with both feet, but to his credit didn't.

"I'll be honest with you, Bruce. I've never really liked thieves," I said. "They erode trust and violate the sanctity of the home and put the whole community at risk. Locked doors, barred windows, suspicious days, and sleepless nights follow in their wake. So no, I don't like you for who you are and never will. But that's not why Sheriff Clark and I keep coming around. It's because your friends keep turning up dead, or missing."

"Who besides Jeremy is dead, or missing?" His voice struck a new chord. Fear.

"Cassandra Hogue and Lori Pitts."

"Missing, or *dead*?" He could barely say the word.

"Missing. For now."

Relief swept over him, as his knees buckled and he held on to the door for support. "Jesus, man, that was low."

"What was?"

"Scaring me like that."

"We can't be sure they're not dead. Neither can you."

He took a deep breath and sat down in the doorway. Bruce Barger was badly in need of a smoke, or a joint.

"So what do you want from me?" Bruce said.

"We want to know who might want to kill them, or whom they might be running from?"

Bruce ran his hand through his hair, then stopped to examine what he found there. "Like I said, if you're looking for answers, you came to the wrong place."

"Apparently we did. Let's go, Sheriff Clark."

Clarkie momentarily balked at that, but he didn't argue.

"Wait a minute!" Bruce yelled as we were leaving. "What about me?"

"What about you?"

"I mean, with what happened to Jeremy and all, could I be in danger?"

"I don't know, Bruce. Are you?"

Clarkie and I didn't wait for his answer.

"Where to?" Clarkie asked once we were back inside the patrol car.

"I don't know about you, but I have a newspaper to put out by tomorrow. You might get ahold of Dr. Airhart and have her go out there with you and see if she can run some tests on that blood we found."

"I'm sorry, Garth. I screwed up again. If I'd gotten that search warrant yesterday, we'd have our answers by now."

"Maybe so, maybe not, Clarkie. Even if Cassandra Hogue and Lori Pitts cleared out on us, which appears might have happened, they sure as hell didn't take the loot from all of those robberies with them. Not on their backs anyway, and not in anything smaller than an eighteen-wheeler."

"Maybe the stuff's not there, or never was there."

"Same difference. We still wouldn't have found it."

We drove past the City Building, made a right down the alley that led past the cheese plant, and came to Gas Line Road. "What do you really think happened out there?" Clarkie said. "Last night, I mean."

"I'm afraid to say, Clarkie. Afraid I might be right."

"You think someone died, don't you?"

"Yes."

"Lori Pitts?"

"Maybe. But she's not my first choice."

"That only leaves Cassandra Hogue. Why would anyone want to kill her?"

"Why would anyone want to kill Jeremy Pitts, or that stranger that we found in Amos Hogue's dump? There's a connection somewhere. We're just not seeing it."

Clarkie turned south onto Berry Street and stopped the patrol car along the east side of the white concrete block building that housed the *Oakalla Reporter.* "Why Cassandra Hogue and not Lori Pitts?" he said. "What I mean is, why do you think that's her blood on the kitchen floor and not Lori's?"

"My real reason, Clarkie? Because I would rather it be her blood on the kitchen floor than Lori's. But then there's the broken window in Lori's truck that I can't explain, and her missing .38. If Lori were already dead or incapacitated, what would be the point in breaking into her truck and taking her gun?"

"Maybe that happened first, Garth, before he went into the house."

"Let's hope not, Clarkie."

I was ready to leave, but he still had a question for me. "Garth, you don't think Lori had anything to do with the robberies, do you?"

"I didn't until today, even though after Jeremy's death it was obvious that something sure had her spooked. But chew on this a while, Clarkie. What better way to move the stolen goods than in an eighteen-wheeler. And who better to drive it than Lori Pitts."

"It does make sense, Garth," Clarkie said.

"I wish the rest of it did."

"What rest of it?"

"All the deaths, Clarkie. I don't see the point."

"Maybe somebody doesn't want to share with his partners. You know, the no honor among thieves bit. At last report, there was close to a half million dollars in cash and merchandise involved."

"But who, Clarkie? Who among the thieves is left?"

"Bruce Barger, for one."

"Who right now is shaking in his shoes."

"Maybe he's faking it, Garth."

"Maybe you're right, Clarkie. Maybe he is the one. Stranger things have happened, I guess."

I climbed out of the patrol car and went into my office, where I called Ruth to tell her what had happened. She was kind enough not to say I told you so, but I knew that she was thinking it.

"What now?" she said.

"For you or me?"

"Either one of us."

"I have to get the *Reporter* out today, so I'm going to be stuck here. But if you have the time, I'd appreciate it if you would go over to Montevideo and nose around the Wisconsin Wesleyan campus to see what you might learn about Christy Morton."

"If I have the time."

"Of course."

"Why there, Garth? Why not have me nose around here some place? Lori Pitts' trail is a lot warmer than Christy's is."

"Because first Christy Morton is missing, and now her look- alike, Lori Pitts, is missing. That's too much of a coincidence to suit me."

"That could be all it is, too, a coincidence."

"That's what I want you to find out."

"And if I don't find out anything?"

"Then we haven't lost anything."

"Only my time."

"Think of it as a learning experience."

"Think of it as overtime." She hung up.

15

I didn't eat lunch, but stayed there at my desk with my fingers on the keys of my Underwood until I finished my column. My topic was the growing length of the Oakalla school year (with the talk of year-round school), which I found appalling. What I tried to say, what I hoped I'd said, was that the idea of lengthening the school year to improve education made about as much sense as lengthening the basketball season to improve the Milwaukee Bucks, or starting spring training in December to insure that the Milwaukee Brewers got into the World Series next year. What the single-minded idea of more school days ignored were the schools, teachers, students, curriculum, and the biggest boondoggle of them all, administration. As always, it was a simple political solution to a complex people problem.

What it also ignored were individuals like Abraham Lincoln, Thomas Edison, and Henry Ford, who, while they didn't spend a great deal of time in public schools, still managed to contribute something to society. Or people like my grandparents, nongraduates all, who could still read, write, work their fractions, and raise their children to be productive citizens; who earned their bread by the sweat of their brows, paid their taxes, kept their noses clean and their neighborhoods secure, and in the midst of the greatest depression that this country has ever known, never once went on the dole, never once stood on Uncle Sam's doorstep with their hands out, expecting something for nothing, just because they happened to be there.

What it further ignored were the kids of Oakalla who, unlike most of the rural kids of my generation, lost the month of May and part of June to formal education. A year of Mays all told when you added them up at the end of twelve years. Which was no big deal at all if you didn't like the out of doors, if you didn't feel "the need of being versed in country things." If you didn't like the smell of lilacs in bloom or the sight of dogwood in flower. If you didn't find the flight of a butterfly or the pop of a baseball as least as interesting as the flight of someone's spit ball or the pop of someone's gum. If you didn't like to fish, or pick morels, or ride your bicycle from here to there just because you finally could. If you didn't like to lie on your back, watch the clouds roll by, and think...wonder...dream. If you didn't like space, peace, quiet, and solitude, the sound of your own heart, the beat of your own drum. If you had the soul of a poet, instead of a bean-counter.

The phone rang. It was Clarkie. "I'm at the hospital, Garth. Dr. Airhart just got through running the test on that blood we found. She says it's human, type O-positive."

"Which includes about everybody in the world."

"That's what she said."

"Is she handy?"

"No. She had an emergency. Some kid with a ruptured appendix. She said she'd try to call you later tonight."

"Thanks, Clarkie." There was a pause, which meant that he wasn't through with me yet. "Was there something else?"

"I just wondered what you thought I should do now?"

I looked out the window and was surprised by what I saw. Another day was about done.

"What do you think you should do now?" I said.

"Grab a bite to eat and go back out to Hogue Valley to see what happens."

"Sometimes you surprise me, Clarkie."

"Sometimes I surprise myself."

"Tell you what. If you can hang on until, say, one or two in the morning, I'll come relieve you."

"I can," he said with assurance.

"I'll see you then."

Two hours later I sat in the Corner Bar and Grill, eating my supper, which included a fish sandwich, french fries, cole slaw, and a Coke. Ruth had yet to call, so I assumed that she wasn't yet home from Montevideo. Either that or she had something on tonight and would wait until morning to tell me what she'd found out.

Four other people, all of them regulars, sat there in the dining room of the Corner Bar and Grill with me. Three of us at the counter, the other two in separate booths, we were the typical Thursday crowd, with nowhere else to go and nothing much to say. But we were comfortable together, like ducks on a pond, or chickens on a roost, each familiar with the other, each secure in the order of things.

Jerry Patterson came out of the barroom and stood surveying the scene a moment before heading my way. I was surprised to see Jerry there at night. If he came into the Corner Bar and Grill at all, it was to eat a quick lunch before heading back home.

"Evening, Jerry," I said, after he'd stopped behind me.

"Evening, Garth."

He didn't offer to move, so I had to swivel around on my stool to look at him. He seemed melancholy, as if all the sadness in his life had finally caught up with him. Even his perpetually young face looked old.

"Have a seat," I offered. "And I'll buy you a beer."

He shook his head. His eyes were red, unfocused. They looked as if he had been on a two-day toot. Either that or he had been crying.

"Got to move along," he mumbled. "Got to move along."

But he still stood there. I could smell whiskey on his breath.

"Was there something you wanted to tell me?" I said, trying to prompt him.

"Something to tell you," he parroted. "Important. About the robberies." Then his face went blank, as the thought slipped away from him. He hung his head and stared at the floor.

"It's okay, Jerry. Maybe you'll remember it tomorrow."

"Tomorrow," he echoed. Then he began a slow shuffle toward the door. "And tomorrow, and tomorrow."

I got up to make sure he wasn't climbing into a car. Instead, he crossed School Street at an unsteady gait and began a slow walk along Jackson Street toward home.

"He make it out okay?" Hiram, the bartender, had joined me at the front door.

"It looks like it. How long has he been in here anyhow?"

"I don't know. He was here when I came in at five. But he was pretty well along by then."

"You serve him anything?" Hiram usually didn't serve anyone that he thought was drunk.

"A double shot of Crown Royal before I realized who it was. He's been on the wagon five, six years now."

"On the wagon from what?"

"His wife's death is what set him off. That and the fact that he lost the home he loved. He got to be in a real bad way there for a year or so, and then he went on the wagon. For his kid, he said. He had to do it for his kid."

"Then what happened tonight to set him off?" I asked.

"It was his anniversary," he said. "Jerry and Janie would have been married thirty years today."

We turned from the door and I followed Hiram through the dining room and back into the barroom. Hiram went behind the bar to get Peachy White a Miller and to fix Norman Haxton another bourbon and water. I stood at the bar and bided my time, waiting for Hiram to work his way over to me.

"Was there something else, Garth?" Hiram said.

"I just wondered what else you and Jerry might have talked about in the two or so hours since five?"

Hiram looked around the barroom to see if anyone else was listening. "You promise to keep this under your hat, Garth?"

"My lips are sealed."

"Because it's not something I'd want to get out. It seems like a breach of ethics, or something to that effect."

"You're afraid you'll lose your bartender's license?" I said with a smile.

"I'm afraid people will lose confidence in me. Which would be a whole lot worse."

"You have my word, Hiram. This is as far as it goes."

"Well, we got to talking about the robberies. You know, anything to get his mind off of his wife. Then he says to me, 'Hiram, I think I know who it is that's behind them. But he'd kill me if he thought I knew.'"

"That's all he said?"

"That was it, Garth. He just sort of drifted off after that into his own world."

"It might have been the whiskey talking."

"That's the way I figured it at first. But an insurance man can hear things, you know, so it seemed like I ought to tell you what he said."

Then I heard the Operation Lifeline siren, which seemed to be coming our way. Hiram and I exchanged glances. I got up and headed for the door.

The ambulance came up Colburn Road, ran the four-way stop, and turned west on Jackson Street. A couple blocks later it stopped. I was already on the run.

The ambulance had attracted a crowd, as several people stood on their porches, and three or four cars had stopped in a line on Jackson Street, unable to go in either direction. Illumined by the lights of the ambulance, Jerry Patterson lay face down in the middle of Jackson Street. One of the paramedics was bending over him. Another was bringing a stretcher from the ambulance.

"What happened?" I asked Ned McFall, whose car was first in line behind the ambulance.

"Damned if I know, Garth. I was just driving along Jackson Street headed for home when I see this big lump, lying right out in the middle of the road. First thing I think of, somebody's dog has been hit. But when I get up close, I see it's not that at all."

"Are you the one who called Operation Lifeline?"

"Darlene Gaylor did. She was already waiting for me at the door when I went to knock."

The paramedics had Jerry on the stretcher and were strapping him in. I didn't see any tubes or bandages, so that was either a good sign or a bad sign.

"How bad is he hurt?" I asked Ned McFall.

"Hard to say, Garth. He was still breathing, but out like a light when I first got to him."

A moment later Jerry Patterson was in the Operation Lifeline ambulance and on his way to the hospital. I wished him Godspeed.

Darlene Gaylor still stood on her porch long after the ambulance had left and the rest of her neighbors had gone inside. I watched the last of the cars in line leave, then went up onto her porch to talk to her.

"A terrible thing," she said before I could say anything. "Just a terrible thing."

Darlene Gaylor was a tall, bony woman, who always looked too thin and never looked quite well. She had operated Darlene's Beauty Parlor there on Jackson Street for as long as I could remember. She didn't have a large trade, and most of her patrons were now over sixty, but somehow she managed to get by.

"Ned McFall said that you were already at the door when he came up there to knock," I said. "Had you already called the ambulance by then?"

Darlene wore only a threadbare sweater over her beautician's uniform. She had to be as cold as I was.

"Yes," she finally said.

"Then you saw what happened?"

Her eyes were large and sad, those of someone who knew that the best of her life was in the past. "Yes."

I waited for her to explain.

"I heard someone singing—loudly, at the top of his voice—some old sad song, 'Danny Boy,' I think it was. So I came to the door to see who it was and what was going on. Right about then he started across the street when, out of nowhere it seemed, here comes this speeding car. I heard a thump, and the next thing I knew, he was lying there on the pavement."

"Did the car run over him?"

"I don't think so. He seemed to rock back just as the car got to him. You know, like he'd lost his balance, then caught it again."

"Then he never saw the car coming?"

"I don't think so, Garth."

"Where did the car go from there? Or did you notice?"

"About three blocks west of here, it turned left. That was the last I saw of it."

"Were its lights on or off?"

"On. I'm sure of it. Otherwise, I wouldn't have seen it."

"Is there anything else you remember about it?"

"No."

"And you're sure it was a car and not a pickup?"

She wasn't sure. I could see the doubt in her eyes.

"I think it was a car, Garth. But no, I'm not sure. Everything happened so fast."

"Thanks, Darlene, you've been a big help."

"Who is he, Garth? Somebody said it was Jerry Patterson."

"That's who it is."

She closed her eyes and shook her head, as if life was suddenly too cruel for words. "Just like his son."

Back at my office I called Abby at the hospital, was put on hold, and hung up. She called seconds later.

"Patient, aren't we?" she said.

"You know better."

"What is it you wanted?"

"Jerry Patterson was brought in there about forty-five minutes ago. I just wondered how he was doing."

"Wait a minute. I'm down here in emergency anyway. I'll check."

While she checked, I thought of all I had yet to do that night. With luck, I'd relieve Clarkie by dawn.

"Treated and released is the word I got. About five minutes ago."

"You mean he's back walking the streets?" I'd sue the hospital for neglect myself if that were the case.

"No. He called a neighbor to come after him."

"Are you sure he's all right?"

"No, I'm not sure," she said with undisguised reproach in her voice. "But the doctor on duty is, and that's good enough for me. Contrary to what you think about your local hospital and ambulance service, they're really quite good for a town this size."

"Not until you came along."

"They saved your life, didn't they?"

She had me there. They had also saved Rupert Roberts' life and Clarkie's life. "Point well taken," I said.

"Then are you through with me, because I'm not yet through with my rounds?"

"How badly was Jerry Patterson hurt, can you tell me that?"

"I can. He suffered a slight concussion, and a contusion on his right hip. In other words, his head might hurt and his butt might be sore for a while, but that's about all."

"Thanks, Abby. You're a prince among men."

"You'd better hope not, dahling."

16

It was nearly three A.M. when I made it to Hogue Valley. I parked Jessie about a half mile north of the house on the hill and walked the rest of the way. One of the reasons I walked was to wake myself up. The other reason was to keep from giving myself away. Despite the zillion stars overhead and the patches of snow on the ground, it was a dark night. If I could stay in the shadows and not kick any rocks on the way, I might make it there without being seen.

Clarkie, however, was conspicuous by his presence. He sat in his patrol car directly in front of the house with his parking lights on and his motor running. He appeared to be asleep. I hoped he hadn't asphyxiated himself.

I knelt down beside the car and tapped on the driver's side window. Clarkie's eyes flew open, and he sat up straight in the seat, like a student who had been caught napping in class. But he still didn't know what was what, not until he rolled down the window and saw me there.

"Garth, is that you?" he whispered.

"For your sake, it had better be," I whispered back. "What's going on?"

"Nothing that I can see. That's why I fell asleep."

"Has anything gone on?"

"Not so that I can tell. I don't think anyone's here, or that anyone's coming."

"You're probably right."

"How did you get here anyway?"

"I left Jessie parked about a half mile up the road and walked the rest of the way."

"Do you want a ride back down there?"

"No. I think I'll hang out here for a while."

"You're wasting your time, Garth. If anything was going to happen, it would have happened by now."

"I can't argue with that, Clarkie. But I still think I'll stay." Then I asked him if he had heard anything about Jerry Patterson.

"Eugene filled me in over the radio," he said. "How is Jerry anyway?"

"I think he's going to be fine."

"Any idea who tried to run him down?"

"Not the first one. But maybe Jerry can tell us tomorrow."

"Do you think I should drive by there on my way home to make sure everything's okay?"

"It might not be a bad idea, Clarkie. And one other thing. Let me get gone before you leave here. If anybody's watching you, they'll see me here when you pull away."

I stayed in my crouch, and using Clarkie's patrol car as a shield from the house made my way over to the side ditch where I found some brush to hide in. A moment later Clarkie pulled away. It wasn't until after he'd left that I realized how cold and lonely the night was.

To move or to stay put? That was the question that I had started asking as soon as Clarkie was out of sight, and was still asking fifteen minutes later. If I moved, I'd be a little warmer and a whole lot more comfortable. But if I didn't move, I'd be a lot less likely to give myself away.

The question was answered for me when I heard Lori Pitts' Peterbilt fire up. I moved.

My only chance was to get there before she got in gear. The Peterbilt was a diesel, and the night was cold, so my chance was better than it might otherwise have been. Heedless of whatever was in my path, I ran straight toward the Peterbilt and got there just as Lori Pitts turned her headlights on. I stood in front of her, frantically waving my arms and hoping that she wouldn't run over me.

Instead, she backed up and started out another way. I ran after her, trying to head her off. I never heard the first shot, but I did see the sparks, as the slug ricocheted off of the Peterbilt's cab and went pinging into the underbrush. The second shot grazed my arm and left a furrow about an eighth of an inch deep that at the time burned like crazy. At that point I gave up trying to stop Lori Pitts and dived for the nearest cover. I heard a third shot, but never saw where the slug went.

Lori Pitts meanwhile had made it to County Road 425 East and was headed north about as fast as the Peterbilt would go. Long after she was out of sight, I could still hear her stacks popping—all the way to Oakalla, it seemed.

My immediate concern, however, was to stay alive. I had never seen my assailant fire, so I didn't know which way to run, even if I was so inclined. Logic said to stay where I was because he couldn't see me any better than I could see him. Instinct, on the other hand, said to make tracks, and the sooner the better. He wasn't Annie Oakley. Already he'd proven that by missing me two out of three times. Also, if I heard right, he was shooting a pistol, perhaps Lori Pitts' .38, which wasn't nearly as accurate as a shotgun or rifle. By staying put, I might be giving him the only real chance that he would have at me.

Bonzi! I was up and running for the road as fast as my legs would take me. Once there, I didn't stop until Jessie was in sight. But either he had run out of ammunition, which wasn't likely, or he had moved on, because he didn't shoot at me again. At first I was relieved. Then I got angry. At myself mainly. For running scared.

I got into Jessie and drove slowly back up to the house on the hill where I parked momentarily while I decided what to do. I then drove on down the hill, past the scene of the hog roast, and came to Alma and Amos Hogue's place. Nothing stirring there, so I went on down the road to where we'd found the stranger's body. There I stayed for several minutes, hoping for the insight that would tell me what to do next. None came.

I drove on clear to the end of County Road 425 East, where it T'd with Davies Ford Road, which continued south along the west bank of Rocky Creek to Davies Ford or turned back north toward Oakalla. Turning left, I headed for Oakalla.

Then I saw the dust hanging low along the road and the taillights of a car about a quarter mile ahead. After giving Jessie some gas, I had begun to close the space between us, when the other driver must have seen us coming and took off.

"Let's go, Jessie," I urged, eager for combat. "Show me what you can do."

True to form, she did show me what she could do, as she always did when I put her through her paces. She hit a chuckhole and broke a tie rod, and she kissed the ditches on both sides of the road before I got her under control again.

By the time we limped back to Oakalla and I parked her in front of the Marathon's big overhead door, the moon had just inched its way over the eastern horizon. I stood a moment watching it, a sharp thin slice of white that was hardly a moon at all. Then I went home.

17

I awakened in pain, thought my arm was on fire, then realized that less than four hours ago I had been shot. Just up, the orange sun was doing its best to promise better days ahead, but I wasn't buying it. Like the pessimist said, they told me to cheer up, things could be worse. So I cheered up, and sure enough, they got worse.

I smelled coffee perking and sausage frying, so that meant Ruth was already up. No sense in postponing the inevitable. I wasn't going to feel any better by staying in bed.

"How is your arm?" was the first thing Ruth asked me when I walked into the kitchen. Though half asleep, she had helped me out of my jacket and then washed and bandaged my bullet wound when I had gotten home.

"I'll live."

"I still think you should have Abby take a look at it."

"When I have time." I poured myself a cup of coffee and sat down at the kitchen table. "What are we having with the sausage?"

"Fried mush."

I cringed, but tried not to let Ruth see me. "We have any maple syrup?" With enough maple syrup, I wouldn't taste the mush.

"The last time I looked we did."

Thank God for that.

"What was that, Garth?"

"I didn't say anything."

"I could have sworn you did."

I stretched and yawned, and scratched myself in a couple places that needed scratching. I should already be at my office, taking my lumps, or my kudos, as the case may be, but I'd have to get there when I got there. Things were getting desperate now that Lori Pitts had flown the coop. She was my best hope of solving this.

"How did it go in Montevideo yesterday?" I asked.

"Surprisingly well," she said.

"Are you going to tell me about it?"

"When you tell me how your day went."

"I already told you. I went running through a cedar thicket at three A.M. and got shot for my trouble. Then Jessie broke a tie rod on Davies Ford Road and I had to nurse her home."

She took the sausage out of the frying pan, put it in the oven to keep it warm, and began slicing the mush and dropping it into the hot sausage grease. Meanwhile I went in search of the maple syrup and found it in the cupboard behind a can of applesauce.

"Before that," she said. "Tell me everything that happened."

So I told her. Meanwhile she finished frying the mush and set it and the sausage on the table.

"Then you've lost Lori Pitts?" she said.

"For now. Maybe forever, but I hope not."

"Where do you think she's headed?"

"Who knows, Ruth? She's got the whole country to hide in and enough trucker friends to hitch a ride with if push comes to shove."

She passed the platter of sausage and mush to me. I took a couple patties of sausage and as small a helping of mush as I thought I could get by with. Then I reached for the maple syrup.

"What do you make of the fact that somebody tried to run Jerry Patterson down?"

Ruth took the maple syrup from me when I was through with it, and soon I could barely see her plate for the syrup. Ruth liked mush about as well as I did, but she still bought some every year for old times' sake.

"I won't know what to make of it until I talk to Jerry," I said.

"Is he in any kind of shape to talk?"

"I'm about to find out."

After breakfast I called Clarkie and caught him at home. He sounded about as I felt, a quarter full headed for empty.

"Where do you think she'll head, Garth?" he asked about Lori.

"Her last run was to Amarillo, Texas. You might start there."

"That seems to me the last place she'd go."

"You figure it out, Clarkie. I can't."

"What is it that we're charging her with? I'll have to know before I put out an APB."

"How about unlawful flight to avoid prosecution?"

"What's her crime, Garth? Has she committed any?"

"Hell, I don't know, Clarkie. She surely has, or she wouldn't be running. Isn't there something called probable cause?"

"Not in her case, I don't think."

"Then forget it for now until I come up with something."

"I'm sorry, Garth, but the law's the law whether we like it or not."

I hung up. For a moment there I thought I was talking to Rupert Roberts.

I then called Jerry Patterson. It took ten rings, but he finally came to the phone.

"Jerry, this is Garth Ryland. How are you feeling?"

"Like a truck ran over me, which I guess is what happened."

"You don't remember any of it?"

"No."

"Then you don't remember talking to me?"

"No. Were you there?"

I glanced outside where a male cardinal was in full song, doing his best to convince a nearby female that spring had truly arrived. In truth, he probably was just trying to get laid.

"Yes, I was there—at the Corner Bar and Grill," I said. "We shared a few words before you left. You said that you had something important about the robberies to tell me."

There was a pause, as if he were trying to get his rusty wheels to turn again. "I'm sorry, Garth. I don't remember."

"Then do you have any idea who might want to run you down?"

Another pause, as he sorted things out. "I didn't know anyone had."

"There's a witness who says that's the case. Teddy's death..."

"An accident, Garth." He cut me short before I could ask. "My son's death was just one of those pointless senseless things that never should have happened, but did."

"I'm sorry, Jerry. I had to ask."

"You're sure you have a witness who says someone tried to run me down?"

"Yes. That much I'm sure of. So if anything comes to mind that you think I should know, get in touch with me."

"If you say so."

"I'm serious, Jerry. Somebody tried to take you out last night."

"Yes. But if I can't remember it, it's like it never happened. Do you know what I mean, Garth? It's not real to me."

"Then try to remember. So it will become real."

"I'll do what I can," he said. But I wasn't encouraged.

I made another phone call. "Abby, this is Garth. What are you doing for the rest of your life?"

"What did you have in mind?"

"I'm running away from home. I'd like for you to go with me."

"Sure. When?" She didn't even have to think about it.

"As soon as you can get dressed and get over here."

"What makes you think I'm not dressed?"

"Are you?"

"No. But that's beside the point."

"I'll see you in a few minutes."

"Better make that an hour."

Forty-five minutes later she pulled up in front of the house in her red Honda Prelude. She wore a gold sweater tucked inside her jeans, a tan insulated vest over her sweater, gray wool socks, and ankle-length hiking boots. Her straw-colored hair came just to the top of her vest and felt clean, soft, and eminently kissable.

"Good morning," she said. "Do you want to drive, since you know where we're going?" She knew how much I loved to drive her car.

"I don't mind if I do."

"Of course, if you'd rather take Jessie...," she teased.

"Jessie's out of commission right now. We hit a chuckhole last night and broke a tie rod."

She climbed into the passenger seat while I sat down in the driver's seat. "While doing what?" she asked.

"Chasing after the man who shot me."

She gave me a look that said I'd better be kidding. "Run that by me again."

I pulled up the sleeve of my sweatshirt to show her my bandage. "It's just a scratch."

"Then why are you grimacing?"

"Because it hurts."

"It should hurt," she said as she lifted the bandage to look at it. "It should also have some stitches in it."

"That's what Ruth said."

"And you said?"

I put the Prelude in gear, made a U-turn, and headed toward Jackson Street. "I said I didn't like needles."

She rolled her eyes and said, "No wonder women live longer than men."

The house on the hill hadn't changed much since last night. Its bricks were still orange, its facade still crumbling, and like an aged dowager, it still commanded respect, if for no other reason that after all of these years, it was still standing.

"What do you think?" I asked Abby, who was seeing it with me for the first time.

"I think somebody should fix it up."

"I hear doctors have a lot of money."

"Not this one. Not yet anyway." We stood in the shadow of the house. It was cool there, compared to the sunlit grounds. "Besides, it's not my style."

"Mine either," I said.

"Then what are we doing back here?"

"Something that I remembered earlier this morning. This was once a station on the Underground Railroad."

"So we're looking for old railroad memorabilia?"

"Yeah. That's it."

"Lighten up, Garth. This is supposed to be fun."

"Tell me that an hour from now."

She raised her brows in question, but I didn't say anything more.

We went on inside the house, which was as cold as its shadow outside, then made our way on into the front parlor. From there to the library, back parlor, and kitchen. We didn't find any trap doors with stairways that led under the house.

"Does this place have a basement?" Abby asked.

"Not that I've been able to find."

She opened the door to the stairway upstairs. "Where does this lead?"

"Upstairs to three bedrooms, or what used to be bedrooms."

"Nothing else?"

"There's a small room and landing about midway up the stairs. But the room's empty."

"You mind if I take a look?" she asked.

"Not if I don't have to go with you." But I wasn't kidding as she thought.

She flipped the switch at the bottom of the stairs, then again to make sure. "It doesn't work."

"You noticed that."

"So how are we supposed to see?"

I took a kerosene lantern from its nail overhead. I didn't remember it being there yesterday. "You got a match?" I asked.

"Not since Supergirl died."

She had a lighter in her pocket, which worked almost as well. I lighted the lantern, then trimmed the wick.

"I feel I'm living a Nancy Drew mystery," she said as we started up the stairs.

"I'd settle for Frank and Joe."

At the first landing I opened the door and showed her the narrow deep room that led back into the belly of the house. "See. Just like I said, empty."

"Don't be in such a hurry," she said, as I started to close the door. "There's a path in the dust there, or didn't you notice that."

I hadn't noticed that. But then I wasn't looking very hard.

"What's the matter with you? You're acting funny," she said as she tried without success to push me into the room.

"I'm claustrophobic, remember?"

"Oh crap! I forgot about that. Why didn't you say something?"

"I just did," I said, as I handed her the lantern.

While she went on into the room, I waited on the stairs. I didn't know if I was a true claustrophobic or not, since I could usually control my fear. But today I felt on the edge and wasn't sure I was up to it.

"Well?" I said when she didn't return right away.

"I think I found something, but I'm going to need your help."

"Shit," I said to myself.

"What was that, Garth?"

"Nothing. Hold the lantern up so I can see where I'm going."

My first couple steps into the room didn't bother me. But with each succeeding step the room seemed to shrink, as it became a contest between legs and will for me to keep going.

"There, that wasn't so bad, was it?" Abby said as she handed me the lantern.

"Speak for yourself."

"Why is it that the stairs don't bother you and this room does?"

"I don't know. It's a matter of perception more than anything else. And feel. I don't like the feel of this room."

"Neither do I, now that you mention it."

She showed me what she'd found, which was a block of wood on the floor and a block-sized hole in the wall at the end of the room. The hole was just about the right size for a handhold, but pull though she might, Abby couldn't get the wall to budge.

I studied it a moment, then said, "Push."

So she pushed and part of the wall began to swing inward as a door. "I'll be damned," she said.

"Close it."

"Why? We just got it open."

"I want to see how it all works."

Reluctantly she closed the door, which when closed revealed no seams to betray its presence. I picked up the block of wood, which had been painted white on one side, and fitted it into the wall, white side in. Because its shadings matched those of the wall, it too revealed no seams unless you knew exactly what you were looking for.

"Now, how do we get it out again?" Abby said.

"How did you get it out in the first place?"

"I didn't. It was lying on the floor."

"It wasn't yesterday. I would have noticed."

"You didn't notice today."

"I didn't have Clarkie's flashlight today."

"You have a knife on you, or a credit card?"

I had both, but that seemed like cheating. "Feel behind that rafter," I said. "There must be something here."

That something turned out to be a silver butter knife that had blackened with tarnish and that Abby had found in the wall behind the last rafter. Meanwhile I stayed where I was. The room seemed bigger with me in the middle of it.

"It works," Abby said as she used the butter knife to pry out the block of wood.

"I was afraid it might. Now put it back in again. We don't need it out to get the door open."

"Why can't we just leave it out?"

"Because I want to see how the whole thing works from top to bottom."

Once she'd put the block of wood back in place again, Abby pushed open the door and started down the stairs behind it. "You coming?"

I had stopped to examine the wood around the opening which, like the door, was yellow poplar. Its edges had been meticulously milled to allow for a seamless fit. A lot of care had gone into the construction of this door, much more care than had gone into the rest of the interior. It was almost as if the house had been built for the door.

"Coming," I said.

Abby held the lantern. I did my best to stay as close to her as possible and not think about where I was.

"How did you know to push on the door instead of pull it?" she said.

"I didn't see any hinges."

"Are there any?"

"Yes. On this side."

The stairs led beneath the house and into a tunnel, which was just big enough to stand up in and to walk two abreast. Every few feet it had been shored up with rough-hewn timbers along the sides and across the top. It appeared to be as old as the house itself.

"I still don't like the feel of this place," I said.

"You sure it's just not your claustrophobia kicking in?"

"The only thing I'm sure of is that I want out of here."

"So why don't we turn around and go back?"

"Because I wouldn't be satisfied with that and neither would you."

The tunnel at first seemed interminable, as we stopped every other step for me to catch my breath and find my courage again. But in truth we probably hadn't gone much over fifty yards. I had to applaud Abby's self control. She was being very patient with me.

"If this was part of the Underground Railroad, they surely went all out to hide the runaway slaves," Abby said.

"That's what I'm thinking."

"What else are you thinking?"

"Nothing. Just that."

Then suddenly we weren't in the tunnel any more.

Abby stopped as abruptly as if she'd run into a wall. I had to grab ahold of her and carry her a couple steps to keep from running over her.

"Sorry," she said as I set her down.

"Don't be."

She held up the lantern as high as she could to better survey the area that we were in. Even with the lantern at its height, we could barely see from wall to wall. However, it was easy to see the wooden ceiling a couple feet above us. Six-inch-wide planks of tongue and groove yellow poplar were supported by logs at least a foot in diameter.

"What do you suppose that is?" she asked, shining her lantern on the ceiling.

"My guess is it's the floor of the old barn."

"There used to be a barn here?"

"The 1910 *Adams County Atlas* shows one."

"Look at all that stuff," she said, lowering the lantern to show me. "There must be fifty thousand dollars in stereo equipment alone."

"At least that."

Someone had covered most of the earthen floor with sheets of black plastic that they had then duct-taped together. On top of the plastic sat televisions, radios, stereos, VCR's, disc players, and speakers. Hundreds of them. More than what could have come from Adams County alone. A long double row of shotguns and rifles stood along one of the earthen walls, and an equally long row of handguns lay each in a clear plastic bag on the plastic in front of the rifles and shotguns.

"There are enough weapons here to outfit an army," Abby said.

"They probably would have, a street army."

"I don't know why that scares me so. It happens every day."

I was walking along a row of televisions, examining each one.

"What are you looking for, Garth?"

"All the jewelry they stole. I don't see any of it lying around."

"Maybe they buried it," she suggested.

I saw a shovel leaning against the dirt wall a few feet ahead of me. "Good thought."

The shovel had been used recently. The dirt on its blade had not yet dried. Now all we had to do was find some freshly overturned earth.

"Over here," Abby said, lifting the lantern to show me the way.

I walked over to where she stood and began digging. The blade cut easily through the soft dirt. A foot down I hit something that squished. When I raised the shovel to examine it, I saw blood on the blade.

"Not the jewels," I said to Abby.

Cissy Hogue, as it turned out.

As the autopsy later revealed, Cissy Hogue had been shot in the head at close range by a .38 caliber pistol. The slug had penetrated her skull and lodged in her frontal lobe, killing her almost instantly. What I remembered about Cissy Hogue was seeing her lying there in her beads, moccasins, and buckskin dress with her eyes and mouth open, a slash wound on her arm where the shovel had cut her, and a small neat hole in her forehead about the size of my little finger.

"I think I'm ready to leave now," Abby said.

"In a minute."

"What's the point of staying, Garth?"

"The point is, we haven't finished what we came for."

"Just keep reminding me of that."

Abby held the lantern down low to the ground so we could look for freshly dug earth. I followed her closely with the shovel. We left Cissy Hogue behind.

We came to a small patch of freshly turned earth against one wall. I approached it in the ready position, but hesitated before pushing the shovel into the ground.

"Cold feet?" she asked.

"Cold feet. I'm almost afraid of what we may find."

I dug into the dirt and was relieved when the shovel hit what sounded and felt like plastic. Not wanting to tear anything up, as I had Cissy Hogue, I got down on my hands and knees and used my hands to scrape away the rest of the dirt. Then I felt something long, hard, and smooth that didn't feel like plastic to me.

"What's wrong, Garth?" Abby asked when I stopped digging.

"I'll tell you in a minute." I saw the lantern flicker and noticed that its flame seemed to be burning lower. "How much kerosene do we have left in there?"

She held up the lantern to look. "Not much."

"Enough to get us out of here?"

"If we start now."

Unfortunately, that was out of the question.

Once I'd freed it from the dirt, I hoisted the bag of jewelry out of the hole and set it on the ground at Abby's feet. The bag must have weighed close to fifteen pounds. It would have kept me in printer's ink for a long time to come.

"Is that all?" Abby asked.

"I wish." I handed her what else I'd found. "I don't suppose you know what this is?"

She had to hold it right up next to the lantern, which was growing dimmer by the minute. "It's a femur. Adult human."

"And this?"

"Tibia. Also adult human."

"Need I go on?"

"Is there a skull in there?" she asked.

I handed it to her.

She bent down to the lantern to examine it. "This is really strange, Garth. This looks like a Negroid skull to me."

I got up off the ground, found another likely looking place near the lantern and began to dig. A couple feet down I again struck bone.

"Two for two," I said.

Another dig, another set of bones.

"Three for three."

The lantern went out.

"What do we do now?" she asked.

"Find a wall and follow it. Here, take my hand."

"I mean about the bones."

"Leave them for now. Cissy Hogue, too. We have a killer to catch." Hand in hand, we began groping for the nearby wall. "Do you have the jewelry? I have the shovel," I said.

"Want to trade?"

She handed me the bag of jewelry and I knew immediately why she wanted to trade. It was a hell of a lot heavier than the shovel. A moment later I heard the shovel hit the ground, as she threw it down.

"There goes our only weapon," I said.

"With luck we won't need it."

Then we both laughed. We knew we neither one had any luck.

We soon found the wall and followed it to the entrance to the tunnel. There I had to stop and have a talk with myself.

"Are you going to be all right?" she asked.

"As long as I can't see where I am."

"There's no danger of that, is there?"

"I mean in my mind."

"Try not to think about it."

"Easier said than done."

Abby led and kept having to stop every few feet for me, as she had on our way in through the tunnel. The reason was that I couldn't make myself go any faster through what seemed to me like the belly of a snake. A living thing that slowly began to constrict around us.

"Is the tunnel getting smaller?" I asked.

"No. I don't think so."

"You're sure we didn't take a wrong turn somewhere?" I was very close to panic.

She flicked her Bic to show me where we were. "I'm sure."

I took a deep breath, knowing that I was never going to make it the way we were going. "Here," I said, handing her the jewels. "I'm going to make a run for it."

"Garth, are you crazy? You'll kill yourself."

"Better than the alternative."

"No!" she said. "We've been walking for hours it seems. We have to be close to the stairs."

"I'm not kidding, Abby, I'm about to lose it," I said, feeling my panic grow.

"Then go ahead. But don't say I didn't warn you."

I took off running. Five steps later I realized my danger and pulled up just before I crashed into the stairs. Then it was only a matter of climbing them in the dark, carrying a fifteen-pound sack of jewelry in one hand and leading a craven coward with the other. But Abby acquitted herself very well.

"What now?" she asked at the top of the stairs.

"Flick your lighter again."

She did. The square of white paint gave me a good target as I used my fist to punch the block of wood out. I pulled, and we stepped back as the door swung open.

Light! What a blessed sight.

18

Abby and I drove slowly back toward Oakalla with the bag of jewelry in the trunk of the Prelude. We had closed the door to the tunnel, replaced the square of wood, and left the house as quickly as we were able. We neither one had much to say to the other. We had to sort our own thoughts first.

Meanwhile the sky had changed while we were underground—gone from sunny blue and puffy white to a curdled gray that stretched horizon to horizon—a cheerless sky if I ever saw one. As we turned onto Galena Road and headed back toward Oakalla, I wasn't sorry to leave Hogue Valley behind. For all of its natural beauty, for every magnificent cedar and pine that topped its rolling hills, there was a drop of blood on the earth below.

"What is it that you think we found back there?" Abby said.

"A mass grave. Likely that of runaway slaves."

"For what end?"

"Genocide. Or to be politically correct, ethnic cleansing. And there's a certain perverse beauty to it, too, when you think that they got a lot of the brightest and the best."

"How so?"

The sky lowered, as if a curtain had been drawn. It began to spit snow.

"Those who loved freedom over life. Those who could not stand to be anyone's slave. To my way of thinking, they're the brightest and the best of every race."

Abby turned away from me. I saw tears in her eyes. "They came expecting safe harbor and found death instead. How cruel is that?"

She didn't expect an answer and I didn't try to give her one.

"So what comes next?" she said.

"As I said, we try to find a killer."

"That seems so small now. When you think about the enormity of the other."

"As Grandmother Ryland used to say, 'Small weeds sometimes have deep roots.'"

"Meaning?"

"Meaning there's no such thing as a small evil."

We drove in silence the rest of the way to Clarence Hogue's house and parked right behind his maroon-and-silver GMC pickup. I was amazed at how some people could keep their vehicles so bright and shiny, even in winter, while Jessie always looked as if she had just crawled out of a cave after hibernation.

Clarence Hogue wasn't home. We determined that after knocking on all three of his doors and peering into every window that we could reach.

At our next stop we caught a break and found Bruce Barger home. Bruce's appearance hadn't changed much since yesterday. He wore the same ratty sweat pants, the same smelly T-shirt. Only his gloom seemed to have grown in the interim, and perhaps the circles under his eyes.

"Good morning, Bruce," I said after he answered the door.

"I've got nothing to say to you. Her either, whoever she is."

"Abby Airhart, Bruce Barger. Bruce Barger, Dr. Abby Airhart."

Abby offered her hand, but Bruce ignored it.

"I'm still not talking to either one of you."

To teach Bruce Barger some manners, I thought about punching him senseless, then stuffing one of his overripe socks into his mouth. But then we would never find out from him what we needed to know.

"It's over, Bruce," I said. "So you might as well call you a lawyer and we'll go from there."

"What's over?" he said, not at all convinced that anything was.

"Cissy Hogue's life, the burglary ring, any hope that you ever had of coming out ahead in this. We found the goods at the end of that tunnel under Cissy's house. That's where we found Cissy, too." I held up my little finger to show him. "She had a bullet hole about this size in the middle of her forehead."

Bruce opened his mouth to speak, but no words came out. He just stood there moving his lips and gasping for air. Abby and I helped him inside and into a chair. I watched Abby's eyes as she surveyed the house. *Bleak*, her unspoken thoughts seemed to say.

"Do you need anything?" I asked Bruce.

He shook his head.

"Then are you ready to answer some questions?"

He raised his head to look at me. All of the fight had left him.

"If I can," he said.

"The first one's easy. Do you know where Lori Pitts is?"

"No. Though I wish I did."

"How about Clarence Hogue?"

"Him either."

"Could they be together and, if so, why?"

He admitted that they could be together, but he wouldn't say why.

"Which one are you protecting?" I asked.

"Neither, and both," he said. "You have me. I know that. But I'm not going to take anyone else down with me if I can help it."

I looked at Abby to see what she thought. She shook her head to tell me that I shouldn't pursue it. I deferred to her judgment.

"Okay, Bruce, answer me this. Even if one of your gang is responsible for the killings, why would he start with Jeremy Pitts? Out of all of you, he seemed the least threatening."

"That's what Cissy and I couldn't figure. Lori either, though I think that she knew more than she let on. Who would want to kill Jeremy? That's what blew us away. He never hurt anyone in his life."

Bruce's voice broke and be began to sob. While we waited for him to collect himself again, Abby went to the sink and returned with a glass of water.

"Thanks," Bruce said, gulping most of it in one swallow.

"You're welcome."

He set the glass down and said, "Then it came to me, who might have killed him, though for the life of me, I can't figure out why."

"We're listening," I said. Abby and I each found a folding chair and sat down facing him.

Bruce hesitated a moment, then said, "What the hell. What do I have to lose?"

I glanced at Bruce and then around his house. Not all that much, I figured.

"About seven or eight years ago—you can check it in your newspaper—I got a call from someone who wanted Jeremy and me to do some business for him. It was easy, he said. All we had to do was to burn down this barn, and there would be three hundred dollars waiting in a mailbox for us when the deal was done. I said we wanted some up front money or no deal. He said he didn't do business that way and hung up."

Bruce finished the rest of his water and then looked at Abby as if he were expecting more. She did her best to ignore him.

"Nothing happened after that for a day or two, so I figured he'd given up on it. But then he calls again, wanting the same thing. Not asking this time, though. Telling me that he knew what Jeremy and me had been up to and threatening to call the law down on us if we didn't do what he said."

"What had you been up to?" I asked.

"We had been dealing a little dope, that's all."

"Locally grown or imported?"

"Locally grown. But he's out of business now."

"If you'll tell me who it is, I promise it will stay off the record," I said.

Bruce Barger shrugged. As he'd said, he had nothing to lose.

"Amos Hogue. He grew it out in his woods, then dried it in one of his old hog houses. He'd been doing it for years."

"Why did he stop? You said he was now out of business."

"You'll have to ask him. He never had much to say to Jeremy and me."

"So you and Jeremy went ahead and burned down the barn?"

He nodded. "We figured we didn't have much choice. It was either that or risk going to jail for dealing drugs."

"Did you get your money?"

"Three hundred dollars, just like he said. It was easy money, once we got by the fear of doing it."

"Where was the mailbox located?"

"There in front of Cissy's house, which at the time was deserted."

"Was that the last that you heard of him, then?"

Bruce reached for the glass, saw that it was still empty, and let his arm dangle there above it. Abby got up and refilled the glass, though I could tell that she begrudged it.

"No. That wasn't the last time we heard from him," Bruce said. "About three or four years ago he called, saying he had another job for us. A thousand this time, five hundred up front and five hundred later. Same way of payment, same mailbox. All that we had to do was to go to a motel, pick up a car, put it somewhere that it would never be found again. He said the keys to the car would be in the mailbox along with the five hundred dollars."

"Which they were?"

"Yes."

"Do you remember where you put the car?"

"A ravine out north of town. We drove it there and then burned it."

"Why didn't you just drive it into Hidden Quarry?" Hidden Quarry was two hundred feet deep in places and well off the beaten path.

Bruce took a drink of water as he thought about his answer. In the meantime Abby watched every swallow. She'd be damned if she'd be Bruce Barger's go-for again.

"The cold! That was it, the cold," he said. "It had been so cold for so long we were afraid that the ice on Hidden Quarry would be too thick for the car to break through."

I tried to think of when in the past four years it had been that cold. Several choices came to mind. I asked Bruce his opinion.

"I don't remember," he said. "All I remember is that the motel where we picked up the car had this big fat plastic chicken standing out front. Jeremy and I remarked to each other that it was about the biggest, ugliest chicken we'd ever seen."

"Something to look for," I said. "Do you remember where the motel was?"

"Off I-94, close to Crystal River."

"Do you remember where the ravine is where you burned the car?"

"Not exactly. But I think if we drive out that way, it will come back to me."

Bruce, Abby, and I got into Abby's Prelude. As we did, I noticed Abby give me a questioning look. I thought I knew what was on her mind. How long would it be before the odor of Bruce washed out of her car?

On our way through Oakalla, we stopped at the City Building, where I got out of the car and took the stolen jewelry into the sheriff's office for Eugene Yuill to put in the safe. I then told him to call Clarkie and have him put out an APB on Lori Pitts. Suspicion of murder, in case Clarkie still had any reservations.

Following Bruce's directions, I drove north on Fair Haven Road to the first side road, turned east, then north again at the first crossroads.

"Nice car," Bruce said from in back.

"I'm glad you like it," Abby answered, not really caring whether he did or not.

"I always thought I'd like to have something like this, but I never had the money. Some people are just lucky, I guess."

"I'll tell you what, Bruce," Abby said. "You put yourself through four years of pre-med, three years of medical school, two years of internship, and two years of residency, and you might get lucky, too."

A decided chill crept into the car. Then Bruce said, "Slow down. We're almost there."

I slowed down, and a few feet farther on he had me stop at a gate that led into a weed field.

"How far is it from here?" I asked.

"Not far."

We got out, climbed the gate, and began walking through the field, which was still knee-high in weeds and soggy from the melted snow.

About a quarter mile later we came to a large ravine that had eaten away part of the field and was partially filled with rolls of old fence and a couple of concrete corner posts. At the bottom of the ravine a burned-out car rested on top of a rusted-out water tank, Oakalla's version of junk art.

Abby and I went down into the ravine to look at the car. Bruce stayed in the field above.

"What are we looking for?" Abby asked.

"Anything that will help us identify either the car or its driver."

"Where are the keys to *my* car?"

"In my pocket. What's the matter, don't you trust Bruce?"

"About as far as I can throw him. Talk about your basic low-life."

We found no title or registration in the car, and the plates were missing, but on the driver's side of the dashboard just beneath what used to be the windshield, I saw a metal plate with an alphabet-long number on it.

"Do you have a pen and paper handy?" I asked Abby.

"What do you think?"

I found a soft chunk of wood and used the blade of my pocket knife to scratch the identification number of the car on it. Nobody but me could read it, but I was hoping that no one else would have to.

We picked up Bruce and walked back to the Prelude. The wind was cold out of the northwest and seemed to be on the rise. Snow showers by night, I bet. If it waited that long.

"Was that the last time you heard from the man, after you'd burned the car for him?" I asked Bruce on the way back to Oakalla.

"That was the last we heard of him until late last Monday night, when he called me again at my house. This time it was with a warning. He said that, if we didn't stop stealing from the good people of Oakalla, we might all end up like the man they found in Amos Hogue's dump." Bruce shuddered. "I didn't doubt for one second that he meant what he said."

"Then the next night Jeremy was killed," I said.

"That's what I couldn't understand." The puzzlement was back on Bruce's face, the whine back in his voice. "He never even gave us the chance to see if we were going to stop or not. We would have, if he'd just let us."

"You were that much afraid of him?" I asked.

"You would be, too, if you ever got a call from him. There's something about him that's just not quite right."

"In what way?"

"I can't explain it. Like he's got no soul, or something."

"You're sure it was the same man who called you each time?"

"I'm sure."

"Was his voice familiar?"

"No. It wasn't his natural voice. It sounded like he was talking through a handkerchief or something."

"You have any idea who he might be?"

I glanced over at Abby, who was just as interested in Bruce's answer as I was. Together we waited while Bruce decided whether he wanted to risk telling us or not.

"Cissy told us that she thought it was her cousin, Amos, that he had some grand scheme to get Hogue Valley all to himself."

We were back on Fair Haven Road, headed for home. "How would burning down his own hog barn help him in that?" I said.

"Insurance money is what Cissy said. He needed the money because he thought that her place was coming up for a tax sale. Then Clarence Hogue stepped in and paid the back taxes on the place and saved her property for her. She went on to say that the only thing that stood between Amos and all of Hogue Valley was her and her one hundred twenty acres, so not to be surprised if something happened to her one day."

Now the only thing that stood between Amos Hogue and all of Hogue Valley was Clarence Hogue, wherever he was.

"What about the man whose car you burned? How did Cissy explain that?" I said.

"She thought he was a dope dealer that Amos double-crossed and killed once he got his money. Amos had quit supplying us, so he must've turned his attention elsewhere."

Five minutes later we stopped in front of Bruce's house. I got out of the Prelude to let him out.

"Am I under arrest?" he asked.

"House arrest. Don't go anywhere without checking with Sheriff Clark or me first."

He shrugged, looking lost. "Where would I go? My two best friends are dead."

"One last question, Bruce. Did Cissy ever mention a Kurt Voege to you?"

"She said he was an old friend of hers. Not to be concerned if he showed up at my house looking for her some day."

"The last I heard, they were together."

"She said that they split up on their way here, that he was in Canada now."

"Thanks, Bruce. I appreciate your cooperation."

"Catch Jeremy's and Cissy's killer," he said with sudden resolve. "That's all the thanks I need."

He went into the house. I drove toward home.

CHAPTER 19

"What's your hurry?" Ruth asked on hearing the door slam.

"Abby and I leave for Crystal River in an hour. That is, if she can get someone to cover for her tonight."

"You had lunch?"

"No."

"Then I'll fix you some."

While she began to fix lunch, I threw my insulated vest on the couch and went into the dining room to call Clarkie.

"Clarkie, this is Garth. Did Eugene get ahold of you?"

"We just got off the phone a few minutes ago."

"Well, I've got a shit-load of other things to tell you, so pay attention. I don't have time to repeat myself."

"You have a bad morning?" he asked.

"That's not the half of it."

As Ruth listened from the kitchen, I briefed him on my morning, then finished by giving him what I hoped was the burned car's identification number. The only thing I omitted was the mass grave that Abby and I had found. I wasn't yet sure what to do with that information.

"I'll get right on this, Garth. Are you going to be there for a while?"

"An hour at the most. Any ideas on Lori Pitts?"

"Not yet. But I'll give it some thought."

"Try Amarillo, Texas, and every state in between."

"I thought we agreed that was the last place she would go."

"You said that, Clarkie, but I think she might head for familiar territory because that's the route she knows best."

"I'll put out the word on her as soon as I find out the car that goes with the number you gave me. What kind of car is it, do you know?"

"A Mercury, I think." I glanced outside and saw that it was snowing hard. But not for long, I hoped. "By the way, Clarkie, I put Bruce Barger under house arrest. If you think he belongs in jail, then put him there."

"What are the odds that he'll skip town on us?"

"Slim and none, if I know Bruce."

"Then we'll leave him where he is for now."

I hung up and went into the kitchen, where I threw away the chunk of wood on which I'd written the Mercury's ID number.

"What was that?" Ruth asked.

"My country tablet."

She retrieved it from the waste basket, gave it the once over, and went on about her business. "Hot dogs okay with you?" she said, taking a bottle of beer from the refrigerator.

"Okay with me."

She would steam the hot dogs in a splash of beer, then drink the rest of the beer with her lunch.

"What did Clarkie have to say?" she asked.

"Not much. Just that he'd try to get the car identified before I left."

"Where are you headed, now?"

"Crystal River. To a motel there."

"You and Abby, right?"

"Right."

She just shook her head and went back to work.

She soon served up the hot dogs and some cold pork and beans, which was the way that we both preferred them, while I set catsup, mustard, and relish on the table and ran us each a glass of water. I'd managed one bite of a hot dog when the phone rang.

"Garth, this is Clarkie. I've got a name for you."

"Fire away."

"The name is Zack Richards. He lives in Superior. He bought the Mercury Cougar there in November 1988."

I wrote that down. "You have an address for him?"

"Just a post office number."

I wrote that down, too. "Thanks, Clarkie. See what else you can find out about him, and I'll check back with you later."

"Will do," he said as he hung up.

I hadn't heard Clarkie that happy or excited in a long time. Not since he became sheriff, in fact.

"Is something wrong, Garth?" Ruth asked as I returned to the table.

I didn't tell her the truth, that I had just realized how miserable I had been making Clarkie by keeping him on the job. Up until now all that I had been concerned about was Oakalla and me.

"Clarkie has a name for us," I said. "Zack Richards. It mean anything to you?"

She had finished one hot dog and was spreading mustard on a second. "I knew a Nelson Richards. He died of a bad heart about three or four years back. But he didn't have any family that I know of."

I started on my hot dog before the phone could ring again, then spooned relish onto a second before even swallowing the first. Ruth meanwhile opened a can of her Aunt Emma's freestone peaches and put some in a dish for each of us.

"Hogue Valley," I said between hot dogs. "Have you heard of any plans to develop it?"

"I've heard talk. But that's all it is, is talk."

"What sort of talk?"

"That a Madison developer would like to put a golf course in there."

"A public course? I don't think that will fly."

"A private course. For those in Madison who can afford it."

"What's holding it back?"

"One guess."

"Amos Hogue and his hogs."

"That's the word I get."

I gave it some thought, but still couldn't figure out what Amos's angle was, if he was working one—unless he planned to either buy or drive everybody else out and then claim Hogue Valley for himself, as Cissy Hogue thought.

"You never told me what you found out in Montevideo yesterday," I said, after starting on my second hot dog.

Ruth sat back in her chair and assumed a thoughtful look. I was reminded of those wonderful Thornton W. Burgess stories when Old Mother West Wind would "put her thinking cap on."

"What I found out was that something out of the ordinary happened the very next day after Christy Morton disappeared. A man, who told the housemother that he was from Manpower and temporarily helping out the janitor, came into the residence hall where Christy Morton had been living. The housemother wouldn't have thought anything about it, except that the first time she turned her back, the man disappeared and she never saw him again after that."

"What was he doing while he was there?"

"Dusting, she said. Around the mailboxes."

"Can she describe the man?"

"No. Just a man from Manpower. That's all she remembers."

I finished my hot dog, then my beans and peaches. I was still hungry, but didn't see anything else to eat.

"Did the housemother tell the campus police about what happened?"

"She tried, but they didn't seem very interested. To their way of thinking, odd duck that Christy was, it just made sense that she had left on her own."

"What do you think, Ruth?"

She went after her purse and brought it to the table. "I might tend to agree with them except for a couple things. One..." She reached into her purse and showed me a photograph that looked as if it had been cut from a high school yearbook. "I asked the housemother if this was Christy Morton and she said yes."

"And it's not?"

"No. It's Lori Pitts. Cousin Agnes gave it to me."

"What's the second thing?"

Ruth studied the photograph a moment, then put it back into her purse. "The second thing is that I walked the route that Christy would have taken from the library back to her residence hall. Even in the middle of the day, unless it was between classes when you can't walk for all the people, there are plenty of places where someone could have lain in wait for her. At night he could pick his spot."

"So it's possible that she *was* abducted?"

"Think about it, Garth. After all of this time and not a peep out of her, I think it's likely."

"Then why hasn't her body shown up?"

"It's a big country. There are a lot of bodies out there that will never be found."

I thought about the mass grave that we had found that morning in Hogue Valley. "Tell me about it."

Ruth's brows furrowed, as her antennae went up. I knew that I had said too much already. So I went ahead and told her what we'd found. When I finished, she looked about as disturbed as I'd ever seen her.

"There's no chance you're mistaken, Garth?"

"There's a chance. But I don't think so."

"What do you plan to do about it?"

"I haven't decided yet. Do you have any suggestions?"

"They all must have family somewhere. Are there markers of any kind to identify them?"

"None that I could see."

"Then I guess they're just as well off where they are for now."

"What if Hogue Valley becomes a golf course? Somebody could end up teeing off right over the top of them."

"We'll cross that bridge when we get to it."

I had to smile. I was a veteran of too many wars. "We always get to it, Ruth. At one time or another."

20

Abby and I rode the first few miles on our way to Crystal River in silence. Like me, she had changed clothes, into black jeans, red socks, and a red ski sweater with white birds flying around on it. Despite her protests to the contrary, she looked a lot better in red than I did.

"I'm sorry for the way I reacted to Bruce Barger," she said. "I think it's because he reminds me of Steve, my soon to be ex-husband. Not that they're anything alike, but in some ways they are."

While I waited for her to elaborate, I watched a sudden snow shower come sweeping across a plowed field toward us.

"It's the attitude that they have toward people, women in particular. We are there to serve them, it's *expected*, and

221

we are the ones at fault if something goes wrong with their otherwise perfect lives." Her eyes were bright with anger. "Unless, of course, they need something from us, whether it's money, sex, or forgiveness. Then they're Mr. Congeniality, and will apologize for anything and everything under the sun; then forget it the minute they have what they need."

She took a cigarette from her purse, lighted it, then cracked a window to let the smoke out. I didn't mind the smoke as much as the cold air blowing around my neck.

"Steve is a good surgeon, maybe even better than I am when it comes right down to it, but as a human being, he's a miserable failure. Yet some day I can see him running a big hospital somewhere, making loads of money with all of these people at his command and under his thumb, and keeping a string of bimbos on the side."

"Are you saying that he cheated on you?"

"Not to his way of thinking. Because to this day, as late as last night even, he says that he still loves me and doesn't want a divorce. That he's never loved anyone else but me."

"Maybe he hasn't."

She shot me a wicked glance, as I tried to steer the Prelude through the snow shower without running off the road.

"Some men are like that," I said. Then I corrected myself. "Some *people* are like that. They know what love is. They just don't know how to practice it. So as long as they're faithful in their heart, that's good enough for them. That's because they think their body has a mind of its own."

Abby took a long drag on her cigarette and angrily blew a smoke cloud my way. "That's convenient bullshit. That's what that is."

"True. But it's also the way of the world."

We came to I-94, turned north, then a few minutes later took the Crystal River exit just as another snow shower overtook us. Seeing no motels with a large plastic chicken in front, I stopped at an Amoco service station to ask about it. The young clerk at the register didn't have the faintest idea of what I was talking about, but the middle-aged woman in line behind me did.

"You're looking for the Chanticleer," she said, then pointed to show me. "It's about a half mile in toward town. But the rooster's not there anymore. It blew down in a windstorm a couple years ago."

"Was it as ugly as I heard?" I said.

"Let's put it this way, at last count twenty-six trucks, three cars, and a bicycle had deliberately run over it before they could get it out of the road."

I thanked her and left.

The Chanticleer Motel was one story, limestone, and had at most eight units, one of which also served as the office. An attached diner advertised an all-you-can-eat walleyed pike supper for $8.95 that included a schooner of Old Style and a salad bar. The diner didn't open for supper until five, and I was willing to bet that by six PM there would be standing room only. Unless of course, the walleyed pike turned out to be carp.

The manager of the Chanticleer was a short round woman named Marla with flat rust-red hair that looked like mine after it had been under my stocking cap all day. It was hard to guess her age. She had a jolly-old-elf look and an elfish twinkle in her eyes that made her seem younger than she was. I guessed her age between fifty and seventy and was surprised to learn that she was seventy-two.

"Seventy-three," said her husband, Ed, who had his back to us and was watching C-span on a large screen TV.

"Well, who's counting?" Marla said.

I had been making small talk with her for a couple minutes while trying to size up the motel. It didn't seem like a pirates' den, where people routinely disappeared and were never heard from again, but I had been fooled before. Abby meanwhile waited for me in the Prelude.

"That your wife out there?" Marla asked.

"No. Just a friend."

"Looking to spend the night, are you?"

Her jolly-old-elf face had begun to harden. She seemed to be growing more suspicious of me by the minute. Then I realized that this wasn't the fifties any more and that terror often rode the interstate in the guise of innocence.

"Are you armed?" I asked.

"Ed is. He keeps a shotgun there on the floor beside him all the time."

"Well, tell Ed that I'm going to reach into my pocket and show you some identification."

"Ed, he's..."

"I heard him."

Ed turned around in his chair. He had a double-barrel shotgun resting across his knees and his right hand over the trigger guard. Small and pudgy with a flattop haircut, and wearing bib overalls over a long-sleeve white dress shirt, he was a dead ringer for George Gobel.

I eased my hand into my pocket, took out my wallet, and showed Marla my special deputy's badge. "You can call Sheriff Clark of Adams County if you want to verify it," I said. "My name is Garth Ryland."

"Don't need to," she answered. "I recognize the name. You're the fellow that writes that column once a week in our newspaper." She turned away from me to speak to her husband. "You know the one, Ed. The one that you said makes darn good sense sometimes."

Ed nodded, then turned his chair back to watch television again. I was relieved to see the shotgun go with him.

"Why didn't you identify yourself in the first place?" she said. "You would have saved us some anxious moments."

"I wasn't anxious," Ed answered. "I knew who he was all along."

"Well, I didn't. So why the cat and mouse business, Mr. Ryland? And who is that in the car really?"

"That's Dr. Abby Airhart, deputy coroner of Adams County. We're investigating at least three homicides, one or all of which might have a tie-in here."

"*Here*? To the Chanticleer? Ed, did you hear that?"

"I heard," he said in that flat dry expressionless voice of his. Apparently it took a lot to get Ed excited.

"And you thought we might be involved somehow?" she asked.

"These days you never know."

"Boy, isn't that the truth? A couple about our age, not more than thirty miles up the interstate from here, let a kid into their house to use the phone, and he shot and killed them both. For what? Fifty dollars and change. And just a kid at that."

"Sixteen years old," Ed said. "About the age of their grandson. That's why they let him into the house in the first place. What's this old world coming to? That's what I'd like to know."

I waited out the silence that followed. As a longtime newspaper man who had done his share of reading in the morgue, I knew that this generation didn't have a monopoly on violent crime. Today's criminals just had better press.

"What we need to know is whether a man by the name of Zack Richards ever stayed here at the Chanticleer? It would have happened within the last three or four years," I said.

"Describe him to me," Ed said.

I waved for Abby and she joined me in the office. Hearing the office door open and close, Ed turned around to check her out.

"I've never seen an assistant coroner up close," he said. "At least not of the female persuasion."

"What do you think?" Abby said, pirouetting to show him all of her.

Ed smiled for the first time, then turned around to watch his show.

"What do you need?" Abby asked me.

"A description of Zack Richards. Have you got any ideas?"

She shook her head. "No. I can't even make one up."

"I'll look through our old receipts," the woman said. "Maybe I'll find him there."

"Don't bother, Marla," Ed said. "Remember? He's the one who made off with two of our towels. The one that I said I didn't like the looks of from the first time I saw him."

"Ed has a way with names," Marla explained. "Once he puts a name with a face, he's not likely to forget."

"You might also remember, Marla, the way the man ate," Ed said. "You remarked to me at the time that you had never seen anyone eat like that before."

"I remember now!" she said as she came to life. "He nearly ate us out of business, that one did. I wasn't sorry to see him go."

"Did you see him go?" I said. "I mean, did you see him leave when he left here?"

My question drew a blank look from Marla. Ed seemed to be thinking it over. "We never saw him go," Ed said at last.

"Did he have any visitors that you know of?"

"I can't say. Mornings and nights are a little busy around here, with the diner and all. So it's hard to keep track of who comes and who goes."

"He had a visitor," Marla said. "I was working the cash register that night in the diner and remember a man coming in and asking for him by name. I thought to myself at the time, Lord God help us if he eats like the other one."

"Do you remember what the other man looked like?" I said.

She shook her head. She couldn't remember. "Ed could tell you, but I can't."

"If Ed had seen the man," he answered.

"What about Zack Richards? What did he look like?" I asked.

"Blond, stocky fellow, about five-ten or eleven," Ed said. "Wore a snarl on his face about nine-tenths of the time he was here."

I glanced over at Abby, who had suddenly become very still. "Did he have any tattoos on his arms?" she asked.

"Never saw his arms," Ed said. "How about you, Marla?"

She shook her head.

"Thanks, folks," I said. "I'll try to let you know how this all comes out."

"You be sure to," Marla answered for both of them.

I used the pay phone outside the diner to call Clarkie. "Paydirt," I said. "Zack Richards was here in Crystal River within the last four years."

"And I've got something else to add to the list," he said with excitement in his voice. "As of January, three years ago, Zack Richards has been missing from Superior. At least he never showed up to pick up his last check, so his employer sent it on to the state."

"Where did he work?"

"Superior Shipping. He was in the merchant marine."

"Thanks, Clarkie. Any other news?"

His hesitation meant yes, but it wasn't good news. "Not over two hours ago, they issued Lori Pitts a speeding ticket just west of Clinton, Oklahoma on I-40. But the dispatcher didn't get the news that she was wanted by us until about fifteen minutes ago. I'm sorry, Garth. I got so involved with Zack Richards that I forgot about Lori Pitts."

"Don't give up the ship just yet, Clarkie. They still might stop her somewhere down the road."

"The problem is, I'm not going to be here for a while to keep a handle on things. Eugene just called from my office to say that he's getting overrun with phone calls, which probably means that he's had three or four. But it does mean that I've got to go out on the street again."

"Part of the job, Clarkie," I said without thinking.

"How could I forget?" he said, as his voice, and then the line, went dead.

"Well?" Abby said as I climbed into the Prelude, this time into the passenger seat.

I told her what Clarkie had told me.

"Does this mean that we're going to Superior?" she asked.

"You're the driver."

She started the Prelude and wheeled out into traffic. "I was hoping you'd say that."

"What about your rounds at the hospital?"

She gave me a smug smile. "I'm covered."

"All night?"

"If need be."

I sat back in my seat and just stared at her.

"I know what you're thinking, Garth, because I'm thinking the same thing. But this trip is strictly business."

"My thoughts exactly."

"Bullshit. And wipe that smile off your face."

"When you do," I said.

We must have been at least thirty more miles down the road before I asked, "What was that question about the tattoos all about?"

"The man in my basement is five ten or eleven with blond hair and a stocky build."

"You're thinking that he and Zack Richards are one in the same?"

"It's a possibility."

"Then where has Zack Richards been for the past three years, and why did someone in Oakalla have Jeremy Pitts and Bruce Barger dispose of his car?"

"That's what we're going to Superior to find out."

21

We rolled into Superior about seven that evening—hungry and underdressed. The wind was right off Lake Superior and showed us no mercy when we got out of the Prelude to ask directions to the nearest and best restaurant.

"Ain't no such thing around here," the man behind the counter at the liquor store said. "Not in this neighborhood."

We were in downtown Superior near the iron ore docks. Few cars were on the street, and even fewer people on the sidewalks.

"Then where do the people around here go to eat?"

"Most of them go to the old hotel there along the docks. It's a pretty rough crowd that hangs out in there now, but the food's good." He was staring at Abby, who was shopping for wine. "I wouldn't advise taking her in there, though. You might have to fight your way out."

Abby brought a bottle of white zinfandel to the counter and paid for it herself. The clerk gave me a knowing eye. I smiled just as if I were the cocksman that he thought I was.

"What did he have to say?" Abby asked when we were back in the Prelude.

"He said the old hotel near the docks."

"What else did he have to say?"

"That if I took you in there with me, we'd probably have to fight our way out."

"Is the food any good there?" she asked.

"He says it is."

"Then I'm willing to chance it."

I didn't say anything.

"Aren't you?"

"I don't know, Abby. I don't like putting you at risk, if I don't have to."

"You're not putting me at risk. I am. There's a difference." She started the Prelude. "Now, where is this place?"

I wasn't encouraged by what I saw at the old hotel. The dining room, if one could call it that, had nearly every table filled, most of them with men wearing denim jackets and navy-blue watch caps. Not a woman in sight, except for one waitress who wore jeans and a denim jacket herself. No watch cap, though. It would have clashed with the white patch over her left eye.

Abby and I went into the dining room, which with its cracked plaster ceiling, steam radiators, and soft wooden floor reminded me of my old high school auditorium back in Godfrey, Indiana. So did the icy draft crawling up my legs and the frost on the inside of the windows.

Seeing no "please wait to be seated" sign, I took Abby by the hand and led her to the nearest unoccupied table. The previous customers had left, along with their dirty plates and utensils, three french fries, two T-bone steak bones, and a dollar tip. Either the food was dirt cheap, the service was bad, or they were the last of the red-hot tippers. As I looked around for the waitress, I saw about thirty pairs of eyes, all of them male, pointed my way.

"Are you intimidated?" Abby asked.

"Scared shitless is more like it."

"You're in luck. Here comes the waitress."

Luck was about sixty years old and wearing a black wig that had been shot twice and then run over by a train. Her one good eye, the one that wasn't covered with the white patch, was every bit as black as her wig, and in its fierceness reminded me of the one-eyed grackle that I had wounded as a boy. The grackle that had stared me down even as I raised my pellet gun to put it out of its misery.

"What can I get you to drink?" she asked.

"What do you have on tap?" I asked.

"Nothing."

"Then bring me a glass of water."

"What about you?" she asked Abby.

"Coffee will be fine."

"Do you want to order while I'm here?"

"If we could see a menu."

She reached across me and produced two menus from behind the napkin holder and slapped them down on the table. "I'll be back with your drinks," she said.

"What a warm woman," Abby said when the waitress left.

"My thoughts exactly."

We'd barely skimmed the menu when the waitress returned with our drinks. Abby and I were still attracting a lot of attention, but not quite as much as before.

"What's good?" I asked.

"It's all good. What are you hungry for?"

"How are the steaks?"

"Good. Like I just said."

"Then I'll have a New York strip, medium rare, American fries, and a tossed salad with blue cheese dressing."

"What to drink?"

"Water, like I ordered."

She let her evil eye rest on me a moment before she turned it on Abby. I was beginning to understand the dollar tip a little better now.

"I'd like perch, french fries, and tossed salad with vinegar-and-oil dressing," Abby said. "And water to drink.

"You could've told me that earlier."

"Sorry. I didn't think of it... Bitch," she added when the waitress was safely out of hearing.

"Well, I'm ready to go. How about you?" I said to Abby.

"And waste this opportunity."

"What opportunity? If you mean to get mugged, I gave at the office already."

"Look around you, Garth. How many blue watch caps do you see? Every one matches the one you found in Amos Hogue's dump."

I wasn't convinced. "You've seen one blue watch cap, you've seen them all," I said. "There are probably hundreds running around Boston just like them."

"Still, I'm staying. At least until we can ask some questions."

So we stayed—long enough for me to eat one of the best steaks I'd ever eaten and for Abby to gush over the perch to whoever was in earshot.

"Aren't you overdoing it a little?" I asked.

"I'm serious," she said, as she pushed away her empty plate and lighted a cigarette. "Those are the best fish I've ever eaten."

I watched the men around us watch us. Their eyes were bright and hard with envy. The fact that Abby smoked seemed to make her even more attractive to them. In a strange and disquieting way, it did to me, too. Perhaps because I'd had such bad luck with nonsmokers.

"Was there anything else?" Evil eye was back with our check. Dessert would be out of the question at this point.

"There is one thing," I said, reaching into my wallet and laying a ten-dollar bill on the table. "We're looking for Zack Richards. Would you check around in here and see whether anyone knows him, or knows where he is?"

"Anybody in here know Zack Richards?" she shouted at the top of her lungs. The whole room went quiet. I could feel every eye on us.

"Guess not," she said. She reached down and in one smooth motion that would have done justice to a pick-pocket, snatched up the ten-dollar bill and left.

While on my way to the cashier, I noticed two men in watch caps rise hurriedly from their table, then go out-side while I was paying for our supper. Abby had gone on to the rest room, so she didn't see them. The one thing besides their watch caps that I had noticed about them was that they were both younger and bigger than I was.

"Ready," Abby said on her return.

"Stay close. There might be trouble ahead."

"Are you serious?"

"As I've ever been."

Before we left, I checked the street and sidewalk. No help there. They were as bare as Old Mother Hubbard's cupboard.

"Here we go," I said to Abby as we stepped outside. "Whatever happens, don't stop to wait on me."

A bitter blast from Lake Superior hit us full in the face. That was the first thing that happened. The second thing was that two large men in watch caps stepped out of a shadow and blocked our path. Damn, I thought, as I balled up my fist. Here we go.

"We don't want any trouble," I said.

"Neither do we. You were asking about Zack Richards."

"Are you friends of his?"

"Shipmates. Zack didn't have any friends."

I felt relieved, but still not entirely out of the woods. "Could we go inside and talk? It's freezing out here."

"Sure. Why not?"

They followed us back into the lobby of the hotel, which had a green-shaded floor lamp in the corner and all of five chairs scattered around its perimeter. There was a hole in the ceiling where apparently a chandelier had once hung and a dark-green plastic bag taped over one of the windows. The bag breathed in and out every time the front door of the hotel opened.

The two men in watch caps gathered four of the chairs into the corner with the lamp. Though they were obviously on their home turf, they seemed awkward, almost backward in our presence, like newlyweds receiving their first real guests.

"Have a seat," one of them said. "It's not much. But we call it home."

"You live here?" Abby asked.

"Part of the year, when we're iced in, like we are now. The rest of the time we're aboard ship."

I glanced at one and then the other. Fair-skinned and blue-eyed, they didn't look over twenty-five. Except for their hands, rough, large-knuckled, workingman's hands, they could have passed for college students.

"You been at it long?" I asked.

"Eight years," said one.

"Seven years," said the other.

"Lifers," they both agreed.

Abby just sat and stared at them, as fascinated as if we were being entertained by Captain Nemo and his crew. They were equally fascinated by her. They stared at her as if they'd never seen a woman up close before. But I doubted that.

"What is it that you do?" they asked me, though they were really asking her.

"I own and edit a small newspaper downstate. Dr. Airhart is our local surgeon."

"You're a doctor?" Her stock just went up that much higher.

"Yes," she said, unable to contain her smile. "I'm a doctor."

"Then why are a doctor and a newspaperman looking for Zack Richards?"

The question seemed as innocent as their smiles, but neither could have been quite the neophyte that he was pretending to be. Not after seven or eight years at sea. I doubted that they intended us any harm, but given a chance at Abby they would have taken it. In a second.

I took out my wallet and showed them my badge. "I'm a special deputy working for the county. Dr. Airhart is deputy county coroner. Zack Richards' name turned up in a murder we're investigating." Along with his body, it was starting to look like.

They exchanged glances. Neither one was quite prepared for this.

"You think Zack's involved in a murder?"

"In one way or another. What do you know about him?"

Again they exchanged glances. Suddenly neither one wanted to be the spokesman. But once you take center stage, it's hard to exit gracefully without delivering your lines.

"Like I said, Zack didn't have many friends," the bookend on my right said. "So I can't tell you too much about him. What I can tell you is that he was expecting to come into a lot of money, so it was no surprise to any of us when he didn't report to ship again."

"What kind of money was he going to come into?" I asked. "Could it have been drug money?"

He shrugged as if he hadn't entirely dismissed that idea. "He never said. Just that he would be set for years to come."

"How long ago was this?"

He did some figuring and said, "A little over three years ago. The ice came in right after he left, so we didn't ship out again until spring."

"Did Zack have any tattoos on him?" Abby asked.

"He had Maggie T. tattooed on one of his forearms. A lot of us do."

As he rolled up his sleeve to show us his tattoo, I could see Abby shrink back in horror. It was as if the man in her basement had suddenly sprung to life. But then the scientist in her took over, as she leaned forward to examine the tattoo. The seaman smiled broadly, proud to show her his muscular arm.

"Who is Maggie T. anyway?" I asked.

"Our ship. The Margaret Thatcher. She's an iron ore carrier."

"Of course," Abby and I said in unison.

Then we rose and Abby and I each shook their hands, which were as hard and strong as they looked.

"Thanks for the information. We appreciate it," I said.

"You sure we can't show you to your car? This is a pretty rough neighborhood."

"Thanks anyway, fellows," Abby said with a smile as she took my arm. "But Garth is all the protection I need."

Then we made a beeline for the door and hit the bricks running.

"What fun!" Abby said when we were safely inside the Prelude. "I've never been so scared in my life."

"I'm glad you enjoyed it."

"Cheer up, Garth. I was the one they were devouring with their eyes the whole time."

"And I'm the one they had to go through to get to you."

"Would you have fought them, really?"

"To my last breath," I said jokingly. But I knew I wasn't joking.

Abby reached over and rested her hand on mine. It was still there when I pulled into a motel an hour later.

"Where are we?" she asked groggily. She had been nodding for the last few miles, drifting in and out of sleep.

"We're at Rice Lake. I can't drive any farther."

"Had you intended to?"

"It depended on how things went. But I need sleep more than I need to get back to Oakalla."

She leaned back in the seat and closed her eyes. "Good choice."

A few minutes later I returned with a key to our room. I handed it to Abby.

"Only one?" she asked.

"That's all they had left. It seems the place is crawling with cross country skiers."

"And how many beds?"

"One."

Her eyes opened a little wider. "We're adults. We'll manage."

Famous last words.

An hour later I lay with both eyes open, staring at the ceiling. I was wearing only my boxer shorts. Abby was wearing only her panties and my T-shirt. There was a thin line of bed between us, one that I'd already crossed a hundred times in my mind.

"This isn't working," I said aloud, thinking she was asleep.

"I know," she answered. "Maybe a glass of wine will help."

"If we could ever get the cork out of the bottle."

"Next time remember to bring a corkscrew."

"What would be the harm?" I said. "It's going to happen sooner or later."

"Sooner, I'm quite sure. I guess I'm willing if you are."

I reached over and turned on the light. She looked so damned beautiful lying there that I could hardly stand it. And still married.

"I should have driven on, found us a big room with two beds the size of Texas in it."

She took my hand in hers. I loved the feel of her. Never had anyone touched me so well.

"But you didn't drive on. So what's it going to be, buster, are we going to make whoopee or not?"

I got out of bed, taking one pillow and the bedspread with me, leaving her the rest. "Not."

"You're sure that's what you want?"

I forced a smile. "No. It's not what I want. But I think it's what we both need."

"Speak for yourself, Garth."

I leaned down and kissed her. Then I turned off the light.

"Good night," I said.

"Good night. I love you."

I laid my pillow on the floor and tried it out for size. "Good."

CHAPTER 22

"Well, how did you sleep?" Abby asked me the next morning after we'd both showered and were dressed again.

"I've slept better on campouts."

Her hair was still wet. She sat on the edge of the bed towel-drying it. "I did okay once I got to sleep."

"You're beautiful, you know that," I said. "I could sit here for hours just watching you."

"And you're hungry, I bet."

"How did you know?"

She smiled. "I know you."

We ate at the motel restaurant and then were on our way again. Abby drove, while I amused myself by looking at the scenery along the way, which was something that I hadn't had the chance to do for a while. It only confirmed my belief that top to bottom Wisconsin is one of the prettiest states in the union.

"Garth, would you look in the glove compartment and see if there is a pair of sun glasses in there? I think I left my others at home."

The day had dawned cold and clear. We were driving almost directly into the sun.

I opened the glove compartment, started to reach in there, then pulled my hand out again. "Abby, there's a gun in there."

"I know. A Smith & Wesson .357 Magnum."

"Is it loaded?"

"It was the last time I looked."

I waited for an explanation.

"When I was in Detroit, at Henry Ford Hospital, I got mugged one night after work. I came out into an empty parking lot, and there was this big black guy standing next to his car, which was parked next to mine. I didn't think anything about it until he pulled a knife on me and took my purse. It happened so fast that I really wasn't scared until I got home and thought about all that could have happened. So I called up this cop friend of mine whom I'd patched up a few months earlier and asked him what he thought I should do. He said to buy a handgun and he'd teach me how to shoot it. I bought the .357 because it felt the best in my hand."

"Did he teach you how to shoot it?"

"Yes. He was a good teacher."

I didn't press for details on what else he might have been good at. "So you left it in your car after that?"

"No. I got a permit and carried it in my purse after that. I only put it in my car after I moved to Oakalla. I didn't think I needed it here and didn't know if Uncle Bill would want it in the house."

I watched a pine thicket close in around us, then open up again. We were leaving the North behind. Soon we would be seeing mostly woodlots, alfalfa fields, and dairy farms.

"You ever find my sunglasses?"

I eased the Smith & Wesson out of the way, lifted a couple road maps, and found a pair of sunglasses. After cleaning them off on my shirt, I handed them to her.

"Here they are," I said.

We passed over the Black River. The North was behind us now.

"You're very quiet," she observed.

"I'm still getting used to the idea that you're a pistol-packing mama."

"Why does that bother you?"

"I don't know. But it does. I guess because I want you safe."

"It's not a safe world any more, Garth, if it ever was. You above all people should know that."

"I do know that. But sometimes I don't like to be reminded of my limitations. If I can't keep you safe, if I can't help keep Oakalla safe, then what's the point in it all? I might as well be selling shoes or something."

"Would you be satisfied selling shoes or something?"

"No." I didn't even have to think about it.

"Then that's the point. I can't save every one of my patients, but I can sure as hell try. And even those I can't save, maybe I can help them live what's left of their lives with some kind of dignity. That's all any of us can do, really. What we do best."

I smiled at her. "Thanks. I needed that."

"Well, it angers me when you get down on yourself, that you think of yourself as somehow a failure. Nothing could be farther from the truth."

"Not a failure, Abby. But not Superman either. God knows there are days when I would like to be." And today was one of them.

An hour and a half later we drove into Oakalla. As much as I loved home and as much as there was to do once I got there, I was sorry to see us arrive. For a few hours Abby and I had had the world to ourselves. I wasn't ready to give that up just yet.

"Well, this is it," she said, kissing me goodbye. "I'm off to the rat race."

"You on your way to the hospital now?"

She assumed a mysterious look. "Soon. There's something at home that I want to do first."

Ruth met me at the front door, which was never a good sign. "It's about time," she said. "Clarkie's about to wear the phone out calling here. Where have you been anyway?"

"Superior. Then we spent the night in Rice Lake."

"You might have called."

"I might have, Ruth, but to be honest I really didn't think about it."

She looked hurt. I thought I knew why.

"And it wasn't because we were so hot to trot that I forgot about it," I said. "We were dead tired, both of us."

"You don't owe me an explanation," she said. But I could tell that she was glad to get one.

I handed Ruth my insulated vest on my way to the phone. "Clarkie, it's Garth. Ruth said you called."

"About twenty times," he said, as upset with me as Ruth had been. "Where in the world were you?"

"It's a long story. But at least we have an ID on the body we found in the dump. Abby and I are both sure that it's Zack Richards."

"That goes along with what I found, then," Clarkie said. "According to their records, the First Bank of Wausau has Zack Richards depositing $100,000 in a savings account three years ago last December 18th and withdrawing a like amount in July of last year. He used the money to buy a condominium in Venice, Florida. I can give you the address if you think it's important."

"Not at the moment, Clarkie. I'm pretty sure of where Zack Richards is right now." I thought a moment, then said, "But it might help if he had a local address?"

"Just a post office box number in Wausau. That's where they sent his bank statement."

"Thanks, Clarkie. Anything else that I should know?"

"No, I don't guess so. There's still no further word on Lori Pitts."

"Are you going to be home for a while in case I need to get ahold of you?"

"For the time being. But this afternoon I've got to take Milt Manning up to Rhinelander for his trial on Monday. I've put it off as long as I can, but if I don't get him up there by today, I'll be in contempt of court."

"It never ends, does it, Clarkie?"

"You can say that again." But at least there was some life back in his voice. Perhaps because he knew he would be off the streets at least until Sunday.

I hung up and went into the kitchen, where Ruth had my vest draped over my chair and a pot of coffee on. She poured us each a cup and we sat down at the table to drink it.

"You say the dead man is Zack Richards?" she said.

"We think so anyway. Why?"

"Well, while you were gone, I did some calling around. It seems that Nelson Richards might have had a nephew by that name. Aunt Emma isn't sure, but she thinks that's his name. In any case, she knows that Nelson Richards had a nephew."

I took a sip of my coffee. It tasted particularly good after a morning on the road. "How is Aunt Emma, by the way?"

Ruth's Aunt Emma was an alcoholic who, drunk or sober, was still a storehouse of knowledge.

"How is Aunt Emma ever?" Ruth answered, not wanting to talk about it.

"So what do you make of that, the fact that Nelson Richards had a nephew?" I asked.

"There's nothing to make of it, in and of itself. Until you add the fact that Nelson Richards' nephew disappeared right after Nelson died and Andy Metzger's granddaughter disappeared right after Andy died." Pleased with herself, Ruth sat back in her chair. "Then you might have something."

"Did either Nelson Richards or Andy Metzger have ties to Hogue Valley?" I asked.

"Not that I can find."

"Then you might *not* have something. Zack Richards didn't disappear. He just changed post offices."

"What about that $100,000 that he deposited in that bank in Wausau, that he then used to buy a condominium in Florida?"

"You've been talking to Clarkie, haven't you?"

"You've got it backwards, Garth. Clarkie's been talking to me."

I glanced outside where the sun had just gone under a cloud. More clouds were on the way, I bet. We'd be lucky to see the sun the rest of the day.

Ruth said, "On top of that, nobody ever remembers seeing this Zack Richards, not in Oakalla, not in Wausau, not anywhere in between in the past three years. Now that won't bother me if you can tell me where he was."

"I can't, Ruth. We talked to two of his shipmates last night. The last time they saw him was December three years ago. He said that he was about to come into a big chunk of money."

"Well, he wasn't wrong about that. But where has he been since, if not here or there?"

"How about Venice, Florida, where his condo is?" I said.

"He's not been there either. I talked to the manager. His condominium's been vacant, except for furniture, since the day he bought it."

While I was trying to make sense of it all, the phone rang. It was Abby.

"Garth, can you come over here right away?" She was

excited, completely out of breath.

"Why? What's wrong?"

"I'd rather not say over the phone. I just want you here."

"I'm on my way."

"Trouble?" Ruth asked, as I hung up the receiver.

"It sounds like it. Can I take your Volkswagen?"

"Be my guest."

The Volkswagen hadn't even stopped rolling when I jerked the parking brake and jumped out of it. Taking Abby's front steps two at a time, I was glad that Doc Airhart wasn't there to see me make a fool of myself. Already he'd had a lifetime of opportunities to do that.

I didn't knock, but went on inside the house. "Abby, where are you?" I yelled.

"Down here. In the basement."

"In the morgue?"

"Yes."

Crap, I thought. I'm not ready for this. But I headed for the basement anyway and was relieved to see Abby coming up the steps. As soon as she stepped into the kitchen, I grabbed her and held her tight.

"What was that for?" she asked when I finally let go.

"That was for scaring the hell out of me. Are you all right?"

A nearly empty wine glass sat on the kitchen table. Abby took the bottle of Zinfandel that she had bought in Superior and refilled the glass. "I think so," she said with a smile.

She sat down at the kitchen table. I sat down across from her. It was strange to sit there without Doc, or without Daisy scratching at the basement door.

"But it's hard coming face to face with the truth," she said.

"The truth about what?"

"Zack Richards didn't die last Sunday as we thought. He died in December three years ago."

"You're absolutely sure about that?" Because it would answer a lot of questions if he had died then, and raise a whole lot of others.

"Absolutely? No. Very sure to positive? Yes. You remember that all along I've said that something didn't seem right about him. His skin for one thing, which was rubbery and not at all what it should be, even though it had been frozen. Then this morning on the way home I got to thinking about what Marla at the Chanticleer had to say about his eating habits. So I had her check the exact night that he stayed there, which wasn't hard because she'd already done that on her own. It was on a Friday, and that's always their all-you-can-eat fish night."

"And Zack Richards' stomach is full of fish." I remembered her saying that.

"Crammed full of fish. I don't know how he did it."

I sat there dumfounded, trying to take it all in. "Then whom did Jerry Patterson see in front of his house last Sunday and where has Zack Richards been the past three years?"

Abby took a drink of her wine. She was proud of herself.

"I can't answer your first question, Garth. But I can deal with your second one. Zack Richards has been frozen somewhere. Probably in someone's deep freeze."

"For over three years?"

"That's what it looks like."

"Then why bring him out now?"

"I don't know. But I'm sure there's a reason."

We sat there in silence, listening to the grandfather clock in Doc's study tick away the seconds. Clarkie, Ruth, and now Abby had all added their pieces to the puzzle. It was about time for me to do something.

"Do you mind if I use your phone?" I said.

"Be my guest. You know where it is."

I called Clarkie at home and was relieved when he answered. "Clarkie, this is Garth again. I've got a very strange request, but I want you to do your best to honor it." Then I told him what it was.

"You're right, Garth. That is a strange request. But I'll see what I can do."

"I'm counting on you, Clarkie." Never had I meant anything more.

Abby watched me all the way into the kitchen. I stopped at her chair and put my arms around her.

"What do you think?" I said.

"I think if you're right we have a whole new ball game."

The phone rang.

"Damn," Abby said. "That's probably the hospital."

"Let it ring."

"I would if I could."

She slipped from my grasp and went to answer the phone. A moment later she came back into the kitchen.

"For you, she said.

"Clarkie?"

"Ruth."

"Damn," I said. "How does she know?"

Abby only smiled.

"Yes, Ruth, what is it?"

"You don't have to use that tone of voice. You have a visitor here. I thought you might want to know about it."

"Who is it?"

"Someone you wouldn't guess in a hundred years."

"Then tell me."

"Lori Pitts."

"Tell her I'll be right there."

23

Lori Pitts didn't look too worse for wear after her thirty-six hours on the road. But she did have dark splotches on her cheeks that magnified her already large eyes and somehow made her appear malnourished. Though for someone on the brink of starvation, she still had a lot of energy. So wired that she couldn't sit still for more than a few seconds at a time, she was making me tired just watching her.

"So you came back to turn yourself in, is that it?" I said.

Ruth and I sat on the living room couch. Lori Pitts paced back and forth, wearing a hole in our carpet. Already she'd drunk two cups of coffee and was on her third.

"That's it. I came back to turn myself in."

"Why?"

She objected to that question, as she had the first time I'd asked it. "I told you. I don't want to spend my life on the run, always looking over my shoulder, wondering who's there."

"And you have no idea who killed Cissy Hogue and your brother, Jeremy, then took a shot at me?"

"No idea whatsoever." She walked over to the mantel, where she had laid her cigarettes and lighter, lit a cigarette, and began pacing again. "I was out of town when Jeremy was killed. And out of sight when Cissy was killed."

"You were up in her bedroom, right?"

"Right. A crash downstairs awakened me. Then I heard the shot and headed for the secret stairway. That's what Cissy called it, the secret stairway, like it was a big deal or something."

"You do know that it was your gun that killed Cissy?"

She momentarily stopped her pacing. I was glad for the rest.

"No. I didn't know. But I wondered when I reached for it and found it gone."

"When was that?"

"The night you saw me drive off. I was too scared to leave the house until then."

"Why did you go out to Cissy's house in the first place?"

She tried to stare me down and didn't succeed. "Why do I feel like I keep repeating myself? I went out there at Cissy's insistence. She was scared and wanted company."

"Then why did you sleep in her bed and she sleep in your sleeping bag on the kitchen floor?"

Lori went looking for an ashtray and found it on the mantel. "Why all the questions, Garth? Why don't you just lock me up and let me do my time?"

"Because I don't know what to charge you with yet. What did you do after you heard the shot and went to the secret stairway?"

She started pacing again, taking the ashtray with her. "Waited for what seemed like hours. Then when I was sure that it was safe, I went downstairs and found Cissy dead."

"Why didn't you call Sheriff Clark at that point?"

"Because, if you haven't noticed, there's no phone in the house."

"Amos Hogue lives just down the road. You could have used his phone."

Without seeming to realize it, she had stopped pacing and was hugging herself. It was something that a child might do when confronted with the bogeyman.

"I didn't think of it, okay. Like I said before, I was scared to leave the house."

"So instead you carried Cissy's body all the way to where we found her buried?"

"Dragged her is more like it. Then cleaned up the blood afterwards."

"Why go to all of that trouble? Why not just leave her there on the floor?"

"So that I could be blamed for her murder? No, thanks. I was in enough trouble the way it was."

"The robberies, you mean?"

"What else would I mean?" she snapped.

I let that pass for the moment. "Then you waited until you couldn't stand it any longer and came out of hiding, only to find Sheriff Clark's patrol car parked out in front of the house."

She put out her cigarette and set the ash tray back on the mantel. "I could have cried at that point. I really could have."

"So you waited him out, saw Sheriff Clark leave, ran to your Peterbilt, and went where?"

She debated several seconds before saying, "Amarillo."

"Why there?"

"Why not there? I knew my way, where all the cops were likely to be. Except I forgot about the one outside of Clinton."

"Where were you headed? Mexico?"

"To be honest, Garth, I never even thought about it. I put the pedal to the metal and went."

I wished I could have believed her. More, I wished Clarkie would call.

"You went alone, right?"

"I told you I did."

"Then you wouldn't happen to know where Clarence Hogue is, would you?"

Something sparked in her eyes, as she saw that I was on to her. But she didn't back down.

"No. I don't know where Clarence Hogue is," she said. "Why don't you ask around and find out?"

"And the four partners in crime were you, Jeremy, Bruce, and Cissy? Except that your part was yet to come, since you were the one who was supposed to haul the stolen merchandise to Chicago, where a fence would be waiting."

"That's right."

"Who was supposed to set up the deal in Chicago once you were ready to move?"

"Cissy knew someone, she said. He was in Canada now, but she knew how to get ahold of him."

"Kurt Voege?"

She feigned ignorance. "That might be his name. I forget now."

The phone rang. Ruth sat stoically on the couch while I went to answer it. How she had endured all of this without adding her two cents worth was beyond me. But she had my everlasting gratitude.

"Garth, it's Clarkie. You were right. She deposited $100,000 in an Amarillo bank in September of last year. She withdrew $50,000 of it in January of this year and the other $50,000 just yesterday evening. There's still a balance of a few dollars, but I imagine that's there for good."

"Until the service charges eat it up. Thanks, Clarkie."

"I'll be going now, Garth. I'll have to if I'm going to make it to Rhinelander and back today."

"Thanks again, Clarkie. You and your computer have done a great job."

"If only the same could be said for me and my shadow," he said sadly just before he hung up.

"Who was that?" Lori asked, seeing by my look that all was not well for her.

"Sheriff Clark. So you can quit lying through your teeth and save us both some time." Before she could protest, I said, "I mean it, Lori. In September of last year a woman who identified herself as Christy Morton deposited $100,000 in an Amarillo bank. In January of this year she withdrew $50,000 and last evening withdrew another $50,000. Sheriff Clark faxed the bank a photograph from your high school yearbook. The teller identified you as Christy Morton."

I glanced at Ruth, who just rolled her eyes and shook her head. She knew the part about the photograph was an outright lie. But Lori Pitts didn't know that.

"I don't believe you," Lori said. "I don't know any Christy Morton."

"Then do you mind if I look in your purse, or whatever it is that you carry your identification in these days? For that matter, do you mind if I search the cab of your truck to see if I can find the missing money? I can impound your truck while we're waiting for a search warrant."

If she had called my bluff and said, "Go ahead, search away," I would have just shot myself in the foot. Instead, she sat down in my favorite chair, pulled her knees up to her chest, and began to rock back and forth.

I sat back down on the couch, where Ruth was fighting a war with herself. The mother in her wanted to go comfort Lori to try to make everything better. The citizen in her wanted the same answers that I did. In the end, the citizen won out. Ruth stayed where she was and, harder still, kept her peace.

I said, "I'll try to make it easier for you, Lori. I'll tell you what I think I know and then you can tell me what you know. Is that fair enough?"

She continued to rock back and forth. I wasn't sure that she even heard me.

"Garth, can't this wait for another day?" Ruth could stand it no longer.

"No, Ruth, it can't."

"Then I'll be in the kitchen." Where she could hear, but not have to see what was going on.

"Here's what I think happened, Lori," I said after Ruth had left. "I think that last September you got a phone call, which involved an offer you couldn't refuse. It was easy. All you had to do, the caller said, was to pick up a check and some identification and open an account somewhere out of state, preferably the farther away from Oakalla the better. Then you were told to sit tight and he'd be in touch. He got in touch in January and had you withdraw $50,000, which you left for him somewhere. Where was that, Lori?"

For the longest time I thought she wasn't going to answer. Then she said, "The mailbox across the road from where the barn burned down."

"You mean there on County Road 425 West below Cissy Hogue's?"

"Yes. That's where I picked up the check and Christy Morton's identification."

"What kind of check was it?"

"I think it was an insurance check. But I'm not sure." She went back to rocking again.

"So after that you thought you were done with it. The rest of the money was yours free and clear whenever you wanted to claim it. In the meantime, however, you had let Jeremy, or one of that crowd, talk you into hauling their stolen goods to Chicago for them. It wasn't something that you had your heart set on doing, but would only do it as a favor to Jeremy."

The tears in her eyes said that I had guessed correctly.

"Except that Jeremy or no one else knew what else you were involved with, and in the end that's what cost him and Cissy Hogue their lives. With Jeremy it was a case of mistaken identification. He had the bad luck to be in the wrong place at the wrong time and got shot instead of you. With Cissy it amounted to the same thing. She got shot while trying to protect her home and you."

Lori's head was buried in her lap. Her sobs racked her tiny frame until it seemed she might break in two. It was then that Ruth charged onto the scene.

"Are you proud of yourself?" she asked as she went to comfort Lori.

"It had to be done, Ruth."

"By all means, truth must be served." She was as angry at me as I had ever seen her.

"Yes, it must. For those of us who serve it."

"At any cost, right?"

By now I was angry. "She's an accessory to murder, Ruth. If you want to feel sorry for anyone, feel sorry for Christy Morton. She didn't have a choice in the matter."

I put on my vest and went outside. Sure enough, the clouds had taken over the sky. There wasn't a patch of blue in sight.

Around the block I went, then around it again for good measure. Not to miss an opportunity, a dark cloud rolled in and peppered me with snow. I flipped it off and kept on walking.

On my return Ruth and Lori were sitting on the couch in the living room, drinking coffee and chatting like old friends. But I brought a chill into the house with me. Neither had much to say with me there.

"Are you ready to go?" I asked Lori.

"Where?"

"To jail for now."

"What about my truck and the money inside?"

"Is the money locked up?"

"Yes."

"Then it will be safe here."

Ruth hadn't said anything to me. But I could tell that she wanted to.

"Yes, Ruth, what now?"

"Are you stopping by the City Building?"

"I plan to. Why?"

"Yesterday you said that you thought Hogue Valley was the key to this whole mess. It got me to thinking. When they first divided that section, Amos Hogue's father got three hundred twenty acres, which eventually fell to Amos. Clarence and Cissy Hogue's father got three hundred twenty acres, which should have fallen to them. Except from everything I've heard and everything you've said, Cissy and Clarence only got two hundred forty acres, or a hundred twenty acres each, which includes the two houses and everything there along the east side of the road up to Amos Hogue's property. What I want to know is, who got the other eighty across the road?"

I was busy adding up acres. Ruth was right. There were eighty acres of Hogue Valley unaccounted for.

"I give up. Who did?" I said.

"I don't know. But while you're at the City Building, it might be worth your while to look it up in the *Adams County Plat Book*."

"Does that mean I'm forgiven?"

"It means that I don't have time to do it myself."

Lori Pitts and I walked to the City Building. It was either that or ask to borrow Ruth's Volkswagen, which I didn't have the guts to do.

"What did you plan to do with your $50,000?" I asked.

Lori easily kept stride with me. After a few minutes with Mother Ruth, she seemed to be feeling much better.

"Buy me a new rig, or at least a good used one. If you haven't noticed, my old one's about to fall apart."

"So what was your plan when you came back here today? Cop a plea for the burglaries, receive a slap on the wrist, and then take your money and run?"

She shrugged. "That's about it. Close enough anyway."

"Do you have any idea who killed Jeremy and then tried to kill you?"

She stuffed her hands into the pockets of her jeans. "No."

"Not even a guess?"

"No. I don't want to take the chance of being right."

"What's that supposed to mean?"

"You're not going to catch him, Garth. He's too smart for all of us. My best chance is to keep my mouth shut and hope he forgets about me."

"He won't forget about you, Lori. You're probably the only person who knows enough to put him away."

Her face became hard with resolve. "I'll take my chances."

Deputy Eugene Yuill was glad to see us. He got out of his chair and limped over to the counter on his walking cast.

"I see you're up and at it," I said.

"Yep. Doc said I could walk on it as long as I didn't overdo it."

"Doc?"

"Dr. Abby Airhart," he said with a note of pride in his voice. Then he noticed Lori Pitts. "You here to pay your water bill?" he asked. "It's overdue."

"She's here to be put in jail," I said. "So before you formally charge her, you need to read her rights."

"What *is* the charge, Garth?" Eugene asked.

"Accessory to murder after the fact, for starters. If I come up with anything else, I'll let you know." What I didn't tell Eugene was that we could never make the charge stick unless we found Christy Morton's body.

While Eugene limped over to pick up the keys to the jail, I unlatched the gate and entered the office, which Clarkie and Eugene shared with the county clerk.

"Eugene, do you know where the plat books are?"

He pointed to show me. "There in that stack somewhere."

"Do you happen to know what township Hogue Valley is in?"

"Madison, I believe. Either that or Washington."

Eugene read Lori her rights, while I sorted through the plat books, looking for the one I wanted. Finally I found it.

"Has Sheriff Clark been by to pick up Milt Manning yet?" I said.

"Not more than ten minutes ago."

"You have any idea when he'll be back?"

"He said not to expect him until late."

Eugene limped out through the gate, took Lori by the arm, and led her outside. It was fortunate that he didn't have far to go. The jail sat just behind the City Building.

I found Madison Township and then had to find Hogue Valley, which took a few minutes, since I had never been an A+ geography student. First I located Amos

Hogue's four hundred forty acres, since by 1985 Clarence had already sold out to Amos; next I located Cissy Hogue's one hundred twenty acres and ran my finger down County Road 425 West until I came to the spot where the hog barn had stood, then swung my finger to the right onto the property across the road. The owner's name jumped out at me, left a large welt on my heart.

CHAPTER 24

When I told Ruth, as I had expected, she didn't believe me. That's why I had brought the plat book home with me.

I opened the book to page 17. "See for yourself."

She saw for herself. "I still don't believe you."

We were in the kitchen, leaning over the table looking at the plat book, like two people about to arm wrestle. "It all fits, Ruth, if you can keep your emotions out of it, which I did on the way home. He's the only one who had all the tools to make it work."

"I don't care what you say, Garth. You can't make me believe that Jerry Patterson is a cold-blooded murderer."

"The evidence says otherwise."

"What evidence? I don't see a thing that links him to any of those murders."

"He's in the insurance business, Ruth, mainly life and property. My bet is that he was both Nelson Richards' life insurance agent and Andy Metzger's life insurance agent, and that he killed their beneficiaries, who were Zack Richards and Christy Morton, and stole their checks."

"Why?" she said, adamant in his defense. "Just tell me why Jerry Patterson would do something like that."

"I don't know, Ruth. I'll have to ask him."

She glared at me. She hadn't forgiven me for Lori Pitts yet.

"I'm sure that's what you're going to do, Garth. Walk right down to his house and ask him. Everything that poor man's been through and now you're trying to put a noose around his neck."

"I'm not trying to put a noose around his neck, Ruth. He's done a good enough job of that himself."

"According to you."

This was getting us nowhere. It was time to put up or shut up.

I said, "Okay, if you're so certain about Jerry's innocence, then call Bass Appliances and ask them where they delivered that extra-large freezer three or four years ago. You know, the one you and Aunt Emma had looked at, the one you wanted to buy for your niece."

Ruth started for the phone, then stopped a stride away. "What do you know that I don't?"

"Go ahead, Ruth. Make the call."

She made the call. I watched her shoulders sag and knew I'd scored a bull's eye.

"Well?" I said after she'd hung up.

"They delivered it to Jerry Patterson's fishing cabin there on Rocky Creek."

"The one on Davies Ford Road, right?" I'd been there just after he'd first built it, but not recently.

"Right. The one on Davies Ford Road."

"Then that's where I'll start. That is, if I can borrow your Volkswagen."

"The keys are in my purse."

"Call Eugene Yuill for me, will you? Tell him that if by any chance Clarkie gets home early, have him meet me out there."

"I still don't believe it, Garth."

She looked devastated. Not for being wrong about Jerry Patterson, but because one of our very own angels had fallen.

"I can't believe it either, Ruth. I probably never will."

I got in Ruth's Volkswagen and drove west out of town, then turned south on Davies Ford Road after crossing Rocky Creek. Jerry Patterson's fishing cabin was along Davies Ford Road about a mile this side of where it intersected with County Road 425 West. I had passed it in the dark early Friday morning on my way home from Hogue Valley. If I remembered correctly, it was right about where I first saw the taillights of the other car.

Not a heavily traveled road to begin with, Davies Ford Road was particularly lonesome that Saturday afternoon. Once I thought I saw a car behind me, half-hidden by my own cloud of dust, but when I pulled over to see who it was, no car was there. Apparently it had turned off somewhere, because while I could see the remains of its dust, I never saw the car again.

Jerry Patterson's fishing cabin was built on two levels. The first level was eight feet of concrete block foundation, built to withstand those rare rises in Rocky Creek that went beyond bank full to full-stage flood. The second level, built of logs and covered with wood shingles, had a cedar deck and railing that overlooked Rocky Creek, a redwood stairway leading up to the deck, and a white pine door, beautifully marked with dark spirals, leading into the cabin itself. On the deck were a couple folded lounge chairs and a gas barbecue grill, remnants of the summer long past, and a short stack of firewood.

I knocked on the door and got no answer. Knocked again, then tried the door. Discovered that it was locked.

The window that faced the deck was about four feet high and six feet wide and not likely to be broken by the head of a kamikaze woodpecker. There was a thick white curtain drawn across it, so I couldn't see inside to know where anything was. What did it matter? I decided, as I picked up one of the chunks of wood stacked outside the door and threw it through the window. Though disappointed in the size of the hole that it made, I was able to follow the chunk of wood inside.

Found myself in the living room or the family room—I'd forgotten what Jerry had called it, where, like the door, the walls were white pine, as were the walls of the attached kitchen, which was separated from the family room by a bar and three padded bar stools. I was facing the fireplace, which was built of native stone, mostly red and black speckled granite, and which occupied the very center of the wall. Behind me were a brown leather couch and a brown leather easy chair that had a smoking stand beside it. A bearskin rug covered most of the floor between the couch and the hearth. An Indian blanket was neatly draped over the back of the couch. Pencil prints of timber wolves hung on the wall on either side of the fireplace.

As I stood trying to decide which way to go, I felt a cold wind at my back. Left, I decided. I'd go left.

The first bedroom that I came to was apparently that of Teddy Patterson, Jerry's son. Its door was closed, and when I opened it, I felt a sense of violation, that I had no business here, and something else equally as strong—the arid poignancy of a life nipped in the bud. I didn't linger, stayed only long enough to hook the white roostertail back into the eye of his fishing rod and blow the dust off of a couple trophies.

The next bedroom down the hall was that of Jerry Patterson. Plain white quilted spread on the bed, no rugs on the floor, a duck-hunting print on one wall, a muskie head on the other, it had a distinctly masculine look to it, but a strangely feminine smell and feel.

In the half-bath off from it, I found two toothbrushes on the sink, two cans of deodorant in the medicine cabinet, two towels and two washcloths on the rack beside the shower. I wondered who, besides Jerry, might be staying here? Or if in fact the extras had belonged to Teddy Patterson, and Jerry kept them around for old times' sake?

Jerry's bedroom was the end of the line in that direction, so I turned around and retraced my steps past Teddy Patterson's bedroom and the bathroom, then went all the way through the family room into the kitchen. From the north kitchen window I had a good view of Davies Ford Road, so I stood there a minute, until I was satisfied that no cars were headed my way.

That first step from the wooden floor of the kitchen onto the concrete stairs that led to the basement jarred more than my memory. Once I was in the basement, there was no way out except up these stairs. It was like walking into a box canyon in enemy territory.

The second step didn't feel any better to me than the first, so I stopped to think things through. What was the very worst thing that could happen to me? Jerry Patterson could arrive on the scene and kill me, that's what. Oddly, that thought didn't bother me as much as having my body put on ice afterward. Or who would do the autopsy when I was found, which I surely would be one day. Abby? Ben Bryan? It would have to be one or the other. I went on down the stairs and tried not to think about it. If it happened, it wouldn't matter to me then anyway.

Nothing in the basement but a sea of cobwebs and a huge white freezer against the far wall. I wondered how they'd gotten it down the narrow basement steps and decided that they hadn't. Once there had been a door on the west basement wall. Now there were only concrete blocks where the door had been.

Waiting at the foot of the stairs, I listened for Jerry Patterson, but heard only the living room curtain flapping and bumping against the couch. I wished now that I hadn't broken the window to get inside. I wished now that I hadn't come inside at all. It seemed to take an eternity to cross those few feet of concrete to the freezer.

Locked. After all that I had put myself through, the damned thing was locked.

Back upstairs in the kitchen, I went from drawer to drawer in the hope of finding a key in one of them. I glanced at my watch and then out the north window of the kitchen. Two more minutes without finding a key and I was out of here.

The key was in the front of the silverware drawer under the soup spoons. In my hurry to dig it out, I knocked some soup spoons onto the floor, but didn't stop to pick them up. With a man-sized hole in his window and a chunk of wood lying on his bearskin rug, Jerry Patterson probably would guess that someone had been here.

I unlocked the freezer, raised the lid, and stared down into a mound of frozen food. Frozen corn, frozen strawberries, frozen peaches, frozen blueberries. Hamburger, rump roast, round steak, tenderloin; chicken breasts, chicken legs, chicken fillets; whole chickens, chicken quarters, chicken livers, barbecue chicken; beef heart, beef tongue, beef brisket, and stew beef. All went onto the floor as I dug through the freezer.

Then I came to a whole chicken that didn't have a chicken feel. Also the package had been double wrapped in brown paper and sealed with glass tape. I had started to unwrap it when I heard the floor above me creak. I set down the package and listened, but heard nothing more.

Zack Richards' head had been severed at the neck just below his chin. His eyes were closed, and he had a slight snarl on his face, like every good trophy head should. There was a bullet hole in the back of his head and some frost in his curly blond hair. All in all, he looked about as I'd pictured him.

I used a package of T-bone steaks to wedge his head against the wall, so that it wouldn't roll underfoot, then continued to dig food out of the freezer. But not all was as advertised. One of the pot roasts turned out to be a foot, and I found both hands in a package of sausage. I should have been satisfied to stop there, but I wanted to see what was under the sheet of black plastic at the bottom of the freezer.

Christy Morton was what. It must have been cool the night she died. She wore a green-and-white plaid wool skirt, thick green socks that came to mid-calf, and a long-sleeve high-neck green sweater that matched her skirt. Her eyes were open. She looked cold and scared.

I sat down on the floor of the basement and picked up the very first thing that I had removed from the freezer. It was a .38 Colt revolver. There were two shells left in the chambers. I put the hammer on an empty chamber, put the .38 in my back pocket, and started for the basement steps.

Once in the kitchen, I took a long hard look at the rest of the house before I left its protection. I was almost home free. I didn't want to screw up now.

The problem was that I didn't move fast enough. Had I known that Jerry Patterson was in the house, I would have hit the couch running and hoped for the best. Since I didn't know, I tried to pussyfoot my way around the broken glass and got caught in the act.

"Hold it right there, Garth," Jerry said, as he stepped out of the bathroom. "If you make another move, I'll shoot you where you stand."

Actually I wasn't standing, I was leaning over the couch with my back to him. But since getting shot in the back didn't appeal to me, I did as he said.

"What now?" I asked. "Or do I stay here forever?"

"Turn around. Slowly. And sit on the couch."

I slowly turned around and sat on the couch. As I did, I heard the .38 crunch against some glass. A small comfort at this point. I'd play hell getting to it before I got shot.

Jerry Patterson wore jeans, a dark maroon insulated vest over his baby-blue corduroy shirt, and carried a .22 rifle that was pointed at my chest. I would have bet a week's wages that it was the same rifle that had killed Jeremy Pitts and very likely the same gun that had killed Zack Richards.

His face ruddy from the cold, his eyes keen and bright, Jerry looked the best that he had in years. Killing agreed with him it seemed. Or perhaps it was the thrill of the hunt.

"So...," I said.

"So...," he repeated.

"I guess my first question is, what's a nice guy like you doing in a fix like this?"

Jerry sat down on the hearth with his back against the fireplace. That way he could rest his arms on his legs and still keep the rifle pointed at me.

"It's a long story, Garth."

"It usually is."

"I'm not sure we have time for it. I want to be out of here within the hour."

"You're going to let me die with all of these unanswered questions?"

"Why should you be different than anybody else?"

I shrugged and said nothing. I wanted to prolong my life as long as possible, but I wasn't going to beg for it.

"I'll make you a deal, Garth. You don't try to escape, and I'll tell you as much as I think you have a right to know."

I really didn't have to think about that. Either I got shot sooner or I got shot later. Later seemed preferable to me, since escape at the moment was out of the question.

"It's a deal."

He relaxed his arms a little, but still kept his finger on the trigger. "Where do you want me to start?" he said.

Then I noticed him cast a hungry look toward the smoking stand, which was rimmed with pipes. Another of Jerry Patterson's secrets. He was a closet smoker.

"Go ahead and light up," I said, thinking that it would buy me more time. "I'll even hold your rifle for you."

"Thanks, but no thanks," he said.

But I could tell he still had his mind on it. Divide and conquer, someone once said.

"Why don't you start with the hog barn and why you had Bruce and Jeremy burn it down?" I said.

He took one last wistful look at the smoking stand and turned his attention to me. "The reason why I had them burn it down was that I needed to sell that eighty acres across from it, and I knew I never could as long as there was a hog barn there."

"Why did you need to sell the eighty acres?"

His eyes had lost some of their keenness and, along with it, their killer edge. "That should be obvious, Garth. I needed the money because of Janie's MS. She didn't want to move, and the only way I could keep us there at home was to sell everything else I had. That eighty acres would have bought us a few more years at home at least."

"But then you still couldn't sell it after the hog barn burned?"

He shook his head. "I couldn't even get a bid on it. Wilmer Wiemer said that, as long as Amos Hogue ruled Hogue Valley, I wouldn't get a bid on it and neither would anyone else who owned property there."

"Do you mind if we back up a step?"

"It's your show. Back up as far as you like."

Apparently I had missed something. If it had really been my show, I would have been the one holding the rifle.

"When Janie got MS, didn't you have health insurance?"

I knew the look he wore very well. Both Jerry Patterson and I had been stung by life's ironies.

"That's the funny thing, Garth. We didn't. When you're young and strong and healthy with seemingly your whole life ahead of you, you don't think about those things. Or at least I didn't back in the 1960's. I could take care of my family, I thought, whatever came along. Then Teddy was born without a hitch, and that only increased my confidence."

His look was one of self-reproach. "Of course, the other side of the coin is that I didn't sell health insurance and, if I couldn't make a buck on something, I didn't want to bother with it, even if it was in my family's best interests. I was quite a hustler in those early days, Garth. You wouldn't believe it to know me now."

A new look appeared on his face. One of guilt. "Then there was that day when Janie fell and couldn't get up again. I wasn't home at the time. I was never home, it seemed. But when she told me about it, even before I sent her to the doctor, I went in the very next day to Glen Furney's office for health insurance. That's when I got the bad news. Janie had a prior. It had been diagnosed by Doc Baldwin as MS at least a year before her fall, so she couldn't be covered on the policy. You see, Garth, I was so busy taking care of business that I wasn't around home enough to even know what was happening to my own wife. That's what

Janie wrote in her last note to me. 'So many years, so precious little time.'"

"And then you tried everything in your power to make it up to her? After you learned she had MS?"

"I tried, but it didn't work out that way. Instead of more time with her, I had less because I was always on the go, trying to make a buck to pay for her illness. It was terrible, Garth. A terrible time for all of us. I don't know how any of us survived it."

I could feel the cold as it pushed through the curtain and ran under the couch at my feet. It seemed pointless to remind Jerry that not one of his family had survived. At least not intact.

"How did you get that eighty acres to begin with?" I asked.

"Old man Hogue sold it to me for a song. He was dying and knew he couldn't hold things together much longer. He said Clarence would never hang on to his share of the farm. He knew Clarence too well. And Cissy he didn't know at all any more, so he had real doubts about her share. And he couldn't bear the thought that everything he'd worked for all his life would fall to his hated nephew, Amos Hogue, so he sold that eighty acres to me with the agreement that Amos Hogue was the one person I wouldn't resell it to. To this day I've kept my end of the bargain."

"Has Amos ever made you any offers?"

"That's not the point, Garth," he said, suddenly pious.

I begged to differ, but I wasn't the one holding the rifle.

"What happened then, after Janie died?" I asked.

"That's when I really hit the skids—the bottle as well. I really didn't give a shit about much of anything until the day I saw myself—really saw myself—through my son's eyes, when I showed up drunk at one of his track meets. That turned my life around, Garth. I had been a lousy husband and father up to that point. But it wasn't too late to try to make things right with Teddy. Remember when I first brought you here I said that I had bought this for him. Well, I made that come true. It was some place where we could hang out together. You know, just the two of us. And you know yourself that I cut way down on my schedule so I could go to all of his track and cross-country meets. And it worked. Those were the best three years of our lives, Garth. Bar none."

He smiled as he remembered them. Then the smile went away.

"I'll never forget that morning when they called to tell me he had been killed. Everything in me stopped at that point, Garth. I think I died right along with him. The best part of me anyway."

I thought I heard something on the deck that sounded a little bit bigger than a squirrel. If Jerry heard it, he gave no indication.

"So that's when you decided to kill Zack Richards," I said.

"Zack Richards was an asshole, the very definition of the word. Nelson Richards, as sick as he was for as long as he was, wrote his nephew a letter at least once a week, and not one letter, not one, did Nelson ever get in return from Zack. I did the world a favor, Garth, when I killed that sonofabitch."

"How did you arrange it?"

"It was easy. I contacted him and told him that I had an insurance check for him, but I would rather deliver it in person than mail it to a post office box. I told my insurance company the same thing, so they sent it on to me. Then I agreed to meet with Richards at any place of his choosing within an hour of here, so when he called me from Crystal River, I went over there, found out where his room was, walked in, and shot him."

"Just like that?"

"Just like that. He was sitting in a chair watching television. He didn't even bother to turn around when I walked into the room."

"It must have been all the fish he ate."

Jerry gave me a questioning look.

"It's a private joke. What did you do then?"

"Wrapped his head in a couple towels to keep from getting blood all over everything, waited until no one was around, threw him and his stuff into my trunk, came back here and called Bruce Barger, and told him I had another job for him."

"You planned all along to put Zack Richards in a freezer?"

"Not all along. But, as cold as it was, I knew I'd never get a shovel in the ground, so I'd have to put him somewhere in the meantime. I was lucky Bass had a big enough freezer. Once they had delivered it to my basement and Zack Richards was safely inside, I took out the basement door and walled the opening closed."

"What did you plan to do with him when you moved to your condominium in Florida? Leave him for the next occupant?"

"I figured I'd work that out when the time came. Except the time came sooner than I expected."

I heard something else on the deck. This was definitely bigger than a squirrel. It sounded like a moose on crutches. But again Jerry gave no indication that he had heard anything. Perhaps because just then the phone rang, startling both of us.

"Don't move, Garth," he warned.

"I wasn't planning on it."

We waited through fifteen rings. We were both on edge when the caller finally gave up.

"Were you expecting a call?" he asked.

"No. Were you?"

"Not hardly. This number's not listed."

I eased up on one cheek where I'd at least have a go at the .38 in my back pocket. The phone had put Jerry on the alert, brought back the killer glint to his eyes. I was afraid of what might happen if it rang again. The best thing to do was to try to keep him talking.

"The reason the time came sooner than you figured, was because of Cissy Hogue and her gang?" I asked.

Jerry relaxed a little, but not as much as before. Time was growing short, I feared. I eased my cheek a little higher.

"Is there something wrong with your leg, Garth?"

"A cramp." I eased back down again. "But I think I worked it out."

"Not that it matters." Jerry was grim. "Don't get any ideas about jumping through that window."

"I wasn't."

"To answer your question, Garth, Cissy Hogue did force my hand sooner than I expected, though I didn't know at the time that she was the one in charge. I figured it was Bruce and Jeremy. So I figured I'd kill two birds with one stone. Get rid of Zack Richards' body and at the same time send a message to Bruce and Jeremy not to do any more burglaries."

"Which by chance were pointing a finger of suspicion at you."

"Nine out of the last ten home owners who were robbed were clients of mine. If anybody started investigating me for that, which you almost did, then who knew what they might turn up?"

"What about the hands, head, and foot still down in your freezer? What did you plan to do with them?"

"There are a lot of bridges between here and Florida, Garth. A lot of swamps and alligators."

"And Amos Hogue got the torso, plus one foot, to thank him for all he has done for you?"

At the mention of Amos Hogue's name, Jerry's face darkened with anger. Amos was a prime target in all of this. Had he not been such a formidable foe, he could have ended up like Zack Richards.

"Yes. To thank Amos for all he'd done for me."

"It was personal, then, your choice of dumping sites?"

"Yes, Garth. Very personal."

I could see Jerry liked having me hear the story of his murderous exploits. He wouldn't have let me live this long otherwise.

"Is that the reason you told me you'd seen Zack Richards alive and well on Sunday? You wanted to throw some suspicion Amos's way?"

"That was one of the reasons. I knew he drove by in his pickup about that time every Sunday. The other reason was that, if anybody ever did by chance identify that body as Zack Richards, I wanted for him to have been alive for the past three years, so no one would suspect me.

That was why I put his watch cap out there the next night, to tie the body in with the person that I said I saw."

"It almost worked," I said. Would have worked had it not been for Abby.

Jerry glanced at his watch, then at me. I didn't like the look he gave me. I leaned slightly to the left, raising my right cheek off the couch.

"It's almost time, Garth."

"A couple more questions and I'll be satisfied."

His look said he didn't much care.

"Jeremy Pitts' death, was that an accident?"

"Yes. I was trying for his sister, Lori, and got him instead. I forgot that he had long hair like hers. My first real mistake of the whole deal."

Like most killers, Jerry Patterson didn't consider murder a mistake.

"The reason you wanted to kill Lori, was that because she was the only one who could link you to Christy Morton?"

Now that I had him talking again, I eased my cheek back down to the couch. It was too much of a strain to try to hold it up. Meanwhile I listened for further sounds coming from the deck, but heard none. Maybe it was a squirrel after all.

"Yes. I had always planned to kill Lori eventually but, with you already at my door, time was of the essence. Lori knew who I was, I thought. She used to baby-sit for us when Teddy was little, and then helped look after Janie when she could no longer look after herself."

"Why did you kill Christy Morton? Why take the risk when you already had your pension coming and your condo down in Florida?"

"Because I wanted a boat, that's why," he said without remorse. "What good is Florida if you've got to stay inside all the time? You might as well be here and shut in as there and shut in. The odd thing about it is, Garth, that when I had them burn down that hog barn for me, I sweated bullets—before, and for months afterwards for fear I'd get caught. And even though Zack Richards was an asshole and deserved to die, and even though I deserved that insurance money for what I'd been through a whole lot more than he did, I still had to justify it to myself, and I still spent some sleepless nights over it. But with Christy Morton, I saw opportunity and took it, without giving it a second thought."

"How did you work that one?" I asked.

"After Andy Metzger died, I told my insurance company to hold up the check because it was September, and I hadn't yet got Christy Morton's new address at school. That gave me a couple days to go down to Wisconsin Wesleyan and scout the territory to see if she could be had or not. When I determined that she could be, I went for it. Told the insurance company to send her the check."

"You killed her on her way home from the library, then went back the next day and stole her insurance check from the mailbox?"

"As simple as that, Garth. She was such a frail, frightened little thing I had no trouble at all killing her on the spot."

"She was her grandfather's favorite, I take it?"

"You take it right. She was the only one in the whole family that really gave a damn about him."

My time was up. He knew it, I knew it. But still I pressed on.

"Then that bit Thursday night in the Corner Bar and Grill was just an act for my benefit? That and your subsequent accident?"

"Just an act, Garth. At least when I saw you at the bar. You were getting too close to the truth, and I had to muddy the waters. Though by chance it really was my anniversary, and that part of it was real. The pain, I mean. The accident was something else."

"Then who was driving the car that nearly ran you over?"

"I have no idea. Some drunk, I suppose."

"One last question, Jerry, and this one I can't fathom. Why? After all you had been through with Janie, why did Teddy's death affect you so?"

"You know, Garth, I asked myself that very question just a few days ago when this whole thing started up again. God knows everything that I went through with Janie, and how hard it was to lost her and everything else I'd worked for. But I could accept that because I was partly to blame. Teddy's death was different, though. You're a man of the earth, so maybe you'll understand. I felt like a farmer who had suffered through years of flood and drought, one right after the other, who'd lost nearly everything he had, but still hung on to his mortgage, hoping for that one good year to set things right again. Then it came. For once he got his crops in on time, and for once the rains came when he needed them, and not too much at that. And for once the prices were where they ought to be, so in August he sold on futures, certain that his crop would make it. Then early in September, long before it should have happened, there came a freak killing frost and wiped him out. Suddenly he didn't care any more. As far as he was concerned, the whole world could go to hell."

He rose then, pointed the rifle at my chest. "It's time, Garth."

I slumped over on the couch and didn't move.

"I said it's time, Garth. Either you move or I shoot you where you lie..."

I didn't move, didn't even try to reach for the .38 in my back pocket.

"You've got to the count of three. One..."

On the count of two, two slugs struck Jerry Patterson. One high on his right shoulder, the other in his heart. One of the slugs came from Eugene Yuill's .38 Police Special, the other from Abby's .357 Magnum. I don't know who fired the shot that killed Jerry Patterson. Ben Bryan does, but he's not saying.

25

A week had passed. Ruth and I sat at the kitchen table, drinking our second cup of coffee after a breakfast of ham and eggs. On Tuesday Jerry Patterson and Jeremy Pitts had been buried a few yards apart in Fair Haven Cemetery—Jerry beside his wife and son, Jeremy beside his parents. On Wednesday, at the very time that Cissy Hogue was being buried in Koster Cemetery, Clarkie and I and a few others were carrying the stolen merchandise from beneath Cissy's house. On Thursday Abby's divorce had become final.

"Where's my ten dollars?" Ruth said. "I think a week's long enough to wait for it."

I reached for my wallet and handed her an Alexander Hamilton. "It seemed a good bet at the time."

"To me, too." Looking very satisfied, she pocketed the money. "So where to today? It seems you haven't stopped all week."

"Here and there. But I hope this is the last of it."

"Have you thanked Eugene Yuill yet for saving your life?"

"I did that on Monday. He said he was playing a hunch, that's all, and it paid off."

"What about Abby? Have you thanked her?"

"I plan to do that later today. She's been busy on some secret project that she won't tell me about."

"How did she know to go out there?"

"She said that, when you called her, you gave her directions."

Ruth blushed the way only Ruth could. "I guess I did, didn't I? But I would have gone myself if you hadn't had my car."

I nodded. I knew that.

A few minutes later I got into Jessie, who now sported a new tie rod, and drove west out of town on Galena Road. The first sunny day in a week, the sunshine promised to hold out at least until noon. I guessed that half a day was better than none.

No further progress had been made on Clarence Hogue's place the past week. The back hoe still sat where it always had, brush still blocked his emergency spillway, and the house itself, though completed, still didn't look finished—if it ever would.

I found Clarence out back piling brush. He worked at the slow deliberate pace of a man who had nothing better to do.

"Good morning, Clarence," I said. "You have a few minutes?"

"To do what?" Clarence had lost all of his country charm. He was a bitter, angry man.

"Clear up some things. Off the record." I began picking up brush and helping him pile it.

"I ought to tell you to go to hell. You haven't done me any favors lately."

"You're not in jail, are you? With everything I know about you, you could be."

He dragged a limb over my foot on his way to the brush pile. "You're blowing smoke, Ryland, something you're good at. If you had anything on me that would stick, I *would* be in jail."

"You're right, Clarence. I don't have anything on you that will stick. That's why this is off the record. But if I wanted to turn up the screws on either Bruce or Lori, I bet I could get something on you that would stick. Bruce talks tough, but we all know he's Jello inside. And Lori has nothing to gain by protecting you because she's going to take a hard fall no matter what."

He picked up a limb, shook the snow off of it, then threw it down again. "Let's go get a cup of coffee. My treat."

We climbed into the cab of his pickup, where he handed me a couple Styrofoam cups and poured coffee out of his thermos into each of them. I handed his to him and took a drink of mine. I supposed that this wasn't the time to ask if he had cream and sugar.

"What do you want to know?" he said.

"What was your part in the burglaries? Were you the front man, the scout, in other words?"

"How long have you been thinking about this?"

"About a week now. I figure you let them know what places were ripe for the picking and what might be had there, and then the days of the burglaries you ran interference for them to make sure that nobody surprised them at their work."

As he turned my way, he wore a look of grudging admiration. "What do you need me for, to applaud? But I want you to know something, Ryland, I never made a dime off of those burglaries. None of us did, except for the money that Cissy kept for her and the boys to live on."

"The boys?"

"Bruce and Jeremy. The boys. Which is what they are and always will be."

"Your share was to go on to this place?"

"Ever cent of it. Now I'm not sure how I'm going to pay for it."

"Pardon me if I don't feel sorry for you."

"I don't expect you to."

I took another drink of my coffee. It wasn't Ruth's, but it would do.

"What did Cissy plan to do with her money?"

Clarence just shook his head. His sister had always been a mystery to him and apparently still was.

"She planned to fix up that old house of hers and then live there. You know, restore it back to the way it was when our great-grandparents had it. I told her that she'd just be pouring her money down a rathole, but once Cissy made up her mind about something, it was made up. Not you, me, or God Himself could change it." He glanced up at the sun which poured into the cab of the pickup and made it drowsy in there. "Take that 'secret tunnel,' as she described it. It was a hell of a lot of work carrying that stuff up and down those stairs and then all that distance to the end of the tunnel. But Cissy wouldn't have it any other way."

Here Clarence paused as tears came into his eyes. Fright tears, they looked like to me—the kind that rise with the hair on your nape when something fearful crawls up your spine.

"Ever since Cissy found that tunnel as a kid, she was fascinated by it. It was almost like she was drawn to it, Garth, that it had some kind of mysterious power over her. I'm not surprised that you found her buried there where you did. That's the way Cissy would have wanted it."

"Lori Pitts is the one who buried her there, remember?"

"Still, Garth, it has to make you wonder."

It did make me wonder, especially since Clarence couldn't have known what else was buried at the end of that tunnel. But I didn't want to speculate about things I had no knowledge of.

"Speaking of Lori Pitts, did you go with her to Amarillo?" I asked.

"Is there any crime in that?"

"No. I just wondered why."

"She needed a relief driver, that's all. She figured that she could never get there and back in a day by herself."

"Did you know what she was going down there for?"

Clarence shook his head. I'd overstepped my bounds. "That's between her and me, Garth."

We finished our coffee. Then Clarence went back to piling brush, and I continued west on Galena Road.

Alma Hogue didn't look much different than the last time that I had seen her. A little thinner, perhaps, a little paler and sadder, a little more weary of life. I sat at her kitchen table, drinking my fourth cup of coffee that morning. I wouldn't need Jessie. I could probably fly home on my own.

Seeing Alma there in her dress and apron, with her hair up and her fingers busy fixing her husband's lunch, I realized what else it was that made her attractive to me. She reminded me a lot of my Grandmother Sprague, who was also tall, thin, and pretty, and who wore a look of perpetual sadness on her face.

"Amos will be here in a minute, if you're waiting to talk to him," she said.

"Actually, I came to talk to you, Alma."

She sagged, as if all of the air had suddenly been let out of her, and she had to lean on the counter for support. She had been waiting for this, had known the moment I'd walked in the door what I'd come for.

"What about, Garth? Those songs I wrote? I think I've about given up on song writing now." She was trying to peel potatoes, but she couldn't get her hands to work right.

"It's about the phone call that you made to Jeremy Pitts the moment he died, the one that makes you an accessory to murder. Unless you acted in all innocence? Did you act in all innocence, Alma?"

When she wouldn't look at me, I thought I had my answer.

"And the phone call that you made to Jerry Patterson's fishing cabin last Saturday afternoon, the one he never answered. And the call that Jerry made to you a week ago Thursday from the Corner Bar and Grill, telling you exactly when he would be leaving, so that you could speed by and fake his hit-and-run, and thus muddy the waters in case I was on to him! And all of those Sunday night worship services that you never made. And the fact that you and Jerry were high school sweethearts, as one of your old classmates was only too eager to tell me on the day of Jerry's funeral."

I watched as she kept flailing away at the potato with her paring knife, cutting far more potato than peeling. "Do you want me to go on?" I said.

She laid the knife and the potato down and rested her hands on the counter. "Does anyone else know?"

"Sheriff Clark does."

"I see."

"I'm sorry, Alma."

As she turned to face me, I noticed that her eyes were dry. I imagine she had cried all of her tears years ago. I pulled out a chair. She sat beside me at the table.

She said, "I've often wondered what might have happened, you know, if I *had* waited for Jerry to come home from the service, instead of marrying Amos. I think we all would have been a lot happier, don't you?"

"I think so, Alma." It was hard to imagine how any of their lives could have been unhappier.

"Stolen," she said. "After I married Amos, every happy moment of my life was stolen. Now I won't even have those to look forward to. I'll die in prison. Won't I, Garth?"

I shoved my cup of coffee aside. It was getting cold anyway.

"You say Amos is in the barn?"

"That's where he said he'd be."

I rose and went to the back door, where I tried to think of something that would make things better for her. But I couldn't think of anything.

She said, "If I had to take anything back, it would be that phone call. The instant that Jeremy Pitts picked up the receiver and said hello, I knew it was the beginning of the end."

"No condo down in Florida. No moonlight walks along the beach."

"It was a good dream, Garth. Don't make light of it. For always, it seemed, Jerry and I had suffered. We both had some happiness coming."

I nodded and left. Met Amos Hogue on his way to the house.

"Morning, Garth," he said, glancing up at the sun. "You come to arrest my dear wife, did you?"

Amos was downright chipper that morning. I thought I knew why.

"Sheriff Clark will be by later to do that."

"Good," he said, as he turned to spit in the snow. "I'll get one more meal out of her at least." Then he reached out and poked me playfully in the chest with his forefinger. "I told you somebody was porking her, Garth. It just turned out not to be you."

"How long have you known it was Jerry?"

"Almost from the beginning. The minute I got suspicious, I started following her. If you know Alma, that wasn't hard to do."

The sun was doing its best to eat away at the inch or so of snow that had fallen in the night. But the manure days were behind us. We in Wisconsin wouldn't get excited again until spring.

"If you knew, then why did you let it go on?" I said.

He spat again, leaving a brown stain on the virgin snow. "I wanted to see where it would lead. If I might not use it to my advantage. But things got a little hairy there when that body turned up on my property, and then queer-boy had the bad luck to get himself killed with a .22 rifle. Knowing Alma and Jerry, I couldn't be sure my rifle hadn't done the deed, so I took pains to remove it from harm's reach."

"Where *is* your rifle, by the way?"

"Back in the barn, where I aim to keep it." He took his chew of tobacco out of his mouth and gave it a toss. "It's funny, Garth, how things work out. For years now I've been plotting and scheming about how to get Hogue Valley for myself and now, thanks to my dear wife and her homicidal lover, and a bunch of thieving misfits, it practically falls in my lap."

"How so?" I said. "The last I heard, your cousin Clarence still owns a hundred twenty acres of it, or will when it's all said and done."

"He'll never hang on to it," Amos said with confidence. "He's never held on to anything worth keeping in his life. Mark my words, he'll have to sell it to pay for that new place he built there west of town. As for that eighty that Jerry Patterson owned, I'll snap that up at the first tax sale."

"Clarence will never sell to you, Amos, not if you were the last man on earth." I thought I knew Clarence well enough to say that.

"No, but he'll sell to Wilmer Wiemer, who in turn will then buy me out. The way I hear it, old Wilmer's got a golf course all lined up for Hogue Valley, as soon as he can get clear title to the whole shebang. I've seen the plans. The clubhouse itself is going to go up on the hill in the old home place that my cousin Cissy was so fond of." He smiled. "Garth, you don't know how tickled I am how things worked out. And I have you to thank most of all."

"You don't plan to stay in Hogue Valley and raise hogs?"

"Not when I can sell out, move to Florida, and raise hell. These Wisconsin winters are starting to wear on me, Garth, all the cold and clouds. I'm long overdue for a little R and R."

I watched the first cloud of the day head directly toward the sun, as if it had radar. But at least I had made one person happy lately. Two, if I counted Eugene Yuill who, before he shot Jerry Patterson and became my hero, had no claim to fame except for his size fourteen feet. I did wonder, however, how happy Amos would be if he knew what was buried there on that hill. But I wouldn't tell him now. I'd save it for much later.

After saying goodbye to Amos, I got in Jessie and drove back to town. Abby met me at her front door with a smile and a hug, then took me by the hand and began to lead me through the house.

"We have to hurry," she said excitedly. "My rounds start in a few minutes."

Where we headed in such haste? I could only hope.

But we veered off through the kitchen and started down the basement steps. At that point, I balked.

"Abby, where are you taking me?"

"The morgue. I have something to show you."

"I don't think I want to see it."

"Please, Garth. It's important to me."

"Okay. Since you put it that way."

What she wanted to show me was a reconstructed Zack Richards. She had sewn his hands, feet, and head back onto his body, then dressed him in jeans, a dark-blue turtleneck sweater, and the watch cap. She had even taken the snarl off his face, though he would have looked more natural with it on.

"What do you think?" she asked, beaming with pride.

"I think you did a magnificent job. Zack Richards never looked better."

"Do you really mean that?"

I took her in my arms and kissed her. "I really mean that. You are one hell of a surgeon, Dr. Airhart, and an even better person."

"You're just saying that so you can jump my bones later."

"Did it work?"

She kissed me lightly on the lips, then slipped out of my grasp, and began to lead me toward the basement steps. "We'll see."

Vice is a monster of so frightful mien,
As, to be hated, needs but to be seen;
Yet seen too oft, familiar with her face,
We first endure, then pity, then embrace.

—Alexander Pope